Tale of a *Train Wreck* Lifestyle

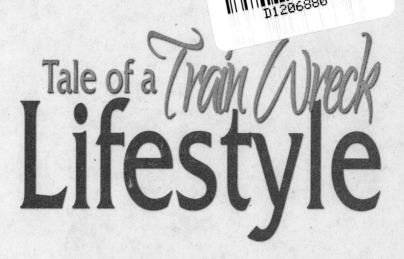

Tale of a *Train Wreck* Lifestyle

by

Crystal Lacey Winslow

Tale of a Train Wreck Lifestyle. Copyright © 2008 by Crystal Lacey Winslow. All rights reserved. Printed in the United States of America. No part of this book may be used or reproduced in any manner whatsoever without written permission except in the case of brief quotations embodied in critical articles or reviews. For information, address Melodrama Publishing, P.O. Box 522, Bellport, NY 11713.

www.melodramapublishing.com

Library of Congress Control Number: 2007943738
ISBN-13: 978-1934157152
ISBN-10: 1934157155
First Edition: October 2008
10 9 8 7 6 5 4 3 2 1

A NOTE FROM THE AUTHOR:

Not quite sure how I went from author/publisher to publisher/author. But somehow the transition is evident. Having said that, I've decided to retire writing for a couple years with promises to come back with exciting characters, juicy plots, and realistic dialogue. I have so many stories within me, yet so little time to execute them properly.

Tale of a Train Wreck Lifestyle is my eighth book, fifth novel. When I sat down to pen this novel, I wanted to incorporate the elements of my surroundings. Both my grandparents lived and died in the New York City housing projects. My maternal grandmother rested her head in Marcy projects. Paternal—Pink Houses. As I began writing this tale I wondered about geography. I thought about how a person's environment can shape their future. That coupled with our parents and the methods they use when bringing up their kids. Some parents are mentally young and don't have the proper tools/common sense/people and social skills to help develop and prepare their children. I thought, How many children born into poverty or unhealthy environments will have a tale of a train wreck lifestyle? I know I had mine.

I hoped you've enjoyed my works. And I thank you for riding with me this long. Until we meet again...

PROLOGUE

Nikkisi Ling

June 2003

IBIZA, SPAIN

I had been living in a small hut on the beach in Spain since I'd fled from America. The scenery was tranquil and serene. I didn't have any visitors and remained a virtual recluse. I grew my own vegetables and washed my clothing by hand. I didn't have any amenities from the outside world. No telephone or television. It was common for people around here to mind their own business.

On this particular morning, I was sleeping peacefully when I heard a noise. Without hesitation, I jumped up and pulled out a butcher's knife I kept underneath my pillow. As the footsteps grew closer I held my breath and expected the worst.

They found me, I thought. I swung the door open and was startled.

"Jesus, Nikki . . . are you going to use that?" Joshua said and smiled his boyish grin. I immediately dropped the knife and jumped into his arms. He grabbed me in a bear hug and spun me around.

"Is it really you?" I squealed. "How did you find me?"

"It wasn't easy, yet it wasn't hard enough," he warned.

"When did you get out?" I asked Joshua as we packed.

"Two weeks ago . . ."

"Why?" I asked.

"Why, what?"

"Why are you here? Why are you putting yourself in the same situation? I'm a fugitive, Joshua. I will never live a normal life."

"Kid, you're all I've thought about for the past few months. I started thinking that I don't have a life in America if you're not in it."

"So you're saying," I paused, "that you love me?"

"I thought you knew how I felt about you."

"I want you to say it!" I demanded.

"I love you, kid," he said and kissed me.

I stared in his blue eyes and said, "I love you, too," and my eyes welled up with tears.

"It's not safe here. We have to leave. If I found you, the authorities can," Joshua continued.

I immediately jumped into action. We ran around my small hut, taking only what we could carry. And the $900,000 I still had left. We crept out quietly and headed to the Republic of China. They don't have an extradition treaty with the U.S. for death penalty cases.

Detective Oldham

"Get your passport, Ripton. We got a hit!"

"Nikkisi?"

"Exactly! A snitch told us she's living in Ibiza, Spain."

"Don't you ever get tired of trailing her?" Detective Ripton asked.

"I will not retire until I have her back in America, facing charges for the murders she's committed!"

PART I:

THE CRISS CROSS

Nikkisi Ling

My tale of a train wreck lifestyle began when my mother committed suicide. My sister, Noki, and I were orphaned because we didn't have any maternal or paternal family. I wish I could say that I always made the best decisions when it came to Noki and I, but I didn't. I was fourteen years old when I turned my first trick. After I had been raped by my foster father, Reverend Daniel, I charged him forty dollars.

I shook my head and grimaced. The past hurt.

I looked in the mirror and she stared back at me. Only I didn't know her anymore. Her high cheekbones were rounded by the recent cheek implants, changing the oval-shaped face into an apple-like roundness. Her Asian eyes were Americanized, and now looked average. Her long, luxurious, jet-black hair was cropped into a short bob and dyed a chestnut brown with ash-blond highlights. The woman in the mirror was me, but after three extensive plastic surgeries, Nikkisi Ling—fugitive—no longer existed. Instead Molly Mathis, an ordinary housewife, stared back at me.

My new life began with the most wonderful, selfless man on this earth. His former name was Joshua Tune. Now he was Matthew Mathis. Matt gave up a life of freedom to live with me on the run, in seclusion and cut off from his family and friends. He did all of this for his love of me. He accepted all of me and my baggage—former hustler, prostitute, and alleged murderess. I was no murderess, though. I mean, yes, I did steal thousands by pick-pocketing my victims. And, yes, I did sell my body. But I never, ever, murdered anyone, unless you counted Noki. I couldn't help but blame myself for her death.

Joshua stepped up behind me and wrapped his arms around my waist. "I need to go back," he stated sternly.

"You can't!" I snapped, unwavering in my stance. I stared him down in the mirror. "They will catch you and you'll go to jail for a very long time." I turned around and looked him in the eye. "I can't lose you!"

Joshua kissed me on the forehead. "I won't go to jail because I won't get caught. It's that simple. You've already bought us several fake passports, two of which we've used and cleared customs without a hitch. You're a pro at this identity fraud thing, and my years as an attorney have prepared me to lie without detection. I can do this," he assured me.

I shook my head. "Why are you doing this? To us?" I asked. I knew why he wanted to go back, and his lack of control concerned me. One slip could get us arrested, or maybe even killed.

"Nik—"

"My name's Molly! You can't even get that right!" I stepped out of his embrace and ran a nervous hand through my bob. "You're gonna slip up!"

"Don't patronize me," he snapped. "I know what to call you in public. You're underestimating me, as usual, and not believing in me to do the right thing."

"Do the right thing? How is going back to the United States where both of us are fugitives doing the right thing?"

"Jesus, Mary, and Joseph," Joshua exclaimed, and then exhaled deeply. His bright blue eyes looked tired and despondent. "Why can't you understand that this isn't a debatable subject?"

"Sonuvabitch! How dare you talk to me like this? I'm your wife!"

"So was she. And she's dying. I have to go back to say goodbye. I owe her that much. With or without your blessing, I'm going back."

Parker Brown-Battle was Joshua's first wife. I hated to admit it, but I was jealous of the high pedestal upon which he put her. I knew in my heart that he still loved her. He always spoke of her in the fondest tones, as if she were a saint. "Parker was a great wife, but I was a lousy husband," he liked to say. "Parker's smart thinking saved me. I could have done years in prison. Parker is raising her rival's daughter, who is stricken with Down's syndrome."

I hated to say this, but Joshua would never truly be all mine as long as Parker was living. Does that mean I wanted her to die?

I shook off that thought. I'd had enough negative karma in my old life, and I was not bringing it into my new one.

I grabbed a sweater and walked down to the beach. We were living in a small, one-room shack in Italy, the most beautiful place in the world. The whole town sat atop a high hill with steep stairs that led down to a beautiful, scenic ocean.

As the waves crashed against the shore, I wondered what I had to do to get my stubborn husband not to risk our happiness by going back to New York. I hated to be so harsh, but he couldn't save Parker. She had terminal cancer, and out of the blue he had received an e-mail from her that read: I need to say goodbye. I have terminal cancer. He wasn't even sure if the message was really from her. We had argued about it.

"This could all be a trap," I said. *"How do you know it's really from her, and not the police?"*

Joshua shook his head, as if by doing so he could shake off my suspicions. "I just know, Nikki. I can't explain it. I just feel it."

"You feel it?" I was so tempted to slap some sense into his thick head, but I resisted. "Your ass will feel the inside of a cold jail cell if this is a trap!" I frowned. "How did she find you anyway?" We'd taken great pains to hide our tracks when we left the United States.

"She took a chance. Throughout our marriage I'd always used the screen name OLDBLUEEYES." He laughed sheepishly. "Guess who still uses that name?"

I just stared at him in disbelief. Surely he couldn't have been that stupid. "What? Why?" I asked, bewildered. "Please tell me that you're not still in contact with your life back in America? Do you know what that communication can do to me? To us?"

Joshua's expression turned mulish. "Nikki, stop speaking to me as if I'm a moron! This is a happenstance situation. I haven't opened communication with my prior life in three years since I gave up that life and went on the run with you!"

"I didn't ask you to," I yelled.

"I never said you did!"

"You didn't have to say it. You implied it. You're always dangling my situation over my head and what you gave up for me, making me feel guilty for a decision that I didn't help make."

"Ciao, bella." The familiar voice snapped me back to the present. It was Alessandro. He had naturally tanned skin, a massive amount of thick, jet-black hair, an athletic body, and he did his best to flirt with me whenever my husband wasn't around. Then again, that could be said of all Italian men. Flirting was their lifeblood.

I didn't want to be bothered.

"I want to be left alone today, Alessandro. Is that OK?"

"You look, how do you say in ummm, English . . . you look . . . like a puppy."

I chuckled softly as he butchered the English language. "You mean, I look sad?"

"Si. What's wrong? You can tell me." He took this opportunity to sit down next to me, although I'd just said I wanted to be left alone. Language barrier or not, I got the feeling that Alessandro had just ignored my request.

I forced a smile. There would be no divulging of family secrets. "I'm just exhausted and want to be left alone."

"Hard day at work, huh? Too much cleaning?" The whole village knew I worked as a housecleaner for the wealthier people in our town. I scrubbed floors on my hands and knees four days a week, although I didn't need to. Joshua and I had more than enough money stashed away. We still had close to eight hundred thousand dollars of my late husband's blood money. Joshua and I both agreed that one way to get caught would be to start throwing money around, and for nosey neighbors to realize that there wasn't a job to support such lavishness. Living impoverished was the best way to stay under the radar.

"Yes, that's correct," I lied.

He cocked his sexy head to one side and intently stared in my eyes. "OK, is that true? I thought maybe you look like puppy over your husband. Maybe he not treat you too good. No?"

"No, you're not correct," I snapped. His constant meddling was making me nervous. What did he know? Was he a snitch, planted to find out anything he could about Joshua and me? There was a huge reward for my capture and my picture, pre-plastic surgery, was plastered on the FBI's Ten Most Wanted Fugitives list.

"OK, OK, don't bite my head," he replied. "I just want to get to know you."

"I'm married, Alessandro."

"So what? We just talk."

I shook my head. "You want to do more than just talk."

"È pazzo! I like you more than umm, sex. No?" He paused as if to make sure he'd used the right words, then continued. "Your husband is no good for you," he said. "He treat you badly and make you sad like puppy!"

"You don't know anything about my marri—"

"Molly?"

I turned to see Joshua standing at the bottom of the clearing of the steps. He looked annoyed. I didn't excuse myself to Alessandro. I just left. As I approached Joshua, I noticed that he and Alessandro were in an intense stare-down. Neither one of them wanted to end their eye-to-eye confrontation. I lightly tugged Joshua's hand and broke his concentration.

"Are you ready for dinner, sweetie?" I smiled up at him.

"Yeah," Joshua said in a short tone. I waved at Alessandro and we walked away, hand in hand. When we were out of earshot Joshua said, "I had a surprise for you. I cooked. But if you want to stay here with your Italian stud, I could eat alone."

I mentally rolled my eyes. Here we go again. "That's not fair," I replied. "Alessandro was just being flirty, as all Italian men are. He's harmless, Matt. Besides, you're the one I'm married to. You're the one I'm with. I love you, so stop with the bullshit, OK?"

Joshua said nothing.

After a dinner of chicken piccata, angel hair pasta, and a salad of roasted red peppers, tomatoes, olives, and mozzarella cheese tossed in olive oil with basil, he said, "I want you to come with me to New York."

I gasped. Had Joshua lost his mind? "Are you crazy, Joshua? You'd really ask such a thing of me? You'd risk my freedom and livelihood, for her?" I couldn't believe his gall, and the strength of their bond further increased my nervousness.

"Well, I don't want you to stay here without me."

"And I don't want you to go!"

"So come with me," he said again.

"I'm facing the death penalty, and all you can think about is your past!"

Joshua sighed. "Well, she's been given a death sentence. I can't abandon her."

"How are you abandoning her, Josh? You made a commitment to me. I'm your future and your wife."

Joshua stood and walked over to the window. "First off, our marriage isn't legal."

A cold sensation spread from the pit of my stomach. "I can't believe you just said that! Legally, Nikkisi Ling and Joshua Tune weren't married, but Molly and Matt Mathis were! You're my husband, and I didn't need a piece of paper to feel like your wife. I thought you felt the same."

"Well then, as your husband, I'm telling you that I don't want you here without me with that gigolo."

"What are you saying? That you don't fucking trust me?"

He snorted. "Don't try to play all innocent, Nik. Remember, I know what you're capable of."

His harsh words cut deep within my soul. Flashbacks of Brian Carter, my first love, came flooding back. He, too, had a low opinion of me because of my past. Brian never thought I was good enough. Did

Joshua feel the same way about me? Had he been masking his true feelings all this time?

"You're an asshole! If you leave for New York, don't come back!" Although I'd said those words, I didn't mean them. I only said them because I was deathly afraid that Joshua would do just that—go to New York and never return.

That night, we didn't sleep in the same bed. When I awoke to the quiet apartment, and the only sound was the crashing of the waves, I knew he was gone. I ran and pushed the refrigerator out of the way, knelt, and carefully removed the plaster that held the secret of our past lives. Inside the tiny alcove was a black satchel. I exhaled. From the onset, everything looked untouched. But after I counted out the money, I realized that Joshua had taken one hundred thousand dollars with him to New York. He was such an idiot. Why would he think he could pass through Customs with that amount of money? He was begging to get busted.

Why would he take so much money unless he planned on never coming back? I wondered. But he could have taken it all, so I guess I should have been grateful.

As the days went by without Joshua, I went through a slew of emotions. I was sad because he left me. Angry because he took my money. Confused because he wanted to see Parker, and bewildered because he came with me on the run in the first place. Grateful because he wasn't apprehended. But ultimately, I began to settle on relieved. Joshua would never fully be happy on the run, cut off from his family. I understood his mood swings as each year passed, although I tried to ignore them because his temper tantrums and outbursts were all because he wasn't happy. Not that they had anything do to with me, I liked to think, but rather with life without his family.

Joshua Tune

The smell of the polluted, thick air felt exhilarating. I was back. Twenty pounds heavier and more alert, but none of that mattered. I pulled my baseball cap down low and began my mission. With a rental car from Hertz, secured using my fake identification as Matthew Mathis, and my overnight bag, I left JFK airport with a laundry list of things I wanted to do and see. The first thing on my list was a hot dog from a New York vendor. I pulled over on Thirty-fourth Street and Eighth Avenue, right next to Macy's, and a million memories came flooding back. I remembered shopping in the department store for gifts for Parker. Then I remembered Lyric. She'd never accepted any gift from there. Honestly, I still missed her sassy self.

"I'll take two hot dogs with mustard, onions, and sauerkraut." I pushed a ten-dollar bill into the Indian guy's hand and couldn't help but notice his filthy fingers. I shrugged it off. It was part of New York's mystique. "And a Pepsi."

The aroma made me miss my former life. I couldn't wait for my chance to get back to it, even if it was under an assumed name and under grim circumstances. I took a huge bite of my hot dog and smiled. This was heaven.

I'd originally decided to check into the Doubletree Hotel, but the hundred grand I'd borrowed from Nikki was burning a hole in my pocket. After years of living like a pauper, I wanted to splurge. I checked into The Plaza, a hotel I'd always wanted to stay in.

The front desk attendant was more than happy to accommodate me. "Well, Mr. Mathis, we have a single room with a king-sized bed available for $359 a night. Would that be acceptable?"

"I'll only be in town for four days. I was looking for something more accommodating. I'd like a suite if you have one available."

She glanced at my left hand. "Sure. That won't be a problem."

The attendant must have felt comfortable enough to flirt because her fingers grazed mine slightly when she gave me the key card to my room.

"Will you be needing just the one key?"

"Yes, only one."

She licked her lips. "No wife joining you?"

"No wife." She'd be disappointed to learn that I preferred black women.

"A good-looking man like you is still on the market?"

I smiled. "Enjoy your evening."

"If you need anything, anything at all, Mr. Mathis, I'm on duty until eight."

I took a nap, showered, and left the hotel around nine o'clock in the evening. My next stop was Parker's place. Briefly I wondered about Nikki. I wondered how she was feeling since I left without saying goodbye. I knew it was a lousy thing to do, but I was so tired of her attitude. Didn't she understand that Parker had been my wife? True, the marriage hadn't worked out, but you didn't share your life with someone for that many years and just expect them to fall off completely. Even though I was no longer in love with Parker, I still had love for her. And she was dying; I owed it to the life we once had together to at least see her and let her know that I still cared for her.

I drove to Parker's house on Long Island, as I'd done so many times in the past. I couldn't help but have sporadic visions of my life with her. Why didn't I see her for who she really was—a strong, black woman who was in love with her husband? I had definitely taken her for granted.

The house had changed in the past few years. I could see that the landscaping was no longer as elaborate and seemed minimal, just enough to look like someone was taking marginal care of it. Most of the house was dark except for a cluster of windows in the far wing of the house—Parker and Steven's suite. As I got out of the car, the sound of the surf pounding against the rocks provided background music to what was sure to be a depressing yet nostalgic evening.

I walked around to the back of the house, savoring the darkness of the area surrounding the house. I went to the back door and felt over the top of the doorjamb for the spare key that Parker and Steven always kept there. I entered the small foyer and followed it through the state-of-the-art kitchen and up the servant's stairs. My footsteps were fairly silent on the Berber-carpeted steps as I made it to the hallway and followed it down the long hall to Parker's suite of rooms.

The door was ajar and soft light spilled into the hallway from the crack in the door. I paused, but heard nothing, so I carefully pushed in the door. Parker was sitting in a chaise lounge by the window, a lamp shining over her shoulder as she read a book. She did indeed look thinner than she did the last time I saw her. Her thick, long, fiery red dreads had been replaced with an ill-fitting wig, pulled back from her forehead and held back with a purple velvet headband. She looked up at the whisper of the door opening and fear crossed her features.

"Who . . . who are you?" she stammered. "How did you get in here?"

"It's me, Parker," I tried to reassure her.

"Me, who?" She pulled the neck of her purple terrycloth robe closed with one hand and the other crept to the side of the chaise. I knew for a fact that Parker kept a loaded .38 pistol on the other side of the chaise since she spent so much time there, reading.

"It's me, Parker. Joshua. Your ex-husband."

The hand reaching for the gun stilled, and Parker stared at me some more. Her eyes roamed over my face in an attempt to find something familiar. Part of her wanted to believe. I could see that. "You're lying. You're not Joshua." Her hand came up and the .38 pointed at me with deadly accuracy. "Now get the hell out of my house before I drop you where you stand." She wasn't lying, either. Parker was a crack shot and used to visit the shooting range regularly.

"You have a birthmark shaped like a duck on the inside of your left knee," I said. "I used to kiss it and quack, and you'd laugh because it tickled."

The gun hand dropped and Parker's eyes widened. "Joshua?" she whispered. Her lips trembled as if she was about to cry. I walked over and knelt beside the chaise. She ran her hands over my surgically altered face, taking in my lightened hair. "The face is different, but the voice . . . the voice is the same." She leaned forward and hugged me tightly. She was only skin and bones. "Joshua," she whispered again. "I knew you'd come."

"So the message was true," I said as she released me from her embrace.

Parker straightened and looked out the window at the nighttime surf. "Yes. I'd been feeling run-down lately, but I put it down to business and the many charity functions I attended. Steven suggested that he run some tests, and then some more tests, then finally exploratory surgery." She turned back to me. "Cancer of the liver, inoperable, and it has already spread to my bones. The specialist gave me less than three months to live."

"Oh, Parker." Tears welled in my eyes at the thought of this strong, brave, vibrant woman succumbing to such a debilitating disease. "Liver cancer?"

"Yes. And I don't even drink! Isn't that ironic?" She snorted and looked back out the window. "When they told me, I knew I had to try to find you. You were one of the best parts of my life, Joshua. I couldn't leave it without seeing you one last time." She cocked her head and looked at me. "Or should I even be calling you Joshua?"

"That's not the name I'm using now," I admitted. It was pointless to lie to Parker. She knew me too well.

"I see." Silence, then, "Was she worth it, Joshua? Worth giving up your life for?"

For once, I didn't have an answer. Yes, I loved Nikki and admired her for all she'd gone through. But the past few years had tested that love, and I had to admit to myself that I'd begun to resent her. Even though she didn't ask me to go on the run with her, she wouldn't have been on the run in the first place if she was doing legitimate work, like normal people. Instead, she began her life as a pickpocket and evolved into a prostitute. Her beauty—coupled with her edgy, seedier side—was alluring, but three years later it'd become stale. And although Italy was beautiful, it wasn't my cup of tea. I missed America. I missed my family.

I must have hesitated too long because she retorted, "I'll take that as a no."

"I love Nikki," I said weakly.

"You loved the rush, Joshua," Parker corrected. "You always have. And then you go on to the next rush when the former one no longer serves." She cocked her head to the side. "You always did have an addictive personality."

Changing the subject, I asked. "Where's Steven?"

"He's working late at the hospital. He isn't taking my illness well. He's such a good man, Joshua, and I don't want to leave him and Mia here alone."

"Is she sleeping? Baby Mia?"

"Yes. We had to hire a nanny to help out around here. I'm so weak all the time that I've been neglecting her too."

"You can't blame yourself. I'm sure they understand."

"How long have you been here?"

"I just got in town earlier today."

"Have you gone to see your parents?"

"No. I don't want to put them in any danger. They're old. If word ever got out that I'm back, the police would constantly harass them. I can't do that to them. I made my choices."

"What is it about troubled, self-centered women that drives you crazy? I was a good wife, and you threw me under the bus!"

"Parker, don't. That's the past, please."

"Lyric, Monique, Lacey, and now Nikki? What did they have over me?"

"I gotta go," I said tersely. "I just wanted to see you before . . ." I let my words fade, not wanting to talk about her death.

"Before I died? How noble," she stated, then grimaced from pain.

I walked back over and gave her a hug. When I moved to release her, Parker drew me into a kiss that reminded me of why I'd loved and married her once upon a time. One thing led to another and soon we were making love on the chaise. I pushed thoughts of Nikki out of my head as Parker's hips moved faster and faster beneath me. She was stronger than I thought she would be.

"Yes! Oh, yes! Fuck me, Joshua!"

I kept thrusting harder until Parker dug her fingernails into my back, making deep scratches. I felt her shake, shudder, and curse beneath me, then I came hard and fast, deep within her. We lay there, sweaty and sated, until I finally roused myself.

"I need to leave," I told Parker.

"Yes, Steven will be home soon," she murmured sleepily.

I was barely dressed before Steven came jogging up the steps. His eyes went from me to his wife, who was lying naked in their bed.

If he was upset or aware of our rendezvous, he said nothing.

"Who are you?" he asked.

"Steven, it's me, Josh."

"Is that you, Joshua?" His medically trained eyes searched out my old features.

"How's it going, Steven?"

"Well, I've been better."

"I know what you mean."

He looked over to Parker as I adjusted my shirt. "Honey, are you feeling better today?" he asked. "Do you need anything?"

"I'm well, thank you. I was just catching up on old times with Joshua. Steven, you have to talk sense into him and convince him to turn himself in."

"You know if you turned yourself in you could still have a shot at a good life," Steven said.

"If they caught me now or later, I'm still facing the same sentence. Let's just say I'm in no rush to sit in somebody's jail."

"Think about it, please, Joshua," Steven said. When I didn't reply, he asked, "I take it you'll be in town a few days?"

I nodded.

"Where are you staying?"

I hesitated. No one knew I was here, and I needed to keep it that way.

"Come on, Joshua," Parker wheedled. "You can trust us. Who are we going to tell?"

I sighed. "I'm at The Plaza Hotel under Matthew Mathis."

"The Plaza." Parker nodded. "You always wanted to stay there, didn't you?"

"You remembered that."

"My memory is long, longer than our marriage lasted," she joked.

"Well, I guess you should be going now," Steven interjected.

"Think about turning yourself in," Parker reminded me.

"I will." I turned and retraced my steps out of the house and back to my rental car. The last thing I saw was Parker's face watching me from the windows in her suite.

✳✳

What are you doing? I asked myself. I was smarter than this. I'd gone down this road before, a long time ago, and it almost cost me my career and did cost me my freedom for a while. So why was I in the heart of East New York, Brooklyn about to cop some cocaine?

As I exited my rental, I looked over my shoulders before approaching a few guys standing on the corner. I'd observed their behavior for an hour. I could have been an undercover narc, and they were clearly and visibly selling drugs hand-to-hand. Maybe they paid for protection from the local cops. It wouldn't be the first time something like that had happened.

The young Hispanic male spotted me first. He tapped the forearm of his partner, an equally young black male. The rest of their crew on the surrounding corners caught the exchange and eyed me warily. The Hispanic guy had shifty eyes that began to dart around, observing his surroundings, no doubt looking for an escape route if I was a cop and about to do a swoop-down. I took my hands out of my goose-down parka and fumbled. Should I take out the money? No, that would be dumb. But I knew it was smart to show my hands, so they knew that I didn't have a weapon.

"Can I help you, partner?" the black guy asked.

I saddled up closely and whispered, "Where can I score some blow?"

His face twisted up. "Call 411, motherfucker! Do I look like I got that type of information?"

I exhaled. I knew this was going to be a bit difficult. "Look, I'm not a police officer. I'm not wired, undercover, or looking to set up anybody. I just need a hit."

I opened my jacket slowly to reveal that I didn't have a gun or a wire. "I know this area. I used to cop back in the day from Be-Boy over in the Pink Houses projects."

"Then go the fuck back there to get your shit!" the Hispanic male spat.

"Are you talking 'bout Be-Boy over on Stanley Avenue?" the black guy asked.

I nodded. "Yeah, that's him."

They all huddled together and began whispering. Then the Hispanic guy said, "We don't got no coke. We got that Chronic, though. It's better than that white shit, and costs less."

I shook my head vehemently. "I know what I like. Can't you get on the phone and make something happen?" My tone was on the verge of desperation. "I'll give you a little something if you can hook this up."

"How little?"

"Huh?"

"How little? I need to know that my efforts will be appreciated."

I thought for a moment. "I'll give you a Benjamin."

His eyes widened. "Word? Hold on. Let me call my man. He might got something for you."

The Hispanic guy turned his back on me and walked a couple yards away as he used his phone. I looked at the remaining hustlers. None of them were older than nineteen, I suspected. The youngest was standing in the freezing cold weather, eating what I guessed was his dinner of four chicken wings and fried rice from the Chinese restaurant. The ringleader came back. "My man got something. How much you looking for?"

I hadn't thought of that. Originally I just wanted a taste to take off the edge of my stress. But then I realized that the last thing I wanted to do was come back in this neighborhood to cop again. One, I could get hemmed up by an unsuspecting raid and get a one-way ticket to jail. Or two, these thugs could hurt, rob, or even kill me. The thought had me shook. It had been a long time since I'd done this, and times had obviously changed.

"About five packs?"

Again he turned his back on me and whispered into the phone. He turned back again and said, "Nah, my man said he only deal in bundles. He don't got time for this petty shit. So you want it or not?"

Damn! They were really trying to dick me. I'd hoped only to spend around fifty dollars and I was steadily approaching much more than that, especially if you counted the hundred I'd promised to the Hispanic guy. "How much?"

"He wants two fifty for the bundle. You get ten packs," the Hispanic guy said with a straight face.

Jesus, Mary, and Joseph! I knew the economy was bad, but there wasn't any way that the price on a pack had skyrocketed to twenty-five dollars. What to do? What to do? Fuck it. I had brought a hundred grand to New York to enjoy myself. Sure, it wasn't truly my money, but I did feel that I had earned it. I'd given up everything for Nikki, and my freedom was certainly worth more than a measly one hundred thousand dollars. I could splurge a little and treat myself, like I had with the hotel.

"This better be some good shit if you're charging me double!" I replied, adding a little bass in my voice. "Don't think I'm some numbnut who don't know shit. I used to run through these streets back in the day."

"Back in the day?" The black guy scoffed as the rest of the crew burst out laughing. "Well, this is a new day, motherfucker, so you best check yourself."

"Calm down, Rambo," the Hispanic guy joked. "You got my word that this is some good shit. Now, do you want it or not?"

"What's your name?" I asked.

He looked at his crew, then back at me. "Perez. Now give me an answer. You want it or not? It's fucking freezing out here."

I looked around. There was a McDonald's three blocks down. I needed to take some precautions. "OK, you and your friend will meet me in the parking lot of McDonald's. I'm in the blue Ford Taurus. When you see me, beep the horn and I'll go through the drive-thru. When I approach the window to receive my food, you'll get in and we'll do the exchange. If you try any funny business, all of it will be caught on camera."

"What the fuck, man? I ain't down with this MacGyver shit. Either we're doing a quick transaction or not."

"You heard what I said. One bundle. Two hundred fifty dollars. McDonald's." I turned and walked away slowly to show no fear, although my whole body was trembling. I wanted so badly to turn around and look over my shoulder to see if I was being followed, but I didn't.

At the McDonald's, I counted out the three fifty, remembering the fee I'd promised Perez. I stuffed the other two grand I'd brought with me into my sock. The anticipation of the coke had me giddy. As I waited, memories of Parker and I making love came flooding back. That scene played like a sweet song in my head.

Finally a burgundy Range Rover, music blaring, came speeding into the parking lot followed by a black S300 Mercedes Benz with extra dark tinted windows. They circled twice until they spotted my rental. The driver's side window of the Range rolled down.

The driver nodded. "Whaddup, homie?"

I nodded back. "What up?"

"Yo, go through the drive-thru. My man's gonna get out and give you what you need. You got that paper?"

I nodded.

Just as we'd planned, I placed my order and when I was about to pay, Perez jumped in the passenger side.

"Give me the money," Perez demanded.

"Show me the shit," I barked back.

He looked around for a moment and hesitated. "Are you sure you're not po-po?"

I looked at him and his eyes showed fear. Briefly, I wondered what had led him to this life. He certainly wasn't built to face what would surely be his future—death or incarceration—if he kept up his current occupation. He probably had a family to feed, or maybe he just liked flashy things, or the job made him feel important. Maybe even a combination of all three. Whatever his motivation, I just hoped he realized the consequences. I had been there, done that, and got the soundtrack.

Four years ago, I was a successful attorney on the come-up. I had a beautiful wife, stable career, and a clean home. I was living the American Dream and I threw it all away practically overnight. Choices were a motherfucker.

"I'm the last man you'd ever need to fear as an undercover cop. I'm just an ordinary man who's a bit wound up. You feel me?" I gave him my trademark grin.

He relaxed. "I feel you."

After the transaction, I sped off. I drove for about ten minutes before I pulled over on Atlantic Avenue, next to the Atlantic Mall, and took my first hit. I inhaled the white, powdery substance into my eager nose, closed my eyes, and sunk into my seat. Within five minutes I felt euphoric. I was absolutely elated! A huge grin plastered my face and suddenly I wanted to dance. I flipped through a number of stations before landing on Hot 97.1. Funkmaster Flex was counting down the Top Eight at Eight. I began bobbing my head to "Crazy" by Gnarls Barkley.

I revved up the engine and drove back over the Brooklyn Bridge toward Manhattan and my hotel. Flex had switched to "Ridin'" by Chamillionaire and I began to laugh hysterically. I hadn't felt this good in a long time—a very long time. I decided that I couldn't wait to get inside my hotel room to take another hit. I wanted to keep the good feelings going.

I pulled over on 23rd Street and the Westside Highway and sniffed two bags back to back. My mind raced. I missed Nikki. I could feel her soft body and long legs wrapped around my waist as I sucked her ripe nipples. I decided that I would go back to Italy tomorrow.

As I cruised down the highway toward The Plaza, I pulled over frequently to sniff my cocaine. When I arrived at the hotel an hour later, I'd gone through all ten bags. No longer did I have the energy of a man half my age. Instantly I was drowsy and staggered into the lobby.

"Good evening, sir," the doorman announced. As he observed my demeanor, he asked, "Are you OK? Do you need to be escorted to your room?"

Vehemently, I shook my head. "No, thank you. I can manage." I stumbled to the elevator and barely managed to press the number to my floor.

Once inside my room, I collapsed on the bed. Four hours later, I jolted awake from my extremely deep yet short sleep. I had to almost pry my pasty mouth open. I'd never had a reaction like that to cocaine before and even though it had been a long time, something felt different. I leaped out of bed and checked all of my pockets, although I knew that what I was looking for wasn't there. It was one o'clock in the morning when I made my journey back into Brooklyn.

If I was certain about one thing, it was that I hadn't been sold cocaine.

Thank God, Perez was still outside. He looked just about ready to leave when I honked my horn. He spun around quizzically and then smiled as he approached my car.

"Listen, wwww-what was that you ssss-sold me?" My voice slurred and I found it hard to keep my eyes open. It was a miracle that I had made it across the bridge.

"Yo, that was good shit, right? I told you."

Again, I repeated, "What wwww-was it?"

"It was that Black Magic."

"Black Magic?" I frowned. "Is that a new kind of coke?"

Perez snorted. "Ahh, nah, my man didn't have any more coke. He don't really fuck with that shit. That was smack. Grade-A heroin."

Jesus, Mary, and Joseph! I knew it. "I fucking trusted you, you fucking idiot! Do you know what you've done?!"

"Watch your fucking mouth!" he demanded. "I'll knock your little white ass out!"

He began to walk away.

"Hold up!" I yelled. I felt the jones coming down something awful. "Can I get another bundle?"

Joshua Tune

The succession of loud, thunderous knocks jarred me back into reality. I heard an unfamiliar voice call out, "Mr. Mathis, please release the safety latch."

I sat up in bed and looked around. I needed to get my bearings. Where was I? Wherever I was, the room was in shambles. I had half-eaten burgers and fries, melted ice cream, cakes, and cookies, and dirty clothes strewn all over the floor. The blinding sun streamed through open drapes and now the incessant banging was more than I could bear.

I leaped from the bed in an effort to quiet the noise. I unloosened the safety latch and flung open the door. I wasn't paying attention to the fact that I was stark naked.

"Yes, may I help you?"

Two men stood in the doorway. Both were well dressed in suits and ties, but one had a more dangerous demeanor. They both looked down at my family jewels and quickly looked away. "Mr. Mathis, I'm George Leventhal, the manager of this hotel," the less dangerous man said. "This is Peter Assam, head of hotel security."

"Uh, hello," I replied. Why were the hotel manager and hotel security bothering me at this time of the morning?

"Sir, we've been calling your room all morning. I'm sorry to disturb you, but you have an outstanding balance on your room that we need to collect."

I shrugged. "Charge it to my credit card." Nikki had managed to get both of us credit cards in the names of our fugitive aliases shortly after we arrived in Italy. This was my first time using mine.

"Well, that's the problem, sir. We've tried and it's been declined."

Declined? Was Nikki so mad about my return to New York that she had gotten the card cut off? "OK, I'll be down later to straighten this out." I tried to close the door, but Mr. Assam stuck his foot in the door to keep me from doing so.

"I'm afraid there will be no later, Mr. Mathis," Mr. Leventhal said. "We've been getting complaints from our other guests that you're keeping them up at odd hours with your television, women guests, and strange noises." He assumed a disappointed expression. "Combined with the decline of your credit card, we have no choice but to ask you to settle your balance and check out today."

What the fuck? Women guests, strange noises, blaring TV? I didn't have any memory of this type of behavior. It was totally unlike me, even if I was glad to be back in New York.

"Well, I'm booked for four days. You can't just kick me out if I can pay my bill. I'll give you cash if there's a problem with the credit card. I have a flight back to Italy on Saturday."

Mr. Leventhal looked at me strangely. "You've already extended your original four-day stay. You've been here for two weeks."

Two weeks? "I . . . ah . . . yes, I know that. I meant that I wanted to extend my stay again, for another four days."

"You have to leave now, Mr. Mathis." He managed a smile. "And reconcile your balance, which is $4,931."

The next thing I knew, I was being shaken awake.

"Mr. Mathis? Sir? Mr. Mathis! Can you hear me? Sir!" Mr. Leventhal looked at me with concern. Mr. Assam, however, gave me a cool look. "Are you all right? Do we need to call a doctor?"

"Huh? What? What's going on?" I felt so groggy that I just wanted to go back to bed.

"Your bill, Mr. Mathis. You need to make payment. Now. Do you have another credit card?"

They pushed me into the room and followed behind me. Mr. Leventhal directed me to the bed, then looked around the room in disgust, although he tried to keep it from his expression.

"Do you mind putting on some clothes, Mr. Mathis?"

I looked down at my naked body. "Umm, yes, of course." I gave an embarrassed chuckle.

I hastily located a pair of boxers on the floor and slipped them on. I ran into the bathroom and splashed water on my face. When I looked in the mirror, I almost didn't recognize myself. My whole face was puffy. I had instantly aged ten years.

I came back to the room a bit more clearheaded, but still groggy and confused about the apparently wild turn of events. "Now, how much is my bill again?"

"$4,931, sir."

I swallowed hard. "Let me see that." I gestured for the bill, which Mr. Leventhal handed over in its leather portfolio.

I reviewed the bill with a frown. Two weeks' worth of room charges, plus room service. And I had no recollection of any of it. "One moment, please. I have the cash to cover the bill." I went to the closet to dip into my stash of cash, only it was no more. For an instant I thought I'd been robbed until I found a half-bundle of smack underneath a few hundred-dollar bills. A quick count of the money showed that I had just over a thousand dollars left.

This couldn't be real.

"Sir?" Mr. Leventhal asked.

"Jeez, stop fucking whining already!" I yelled. "How could you allow my bill to get so fucking high without coming to me earlier? You think money grows on trees?"

"Mr. Mathis," Mr. Assam said in a deceptively calm voice, "if you don't lower your voice, I'll be forced to detain you until the authorities come. You have two minutes to pay this bill and thirty minutes to vacate the premises."

Reluctantly I handed Mr. Leventhal the remainder of my money. He counted the cash and said, "While we appreciate this attempt to settle your bill, we'll need the balance within the hour. If we don't have payment in full, we will call the authorities and have you arrested for grand larceny." He cleared his throat. "We'd rather not have to resort to such measures, Mr. Mathis, as we feel they would be totally unnecessary."

"They won't be necessary. My wife will call the front desk with her credit card number."

Mr. Leventhal looked at Mr. Assam and nodded. "Very well, sir. I hope you've enjoyed your stay at The Plaza Hotel." They turned to leave, but not before Mr. Assam gave me a pointed look.

Once the door closed, I panicked. What the hell happened? Why couldn't I remember? And what was I going to do for money, since I gave Mr. Leventhal the last of what I had on me? Parker! Parker will give me some money.

I picked up the phone to call her and my eyes lit on her obituary, which rested on the nightstand. Memories came flooding back. I had received a phone call from a hospice nurse. Parker's cancer had been worse than she let on. It was so far gone, and spread so rapidly, that she'd gone downhill shortly after I saw her and was not expected to last a week. She went into a hospice on Friday, the day before I was to fly back to Italy. She died on Sunday. I immediately went back to East New York to find Perez and some more Black Magic. And that was all I remembered until Mr. Leventhal and his well-dressed goon banged on my door this morning.

I didn't know what else to do. I reached for the telephone and made the international phone call, praying that Nikkisi would keep her wrath contained until after she bailed me out.

"Matt?"

"Nikki!"

"Joshua? What's wrong, baby?"

"Nik, baby, I need you! I need you, kid," I screamed into the phone. My heart was palpitating from fear.

"Oh, my God! What's happened?"

"The money . . . Parker is . . . and then I . . . and when . . ."

"Joshua, slow down," Nikki ordered. "You're not making sense. Slow down and tell me what's wrong."

"Parker's dead and I've run out of mone—"

"All of it? In two weeks?" she screamed.

"Nikki, please." I swallowed. "I'm going to get arrested."

"What?" she shrieked. "Where are you?"

"I'm at The Plaza Hotel, and I owe them another three grand. They're calling the authorities."

"The Plaza? Where . . . what . . . Joshua, where are you calling me from?"

"My hotel room."

"Are you crazy? Don't you know that if anything happens to you, they will trace the call? If you get busted, then so will I, and then it will only be a few days before they find me! Italy has a solid extradition treaty with the U.S. How could you do this to me?"

"It's always about only you!" I exploded. "You're a selfish bitch, and I'm calling because I need you!" I took a deep breath and pressed the receiver against my forehead. "Nikki, help me! What should I do?"

"Leave the fucking hotel, Einstein!" Click.

She hung up. I had begged for her help, and she hung up on me. I looked at the clock on the nightstand. I had thirty minutes before Mr. Leventhal returned to check on me, and Mr. Assam would more than likely be with him. I had to get out of there now.

I tossed the rest of my things into the duffel bag that once held the hundred thousand dollars, and I took the stairs down to the basement level where I crept into the garage. After a scary fifteen minutes I found my car, managed to find enough money in my wallet to bribe the valets to say they had not seen me, got my keys, and drove carefully out of the garage. I looked to my left and then to my right—no signs of police. I was in the clear. For the moment.

Nikki Ling

I touched down at LaGuardia Airport in a fit of nerves. As furious as I was with Joshua for getting himself in this position—and, therefore, getting me in this position—I was worried about him. I heard the panic in his voice and wondered about its origin. Joshua could only take the weight of certain things, and if this Parker thing turned out to be true, it may have sent him over the edge, and that was not a good thing. Joshua had managed to kick a cocaine habit shortly before we met, and while he'd managed to stay clean for the entire three years we'd been together, I always knew in the back of my mind that it wouldn't take much to get him back on the white.

I watched the seatbelt sign turn off and I stood to retrieve my carry-on suitcase from the overhead compartment in first class. An older gentleman in the seat on the opposite side of the aisle rushed to get it down for me. I shot him a grateful smile as I wheeled the suitcase off the plane. The flight attendants gave me a warm goodbye. I walked off the plane and into the concourse, nerves taut, sweat trickling down my spine. So far, my fake passport as Molly Mathis had held up nicely, and my surgically altered appearance certainly didn't match any picture the police or FBI would have in their databases of Nikkisi Ling, fugitive murderess. I made it through the airport and to the taxi stand without incident and breathed a sigh of relief.

"The Plaza Hotel, please," I instructed the taxi driver. He nodded and pulled off. Thirty minutes later I was at the hotel. Under normal circumstances I would have gone in and inquired of his whereabouts, but since Joshua had skipped out on his bill, the heat would immediately turn up on me as his wife. How was I supposed to know where Joshua was now? We didn't have any cell phones here in the United States. How could I find him?

"Wait here," I instructed the cabbie and gave him twenty dollars as incentive. I got out and walked until I passed the entrance to the hotel garage. Two valets sat around talking. They barely glanced at me until I walked up to them. "Excuse me," I said.

The taller of the two stopped the conversation. "Yes?"

"I'm looking for a man that was here yesterday. White guy, about five nine, brown hair, slim build." I pulled two twenty-dollar bills out of my purse and held them up in the air.

The men began to jabber in what I figured was an Ethiopian language before the shorter one answered. "Oh, him. Yeah, he was here yesterday," he said in accented yet clear English. "He said that you might stop by."

Fear froze my insides. "He said that I might stop by?"

"Yes," the taller one added. "He said that his wife might stop by and ask questions about him. He left this for you." He pulled out a folded piece of paper and gave it to me.

I quickly unfolded it and read. The note simply said Bourne Identity. It was cryptic to anyone who didn't know Joshua and our history, but it made perfect sense to me.

"Thank you," I said to the two valets. I gave them each a twenty and returned to the cab. "Sunlight Cinema on Twelfth Street, please," I told the cabbie.

Once I arrived at the theatre I bought a ticket to the latest action flick and entered the darkened theatre. Joshua loved action flicks. I examined one theater, then left and examined another one where there was another action flick playing. I found him near the back, in the corner, clutching a large duffel bag, his eyes glued to the screen. I slid into the seat next to him. "Joshua?" I whispered.

He jumped, then peered closely at me. "Nikki?"

"Hey, baby."

"Oh, my God! Nikki!" He hugged me fiercely. "I'm so glad you're here!"

"What is going on, Joshua? I'm so worried."

"It's been too much, Nikki." He wiped his nose with the back of his hand. My intuition kicked up a notch as I wondered if my suspicions were correct. "Parker's dead."

I closed my eyes and said a quick prayer for her spirit. "When?"

"I guess two weeks ago. I saw her the day I came in, and she went downhill right after that. She died the day after I was supposed to come back to Italy."

I nodded. "What then?"

Joshua turned his attention back to the screen. "Um . . . I don't remember," he said sheepishly.

"Why don't you remember, Joshua?" When he remained silent, I hissed, "Are you back on that shit again?"

"I just needed a little to get me through," he said defensively. "This has been a tough time for me."

"Joshua, you can't afford to make mistakes like that! You are still wanted for aiding and abetting a fugitive, obstruction of justice, and a whole lot of stuff they can just make up as they go along. You need to be clear-headed right about now." He hung his head and I sighed. Joshua was just a little boy in a man's body. If anyone needed a keeper, it was him. "So what are you going to do?"

"I don't know." He wiped his nose again. "I mean, I want to go back to Italy." He looked at me. "Do you have any money?"

I nodded. "I have enough to get us back to Italy but, Joshua, what ID did you use at the hotel?"

"The Matthew Mathis one."

Shit. If the hotel reported Joshua's skip to the police, a warrant in the name of Matthew Mathis would be issued. And even though the crime was petty, anyone going through Customs using the name Matthew Mathis would be flagged, which meant that he—and possibly I—wouldn't be able to get through the security checkpoints.

I only had nine thousand dollars with me, but I'd made a risky, quick decision while back in Italy. I couldn't leave over a half million dollars hidden in an unattended apartment, not knowing if it would be safe or if we'd even go back to Italy, so I had FedEx overnight the money to the Marriott by the LaGuardia Airport in Queens, where I'd booked a room. I had to do this because you couldn't travel with more than ten thousand dollars and since September 11, security at airports was heightened. With FedEx, they only scanned the packages and had dogs sniff for bombs and drugs. Unless they lost my packages, I should have all my money by the next day. From there I'd buy Joshua and me new passports and we'd take flight to another continent, preferably South Africa.

"Well, we can't fly out of New York right now. I'm having our money shipped overnight by FedEx—"

"Is that safe?"

"Did I have a choice?"

Joshua shrugged.

"We'll need to lay low for a few days until we get new IDs, and then fly out of here. I've booked a room at the Marriott in Queens. Come on, let's go."

The next morning, when I woke up, Joshua wasn't there. I looked at the mahogany desk near the window and saw that his bag of food from last night was still untouched. Where the hell could he be? I jumped up, ran to my purse, and looked for the small makeup bag I carried, into which I'd shoved about seven thousand dollars of the money I'd brought with me. The makeup bag was empty.

"Damn you, Joshua!" I said aloud as I sat back in anger and disappointment. He'd stolen from me to cop drugs. How dare he? I risked my neck to fly across the damn globe to bail out his ass, and he repaid me by taking my money and using it to buy drugs. Oh hell no. I was just glad I'd had the foresight to keep the rest of my money in my bra and panties, and I'd slept in them both last night. I had a feeling that Joshua might pull some shit like this. If my money didn't arrive safely via FedEx from Italy, my life would be over.

I must have called down to the front desk eight times asking if I had any packages, only to be continually told no. I hopped online and put in my tracking numbers, and it stated that one package was signed for two hours ago. But where were my other two? The only information was that they were still in transit.

I charged downstairs and tried to remain calm.

"Hi"—I read her name tag—"Gloria. My name is Mrs. Mathis. I'm in room 2024. I've been calling regarding three important packages."

"Yes, I've told you that they haven't arrived," she stated dismissively.

"Where's your manager?"

She looked up from her computer impatiently. "My manager will tell you the same thing I'm telling you. Your packages haven't arrived. When they do someone will buzz your room."

I was frantic. Had my packages arrived and were inadvertently opened? Was my money stolen? I began to perspire. A light film coated my underarms and swept across my forehead.

"I reed to speak to your manager. Now!"

The elderly black woman turned around and proceeded toward the back. A few moments later she came out with a handsome, thirtyish looking white male. She pointed toward me. "She needs you, but I already told her that her packages haven't arrived."

"Sir, I'm expecting important documents for an early morning meeting that were over-nighted from Italy," I said. "I've called your front desk continually and spoken to Miss . . . ummm . . . Gloria, and she keeps telling me that they didn't arrive. Only I've tracked the packages and they arrived hours ago."

"I'm sorry for your inconvenience, Mrs. Mathis. I'll take a look." He punched in a few things while keeping his eyes glued to the scene. Then he turned toward Gloria. "Her package did arrive as she states."

"Let me see." Gloria looked at the screen as if it would tell her something different.

"Mrs. Mathis, I'm sorry for your inconvenience. What can I do to make your stay at the Marriott more comfortable?" the manager asked.

"You can get my other packages."

"Well only one arrived, and"—he paused—"Gloria, go get her package. It states you're here for two days, Mrs. Mathis. I'll comp one of your days for your troubles. Would that be OK?"

"That would be nice. Thank." I didn't care about a free night. I cared about my money.

Once upstairs in my room, I ripped open my box and it contained the few remnants from my past that I couldn't stand to part with: Noki's Kokeshi doll my mother had bought her, the torn picture of Noki as a child, pictures of Joshua and I pre-plastic surgery, and greeting cards. Now faced with being broke, those items didn't mean as much to me at the moment. I needed the other two boxes, the boxes that contained my money.

After being on the telephone with FedEx for over an hour, they assured me that they were tracking my packages, and as soon as they located them, they would either send them to the Marriott, or if I checked out, I could pick up the packages at a FedEx location. If I didn't pick them up, then they would be returned to Italy. I was livid. Why was it that whenever something could go wrong, it did?

Nikkisi Ling

I stayed at the Marriott until my credit card was drained, which took about two weeks with me running up a heavy room service bill. On the eve before I checked out, Joshua came strolling back as if he knew I'd sit around and wait on him. He was sadly mistaken. Had I had my money, his return to the Marriott would have been in vain.

As I sat watching *Thelma and Louise* on HBO, I heard a faint tap on the door. I glanced at the clock—three-ten PM. Housekeeping had come and gone early this morning.

"Who is it?" I asked.

"It's me, Matt."

"Go away!"

Tap, tap, tap, tap, bang, bang bang!

"I said go away!"

"Come on, Nik! Open the fucking door. Jesus, Mary, and Joseph, I'm tired! Don't make me make a scene!"

Sonuvabitch! I flung open the door and stared at a pitiful sight. Not only did he look horrible, he smelled even worse. As much as I wanted to scratch out his eyes and spit in his face, I couldn't. He was my man and he needed me.

The next morning we left the Marriott and rented a room at a small motel, Executive Motor Inn off the Belt Parkway in Springfield Gardens, Queens that accepted cash and didn't ask too many questions. The room was barely adequate, but it would have to do. We were only going to be there a few days, hopefully, until FedEx found my packages. I got a cell phone and gave my telephone number to the customer service representative from FedEx so she could call me as soon as my packages were located. I had to believe that they would be found. My livelihood depended on it.

Joshua took a look around and curled his lip in disgust. I shook my head as I tucked our bags away in the miniscule alcove for clothes. We were not too far from my old neighborhood, and memories of Noki, Kayla, and my mother came crashing back through the wall I'd built in my mind to keep them at bay.

While Joshua crashed on the bed, I went into the surrounding neighborhood to get us something to eat. I placed my order and waited on the bench next to a young girl who favored the late singer Aaliyah. She sat with her head down, staring at the grime on the floor. When she looked up briefly as I sat down, my heart lurched. Something in her eyes reminded me of Noki.

Soon her order was called and she went to the bulletproof window to retrieve it. I saw her slowly count out some crumpled dollar bills and change, then dig deeper into her pockets. When she turned slightly to look in her purse, I noticed the panicked expression. Apparently she didn't have enough money to pay for her food. The person behind the glass eyed her warily, his hand on the turnstile as if to spin it back around and take back her food. I felt sorry for this young girl for some reason. I stood and walked up to the window.

"Add this to my order," I instructed the man behind the window. I slid him a twenty-dollar bill and he nodded, then slid my change back to me via the turnstile. The girl looked at me with gratitude.

"Thank you," she whispered as she grabbed her food.

"You're welcome." I watched as she gave me a shy smile and left the restaurant. Soon my order was ready and I returned with it to the motel where Joshua was still asleep. I ate my food and thought again about the girl, and Noki, and things that happened that shouldn't have, but did. When Joshua still didn't wake up, I went to sleep.

I had no idea where he went to cop, or when he'd get back, so I got dressed and went back out to get something to eat. I'd bypassed the Chinese restaurant when someone came out of a doorway and ran into me. I stumbled and grabbed the other person to right myself, and realized that it was the same girl from the Chinese restaurant. Her eyes were still worried, and in broad daylight I could see her rounded belly sticking out slightly.

"Excuse m—oh!" She recognized me. "You're the lady from last night, the one who paid for my food."

"Yeah, that's me."

"I really appreciate your help. I didn't have enough money on me. I'd left the rest of it at home on my dresser."

I accepted the lie for what it was and played along. "No problem. I do that sometimes." I looked over at the writing on the window of the store she'd just exited—B&G Pawn Shop. "Hey, I was going to get some breakfast. You want to join me?" I asked. When I saw her hesitate, I said, "It's my treat."

"You don't have to buy me another meal," she protested.

"Don't worry about it," I said. My mothering instinct, which had been honed by practically raising Noki, told me that the girl needed to be treated to a few meals. She didn't look any older than eighteen, but the story in her eyes said something else.

She nodded. "OK. Thank you. I know a good place."

"Great."

"I don't even know your name."

"It's Molly."

"Hi, Molly. I'm Lisa."

"Nice to meet you," we said in unison, then laughed.

We walked three blocks until we reached a diner. I ordered sausages, scrambled eggs, hash browns, toast, and coffee, and sipped the latter as I looked around. The girl gave an identical order, except she had bacon instead of sausages. We both sipped coffee, lost in our own thoughts. I looked at her and once again was reminded of my late sister Noki.

"When are you due?" I asked.

"December." She smiled, but a tear ran down her cheek. "I'm sorry," she said as she took a napkin from the dispenser on the table and wiped her face.

"You look like you could use a friend."

The tears came faster. "I used to have a friend, a best friend, like my sister. She was shot and killed last year."

"I'm sorry to hear that. I know what it's like to lose a sister."

The girl sniffed and looked into my face. "Really?"

I nodded.

"What happened?"

"She was in a motorcycle accident."

"Damn. That's messed up. You know I'm really not an emotional person, but I guess it's my hormones."

"Yeah, you might be right about that."

The waitress brought our orders, refilled our coffee, and we began to eat. I figured that she wanted to talk but didn't know how to start, so I tried to start it off for her. "Do you know if your baby is a boy or a girl?"

"I don't know yet. On one hand, I hope it's a girl. But on the other hand, I kind of wish it's a boy."

"What does the father want?"

The sad look crossed her face again as she played with her eggs. "He doesn't know," she said finally.

"Oh." I took a sip of my coffee. It was really none of my business, but her tale was more common than people thought, especially in this neighborhood.

"Right now I'm transitioning and trying to raise enough money to get a place for me and my father," she said. "I'm renting a room from a homeowner a few blocks over."

"That's good. Family is important."

"Yeah."

We didn't say much more as we finished our breakfast. I paid the bill and we walked outside. She turned to me and said, "Thank you for breakfast." She laughed slightly. "I hope to see you around again."

"I'm only in town for a few days, but maybe I'll see you before I go."

"OK." She gave a slight wave and walked away, her gait giving away her pregnant state. I figured she lived somewhere in the neighborhood and silently wished her well. I turned around and headed back to the motel, hoping that Joshua had returned.

PART II

SERIES OF BAD DECISIONS

Lisa Henderson

1996–Age Ten

People often think I'm telling a tall tale when I state that I can remember my childhood from as early as age three, but it's true. I remember the good, but mostly the bad.

I grew up in a lower middle-class neighborhood. My father was an accountant for the city, and was also in the Marine reserves after serving his country for six years. My mother was a housewife, or at least that was what she was supposed to be. My long list of chores enabled her to sit around and watch soap operas all day. That left me, my brother John, and my sister Jackie to look out for each other.

My mother always had a lingering resentment toward me. Her eyes always stared with disdain when she thought no one was looking. I knew she hated me, and although I loved her, I had no choice but to hate her right back. The ongoing joke—or it would be, if it were funny—was that I was the milkman's baby. Instead of leaving milk, he left me on the doorstep of my parents' home. As a child this never made sense to me because we bought our milk from the store. Nobody ever came by the house and brought it to us. However, I used to privately wonder as I grew older if I was indeed my father's child, because I was the lightest in my immediate family. Now that was ironic—I had the lightest skin, but I was the black sheep.

From day one, I always had to fight for my rights. Being the youngest of three, my ass stayed getting whipped. The behavior of my brother and sister wasn't too alarming. We were kids, and we were siblings, so fighting was normal. It was my mother, Julie, who hurt me the most. To say she had a temper was putting it mildly. She always felt that the best way to deal with disobedient kids was at full volume, accompanied by a choice sprinkling of curses and cutting remarks. She had issues with me that she never had any qualms about explaining with the sharp sting of her belt or the heavy pound of a closed fist. Even though I was young, I knew something wasn't right about my relationship with my mom. My Auntie Brenda, on my father's side, simply said, "There was your father, your mother, and two children—a boy and a girl. Then you came along and spoiled your mother's American dream." She sighed. "I'm telling you, your mother is crazy!"

I wasn't quite sure what Auntie Brenda meant about my mother being crazy, but whatever it was, it was enough to cause my father to seek company elsewhere. His relationship with a woman—I later learned her name was Michelle—made him leave me, my mother, Jackie, and John to live with her for two years. Then one day Daddy showed up in our house again like nothing happened, and our life went on like it was before. Well, not quite like it was before. Mama gave him an extra hard time for a while, and he bought all of us all kinds of gifts like jewelry, flowers, toys, candy, and clothes. So in a way, life was better than before he left us, so good that I hoped that it would stay that way forever.

I remembered the fights between my parents, and being violently awakened from my sleep with bouts of yelling and screaming. I feared for my life as I heard doors being slammed and fixtures being broken.

My worst memory, though, was of the time when my father and mother separated for the second and final time. I was ten years old and tired of their grown-up shenanigans. Once again, my parents' shouts woke me from a sound sleep. A huge knot formed in my throat as I stared at the ceiling and listened to them having yet another argument. They'd been back together for two years, and I was afraid that they were breaking up yet again. I looked at the big red letters on the digital clock on my nightstand—2:45 am. I looked over at Jackie in the other twin bed. She was sleeping fitfully, as she usually did, and I didn't want to wake her. When she was asleep, I had a little bit of peace.

Quietly I slid off my bed and crawled to my bedroom door, which was cracked open. The hallway light was on, illuminating the second floor and I could see that my parents' door was slightly ajar. They weren't even trying to whisper. The heat of their argument had escalated and their tones increased.

"We can't keep the house because I can't make mortgage payments from where I'll be," my father stated.

"What am I supposed to do with three kids and no money?" my mother shot back. "Where are we going to live? I don't have a job. I don't know how to do anything except be a wife and mother!"

"Julie, calm down. This will all blow over—"

"Blow over? You'll be away for seven years!" My mother's voice bounced up and down the hallway.

I heard my father's heavy footsteps pacing their room. "You don't have to remind me of the obvious," he snapped. "I've always taken care of my family and when I get back, things will return back to the way they were. I've always kept a roof over your and my children's heads, haven't I?"

My mother was not appeased. "That's what you promised to do

when I married you. You're my husband!"

His footsteps stopped. "That I am," my father agreed, "and as my wife, I'll expect your loyalty while I'm away."

My mother snorted. "Loyalty? Don't come in here preaching about loyalty! Where was your loyalty when you left your wife and kids for a girl half my age?"

My father's footsteps started up again. "Don't start that again. No matter where I went, I always took care of you. Neither you nor my children ever wanted for anything!"

"They wanted for their father," my mother screeched. "And I wanted for my husband! This isn't about money!"

A heavy sigh. "Look, Julie, the past is the past. I can't change anything. I'm just asking that you keep our family together until I come back, and I promise you that I'll buy you an even bigger house when I come home."

My mother's screeches turned to screams. "Now everything is all about me? Now that the stupid, young slut you were fucking—"

"Watch your mouth!" my father hissed. "Don't wake the kids!"

"I'm not doing a motherfucking thing!"

I huddled near the door, filled with anxiety. I'd never heard my mother speak to my father like that before.

"Now it's all about family values because that trick-ass bitch won't hold you down while you're away," my mother continued. "You done tricked off all your money on her and now you're broke! You didn't even save anything for your kids! Now I gotta go back to the fucking projects and get on welfare to put food in my kids' mouths, and you talking as if I should just understand?" Drawers slammed, doors slammed. The room was a flurry of unseen movement.

"I never loved her."

My mother snorted. "Oh, really? You put that bitch in a three-bedroom colonial! If that's not love, I'd like to see what you do for bitches you just like." She paused dramatically. "Oh, that's right, you leave them and your kids for other women."

My father was suddenly very quiet, so my mother continued. "Oh, you didn't think I knew about the house you bought her? I also know that she's moved on. Used you for all you had and kicked your old, wrinkled ass to the curb!"

"Julie, you have a right to be angry, so I'll let you disrespect me." He sounded weary, like he did when he'd come home from a long day at work. "The only thing I can do is promise you that when I come back home, I'll make it all up to you. You can believe me or not. All I need to know is, will you be there for me? That's all I want to know."

It was my mother's turn to be silent. "Do you love me?" she finally asked.

"Of course I do," my father assured her.

Soon my parents were making grown-up noises. I crawled back into my bed and began to cry. Here we go again, I thought.

Five weeks later my father was gone again, but not before he helped us move out of our house—the house I'd grown up in these past ten years—and into my grandmother's two-bedroom Marcy Projects apartment. Uncle Billy, my mother's brother, wasn't too happy about the move. He lived with Nana, and there was barely enough room for the two of them. In fact, no one was happy. We weren't moving on up like the Jeffersons. We were heading into Good Times territory—literally. That small, cramped, low-budget apartment would be the setting of plenty of arguments and fights, and it would take my life in a direction I'd never anticipated.

Once all our bags of clothing were stuffed into Nana's apartment, my siblings and I huddled together in the living room. We were afraid to sit down. Nana's attitude wasn't exactly welcoming.

"What y'all standin' 'round here lookin' foolish for?" Nana screamed. "Git in here and start unpacking this shit!"

"Yes, ma'am," we said in unison and then skulked into the small bedroom that once belonged to Uncle Billy.

Uncle Billy's new bed was the living room sofa. Although Uncle Billy graciously offered us the room, my mother said that he didn't have a choice. She told us that when Uncle Billy protested at the thought of giving up his room, Nana brought him back to reality.

"Your room?" she asked him. "You ain't paid no rent since you been here, so technically it ain't your room. It's my room, and I can do with it what I please. Now move your shit so them children can put theirs in there." Uncle Billy apparently quit his whining—at least to Nana's face—and did as he was told.

I guess I really didn't pay any attention to the two twin beds in our bedroom until it was nearly bedtime. My mother went into the hallway storage closet and retrieved an extra twin bed—what my Nana called a cot—and rolled it into our room. We all showered and began to pile into the twin beds.

When I climbed into the bed that I assumed I'd be sharing with my sister Jackie, she snarled, "You not sleeping in this little itty bitty bed with me! Your big feet and head would take up all the room!"

"Lisa, you're sleeping in the room with Nana," my mother explained.

"What? But why?" I whined. Being in this situation was bad enough, and Jackie could be really mean, but she was at least familiar. I needed all of the familiarity that I could get.

"Why do you always got to question everything I say? Just go in the other room!" Her deep voice resonated throughout the small apartment.

"But I don't wanna sleep with Nana. Why can't I sleep with Jackie, or you?"

"Because I said so!" my mother screamed. "That's why!"

I rolled my eyes. "It's not fair—"

Her hand landed against my cheek and snapped my head back. I lashed out in anger and began punching her. My mother picked up my lanky body and tossed me onto the hard, cold floor. My bottom lip split open upon impact with the dirty tile and I swallowed blood. I screamed in agony as I continued to kick and fight my mother, letting loose my pent-up frustrations of Daddy leaving us, and us leaving our nice house to go to this godforsaken place. But I was only ten and my fists were no match for my mother, plus my father wasn't around anymore to regulate her beatings. She punched and slapped me until her arms were tired, and then she got her belt to finish what she started. Through my pain-induced haze, I heard Jackie egging on my mother.

"Get her, Mama!" she yelled with glee in her voice. "It's good for her."

"She's too grown," John added from his bed. "She needs her butt beat."

Finally Nana came to save me.

"Now that's enough," she stated with a stern look at my mother. "You better stop beating on that chile like that. You want ACS to come here and lock us all up?"

"I'ma kill this girl one day," my mother threatened. "I swear to God, I'ma kill her!"

Nana shook her head and pulled me off the floor. "Chile, git your stupid ass in here and take your tail to bed. 'Cause if I hafta git my belt, I'ma show you what an ass whipping is really like!"

Bloody, bruised, yet still defiant, I ran into the bathroom and locked myself in. I looked in the mirror and was horrified. My right eye was almost closed shut. Blood crusted my swollen lips from cuts inside my mouth from where my teeth made deep contact with the insides of my cheeks. I took off my pajamas and saw that every inch of my body was discolored with marks. A tear crept down my face. Where was my daddy when I needed him?

No one bothered to knock on the door and beg me to come out. At first I sat on the toilet bowl and watched the roaches crawl up and down the dingy walls. When my back began hurting, I slumped on the floor until I got tired of my head hitting the side of the toilet when I nodded off to sleep. Finally I crawled into the bathtub, but the constant drip of the faucet water kept me awake. Hours later I gave up and came out of the bathroom. I should have stayed in there because my punishment got worse. Instead of sleeping with Nana, my bed became three kitchen chairs set closely together with a makeshift mattress made out of old rags and pillows. That was where I'd sleep that night, and most nights thereafter.

Lisa Henderson

2001–Age Fifteen

I wouldn't say that living in the projects had hardened me. I was already a tough girl. I had to be in order to survive my mother. I would say that my new address helped hone my rebellious attitude. At school I'd joined the debate team and my new hobby was debating the whole household whenever I felt that I was being treated unfairly.

I came home from school one day on cloud nine because I had gotten As on all of my tests, only to be told I had to go food shopping with food stamps! I knew we didn't have much money, and that food stamps were a necessary evil, but still, the stigma of being on government assistance was too much for me to deal with directly. Even though paper food stamps had long since been replaced with the EBT debit card, I still felt shame whenever I went to the store for my mother. I felt like people were staring me down when I swiped the card through the reader. Like they knew.

"Why do I always have to go?" I whined. "Why can't Jackie or John go?"

"Don't question me!" my mother screamed. She'd begun smoking again, and her inner ugliness was now enhanced by her bedraggled outer appearance.

The truth of the matter was that my mother was too proud to use the EBT card. She had always lorded her good fortune over her old cronies in the Marcy Projects, where she grew up, so many were quite gleeful about her apparent downfall. Using the EBT card was yet another painful reminder that our father was gone and she couldn't hold things together as well as she thought she could. Of course, my mother would never allow my brother John to do grocery shopping because "that wasn't a man's place," and he was the "acting man of the family" until my father came home from the Marines. Yes, she still explained his absence as being due to his military duty, although I was starting to suspect otherwise.

"But, Ma, I can't understand why I'm always chosen for the humiliating tasks. This is embarrassing!" As a result of the debate team, which awakened in me a pleasure for reading, my diction and vocabulary were much more polished than one usually heard in Marcy. I loved throwing around big words. They made me sound smart, and I knew that my family wouldn't understand much of what I said. It was a small sense of power, but it was big enough for me at that time.

"What?" My mother stared at me in disbelief.

"Why do I have to be the one charged with the unpleasant tasks? I mean, if you don't like being seen using the EBT card, then why can't you go in the early morning when people are at work or school, since you're not working? Nobody would see you then."

Unemployment was yet another sore spot with my mother, especially since Nana was on her case every day about getting a job. My mother's nostrils flared with rage. "Who the hell are you to question me and what I do? Girl, I will smack you into next week!"

I swallowed the small lump of fear in my throat and pressed on with the determination of the self-righteous. "Why are you always using violence to solve your problems? Especially with me? You're nothing but a bull—"

I didn't get to finish my sentence. It was hard to talk after the force of my mother's hand sent my head banging into a nearby cabinet. I tasted blood. I'd accidentally bit my tongue. After my mother went upside my head, I took the EBT card and went to the local bodega up on Nostrand Avenue. Even though I was told specifically to go to the Associated supermarket where the prices were cheaper, I rationalized that if I continued to fuck up and disobey then (hopefully) my mother would realize that food shopping wasn't the chore for me.

As I walked toward the bodega I saw Shiniqua Ship, one of my new girlfriends. The hood considered her family to be somewhat famous— or should I say, infamous. The legend was that her great-grandfather, Roybal "Slim" Ship, fathered over one hundred children by forty-two women, all of them boys. Those boys went on to father more boys and girls until the Ship family overran the Marcy Projects like the roaches that were such an integral part of the interior landscape. Since Shiniqua had such a large family, no one in Marcy ever messed with them for fear of repercussions, which were usually violent.

Shiniqua stood at the corner as I walked briskly toward her. As usual she had on the latest gear—Seven jeans, a rhinestone-studded, red Baby Phat baby tee that hugged her ample C-cup breasts, and red Prada sneakers. I was in awe of Shiniqua's wardrobe. Even when we lived in our comfortable Queens home, my parents never splurged on high-end clothing. I mean, we had nice clothes, but in Queens we didn't focus on brand names as much as the people did in Brooklyn.

When Shiniqua and I first met a few years after we moved to Marcy, I was amazed that she wore such expensive clothing at such a young age, especially when I went to her apartment and saw that it was just as crammed as ours. There were ten people living in her three-bedroom project apartment, but they were smart. They had bunk beds and a pull-out sofa, so no one was too uncomfortable. Plus, not everyone was home at the same time, so it allowed some flexibility in the sleeping arrangements.

I loved going over to Shiniqua's apartment because they had large televisions in every room that were hooked up to cable, a real leather living room set, and lots of food in their refrigerator. I couldn't help but compare their lives to the miserable one I lived, two buildings over. I longed for my previous comfortable, middle-class existence in Queens and the return of my daddy.

Shiniqua explained that her family afforded all those luxuries because all four of her brothers sold drugs. Timothy, the oldest at twenty, was the ringleader and was quickly moving up from his small-time status. Shiniqua was the baby of the family and the only girl, so she was definitely spoiled.

"What's up, girl?" Shiniqua beamed, displaying her super-deep dimples as I finally approached. Her long, dark hair was wrapped around her head and secured with bobby pins. She must have just come from the Dominican hair salon. Her smooth chocolate skin maintained its usual glow.

"Nothing much," I sulked.

She gave me an understanding look. "What's wrong with you? Julie?"

I was glad that Shiniqua knew everything about me and I didn't have to lie to her. She was fifteen years old, but looked twenty and was wise beyond her years. She was the one who had told me that my father wasn't in nobody's Marines and was most likely in jail. Since this fit his long-term absence and our lack of a home and income, I began to accept that my mother had lied to us.

"Yeah. She's sending me to the store with food stamps again!"

Shiniqua shrugged. "That's fucked up, but fuck it. Ain't shit you can do about it. Besides, most all these motherfuckers out here are on food stamps anyway, including my family."

"But you don't get clowned, 'cause y'all got money."

"True." Shiniqua nodded. "That, and they know that they'd get a quick beat-down."

I'd had plenty of fights during the five years we'd been living here due to the project girls who despised my light skin and long, thick hair, and the project guys who liked me for the same reasons. "You think you cute," the girls would growl as they lined up to beat my ass over things I had nothing to do with. Years of living with Julie, Jackie, and John ended up being good for something as I managed to hold my own, and even win some fights.

"Well, I been handing out beat-downs myself, but it won't stop them from clowning me once they see me pull out this EBT card."

Shiniqua laughed. "Lisa, you don't need to get in another fight. You done fought all of Marcy, and Tompkins, and Sumner!" She held out her hand. "Give me the card. I'll pay for your food."

Shocked, I replied, "You'd do that for me? But you don't even have to go shopping for your family, with or without food stamps!"

"I just said I would, didn't I? Besides, you're my best friend."

It felt good to hear someone call me that. Shiniqua felt more like my sister than a friend, more like my sister than Jackie. We both walked to the bodega and picked out the groceries on the list. When we got to the register, it seemed like the store suddenly filled up with our whole neighborhood. For a second I thought Shiniqua would change her mind because everyone was calling out her name and saying hi. She returned the greetings even as she pulled out the EBT card and paid for the food. I grabbed half the bags, and she grabbed the other half, then we left.

I was filled with relief as we walked back to my building. "Hey, I totally owe you my life," I said.

"You don't owe me shit," Shiniqua replied.

Just as we walked out of the store, we ran into Crystal and Ta-Ta. They were Shiniqua's friends, but they were cool with me too.

"What's up, bitches?" Shiniqua asked.

"Shit. We gotta run in here for my moms and then we gonna be back on our side. Why? What's up for today?" Crystal asked.

"We just gonna chill in front on the bench," I replied.

"Did y'all hear the dirt?" Ta-Ta asked.

"About what?" Shiniqua asked.

"Sean and his crew came off with mad jewelry. Rolex watches and diamond rings and shit like that."

"Where you hear that from?"

"He gave his sister Bambi a diamond bracelet this morning and she told me that they robbed a jewelry store in midtown Manhattan yesterday."

"Oh shit! I saw that on the news," Shiniqua said.

"Well, they running around trying to sell that shit. I wish my man had paper, 'cause a chick need some bling. You feel me?"

Shiniqua and I walked back to my building in silence, both of us apparently thinking about expensive watches and diamond earrings. When we got to my building we sat on the narrow front steps until the elderly people started to complain that they couldn't get through, so we moved to the benches and sat there. From that angle we could see the movements from four buildings.

It was a warm spring day and school was almost over for the year. In the fall, I would be entering my junior year and if I kept up my 3.6 GPA, I would be graduating with honors and maybe even attending college. I'd gotten applications to Fordham University, Baruch College, Iona College, and Medgar Evers College, but hadn't filled them out yet.

I didn't bother to take the groceries upstairs. I didn't care that the milk was getting warm and the margarine was melting in the heat. I felt most comfortable either out in the streets or at Shiniqua's house. John and Jackie hadn't taken to the project lifestyle as I did. Every day they came straight home from school and retreated to the cramped room that they shared until John graduated and enlisted in the Marines. Even when he left, I still was not allowed to sleep in the room with my mother and Jackie. But I was finally able to pull the cot into the living room on the rare nights when I hadn't gotten on my mother or Nana's bad sides.

Since I didn't have a room, I had no real incentive to stay in the house, so I learned all about the streets. I observed the dice and domino games, the girls playing double Dutch, the lookout boys on the corners who always watched for the police, and the drug deals. Sometimes people even had sex in the stairwells of the buildings. Then there were the occasional drug raids by the Narcotics detectives, and sometimes there were shootings and stabbings. New people moved in to replace the dead, and they brought new drama with them. It was all part of an urban soap opera that ran twenty-four hours a day, and I was addicted to it. I hated to miss even half an episode.

After talking for a little while on the bench, I asked Shiniqua if she wanted to play Scully, a game played on the sidewalk where you basically place your bottle-top on the first box, and each player sequentially shoots their chips. The first player to go from one through thirteen, and back to one, wins.

She shook her head. "Nah, it's too hot. Plus we too grown to be out here acting like little kids." She pulled a tube of M·A·C Lipglass from her Louis Vuitton purse and applied a thick layer of chocolate-colored gloss to her full lips. I had no clue why she liked her lips all glossed up. I was mostly ignorant about girly things, because neither my sister or my mom paid any attention to me.

I really wanted to play Scully, which was my favorite street game, but I decided not to challenge her. Besides, she was my best and only friend, so if she didn't want to play Scully, then we wouldn't.

"So what we gonna do?" I asked.

"Just chill." She replaced the gloss in her purse and turned her attention toward the nearby parking lot.

I was confused. "Chill, as in just sit here?"

"Yeah."

Sitting outside all day was the last thing I wanted to do. "I don't wanna just sit here in this hot sun. Let's go up to your house and watch videos," I suggested.

I wasn't really interested in watching videos. I really just wanted to watch Timothy, Shiniqua's brother. Secretly, I had the biggest crush on him. Each time I was over Shiniqua's place, I watched as he came in with his brown paper bags filled with money. His cologne lingered throughout the apartment. He always wore a new pair of white Air Force Ones, Sean John jeans and a crisp, white tee, which matched his sneakers. He had different colored shirts and sneakers, and they were always coordinated. He was so cute, and he didn't even notice me.

Shiniqua faced me. "Lisa, we're not just sitting here to sit here. Look!" She tossed her head toward a nearby chain-link fence and I suddenly understood.

Shareef, another local drug hustler who worked for Timothy, was leaning against the fence. He was nineteen, light-skinned with dark curly hair, and Shiniqua was in love with him. The hot sun glinted from the platinum, diamond-encrusted chain with the letter "S" hanging from it. Shareef never took off that chain, not even in his sleep, from what Shiniqua told me.

Last month, Shareef took Shiniqua's virginity up on the rooftop of her building and he hadn't paid her any mind since. Instead, I'd seen him sniffing around my sister, who had graduated from high school last year and was working at Conway.

"So what you gonna do? Are you gonna say something to him, like ask him why he hasn't called you?" I asked.

"I can't ask him that!" Shiniqua exclaimed. "I'll sound childish. A man in his position is busy making money for his fam."

"Well, he has time to be all up in Jackie's face." Granted, Jackie was cute, but not cuter than Shiniqua. For some reason, all the guys in our neighborhood thought Jackie was a prize because she had a really big butt and hazel eyes, compliments of our mother.

Shiniqua immediately grew upset at my comment. "I hate that bitch!" she stated. "I know that's your sister, but I still hate her big-booty, no-titty ass." She stood and pulled me up with her. "Lisa, walk with me over there. I'm going to tell him that he should buy me a pair of earrings or a watch from Sean."

Always loving drama, especially when I wasn't a part of it, I didn't hesitate to fulfill my friend's request. I picked up my groceries and prepared to follow her.

"Leave those here," Shiniqua instructed. "We're gonna look stupid, lugging bags."

"But . . ." My mother would beat my ass for sure if our groceries went missing.

"Won't nobody touch them," Shiniqua assured me. "And we'll keep an eye on them since we just going over there."

We both stuffed the grocery bags underneath the bench and began our journey toward Shareef, his crew, and Jackie, who had materialized within the seconds between Shiniqua's decision to approach Shareef and our movement toward him. We put as much switch in our hips as we could, and for a moment I felt grown.

Shareef saw Shiniqua coming and turned his attention back toward Jackie. I cringed, but that hint didn't faze Shiniqua.

"What's up, 'Reef?" Shiniqua asked as she stopped directly in front of Shareef. She put her hands on her already sizeable hips and looked Jackie up and down before giving him what she thought was a seductive look. Jackie ignored me, as usual, and looked at Shiniqua, then Shareef.

"Ain't nothing," Shareef replied nonchalantly, giving her a brief glance. "Just tryin' to maintain. You?"

"I'm chillin'. You know Lisa, right?"

Shareef shifted his eyes a fraction toward me, then back to Jackie. "Oh, yeah. This is your sister, right, Jackie?" He gave me a brief nod. "What's good, fam?" The disinterest was plain, though he tried to put on a good front to impress Jackie.

"It's all good," I replied. God forbid I gave Jackie a reason to beat me up when we got home.

Tank, Shareef's right-hand man, asked, "Shiniqua, what's up with your friend?"

Shiniqua sucked her teeth. "What do you mean, what's up? She's standing right here." She gestured to me. "Ask her!"

Tank looked me up and down, but said nothing. I felt uncomfortable. There was something in his look that was out of my scope of experience.

Shiniqua turned her attention back to the matter at hand "Shareef, what's up? When you gonna take me to the movies?"

Surprise crossed his face. "Movies?" He laughed and looked at Jackie, then back at Shiniqua. "I can do that. When you wanna go?"

"Shareef, I know you're not trying to play me!" Jackie snapped.

"Calm down!" He smiled at her. "It's all good. I got this."

"Yeah, she better calm down!" Shiniqua said, glaring at Jackie. Jackie glared right back.

Jackie was good with her hands when it came to fighting and in a one-on-one fight with Shiniqua, Jackie would probably win, but Jackie wasn't a dummy. She knew that if she whipped Shiniqua's ass, she'd get jumped by at least thirty-eight of Shiniqua's cousins that actually lived in Marcy, and that wasn't counting the ones who would come out the woodwork from the surrounding neighborhood. Jackie took the safer route and focused her anger on Shareef instead.

"I thought we were exclusive," she said.

Shareef reveled in the attention from the two good-looking women. He chuckled. "I ain't never said no shit like that."

"Really?" Jackie's voice was laced with sarcasm, but you could see the hurt in her eyes.

"Look, ma, it is what it is."

"So when we going?" Shiniqua interjected. She felt the shift in Shareef's affections and pressed her advantage. She rolled her neck at Jackie and moved closer to Shareef. He gently pushed her back with a frown.

"Chill, shorty," he warned.

At that moment, a masked gunman on a bicycle rode by and sprayed bullets from a small-caliber gun. Pop! Pop! Pop! rang through the air as everyone screamed and ran for cover. Jackie took off first. When I got safely inside my building, I realized that Shiniqua wasn't beside me. I ran back outside and saw her kneeling next to Shareef and cradling his head in her lap. She was covered in blood.

My heart stopped. "Are you shot?" I screamed.

"Lisa, look what they did to him." She cried, tears running down her cheeks. "Look what they did to my man..."

I looked down and saw that Shareef was struggling to keep his eyes open. Blood oozed from multiple holes in his chest. I dropped to my knees beside Shiniqua, careful to avoid the widening puddle of blood beneath Shareef.

"Did anyone call the police?" I didn't know what else to say.

In the background we could still hear screams. People were looking out of their windows and yelling, "Who's dead? Who's that on the ground?"

"Shareef, don't die, OK?" Shiniqua begged in a tear-streaked voice as she wiped a dribble of blood from the corner of his mouth. "I love you! I love you so much," she sobbed.

I didn't know what to do, so I did what I did best. I asked questions. "Who was that on the bike?"

Shiniqua continued to sob as Shareef's life slowly ebbed away. "We were gonna go to the movies!"

I'd never seen anything like this except in the movies. Where was the ambulance? I listened for the sounds of sirens, but all I heard was screaming and shouts for more information on the shooter and the person who'd been shot.

"Do you think the hospital will be able to fix him?" Shiniqua looked me directly in my eyes, silently pleading for reassurance.

Shareef looked like he was dead already, but I decided not to mention that. "Maybe we should put pressure on his wound," I suggested. I leaned over and pressed my hands against his chest in a feeble attempt to stop the blood. We were both shocked when he began to sing.

"Like sweet morning dew . . ." He mumbled a tune that neither of us knew. If he could sing, that was a good sign. Maybe he wouldn't die after all. Shiniqua sobbed louder and leaned down to place a kiss on his forehead. I just sat there with my hands still pressed against his chest, feeling his slow heartbeat.

It didn't take long before the projects got word to his brother and mother. They came running down the narrow pathway as fast as lightning. Shareef's mother shoved Shiniqua aside and became hysterical, "Oh, God, not my baby! Who did this? Wh-wh-wh-wh-who?"

Her sobs finally caused me to cry. I looked up at Shareef's older brother, Rakeem, who just stood there and watched his little brother fight for his life. His hands were tucked deeply inside his pockets and he just kept shaking his head, like he was in a trance.

It seemed like hours before the ambulance finally crept up the narrow driveway. Miraculously, Shareef was still holding on. Once he was carted away, everyone stood around and gossiped. Shiniqua and I sat on the bench for hours and listened to speculation on who wanted Shareef dead and why. The names Little Paul and Havoc from the Sumner Projects kept coming up, and almost all of Shareef's boys' vowed revenge.

It was close to midnight before my mother, Nana, and my brother came looking for me. Jackie was nowhere to be found. As they came progressively closer, Shiniqua said, "Oh, shit, Lisa! That's your mom dukes coming."

"No shit, Sherlock," I replied. I looked for the bags of groceries that I had left hours earlier, only to find them long gone. Someone must have swiped them in the commotion. I was up shit's creek.

"Where you been?" my mother asked when she got in front of me. I could see the belt in her hands. My heart began to flutter at the impending beating I was about to get in front of the whole projects. Think fast, Lisa, I told myself. But what could I say?

I stood and showed my mother all the blood on my hands and clothes, hoping to elicit sympathy.

"You sent me to the store and I got jumped and robbed for the groceries," I lied. "They beat me bloody . . ." My voice trailed off as I looked around for someone to back me up.

"Whip her ass!" Nana demanded.

The belt, which was actually an extension cord, came down on my arm like a lash of fire. As my mother whipped me on my upper body, I could sense she was trying to catch me in my face with the skinny cord. I managed to get down on the ground in a fetal position and cover my face. Suddenly there was a pause in the delivery of the next lash. I peeked up to see that Shiniqua had jumped on my mother and they were tussling over the cord. Shiniqua, who was much younger and more determined than my mom, grabbed the extension cord and whacked my mother with it.

"How does it feel?" she yelled, the emotions of the day boiling over in a rage. "I'm tired of you always hitting her, bitch!"

My mother was shocked and took two steps back at the look in Shiniqua's eyes. Shiniqua's actions gave me courage and I rushed my mother. My pent-up rage swelled and I swung at her with all my might while Shiniqua backed me up with the extension cord. My mother was on the ground, screaming and pleading for us to stop, but we kept hitting.

Nana was gesturing and screaming, "Somebody break that shit up! Break it up, I said!" No one listened. The need for drama was much greater than the well being of one person. Finally, Uncle Billy showed up, grabbed Nana and my mother, and they retreated back to the safety of Nana's apartment. Nana turned and told me, "Lisa, you're going to hell! God don't like ugly. The Old Testament says you are to honor thy mother and father—"

"Shut up, you old bitch!" one of Shareef's crew yelled. "Honor these nuts!"

We all burst out laughing. At that moment, my friendship with Shiniqua was sealed. I knew that my family wouldn't let me back in the apartment, especially after I shamed them in front of the entire projects, so Shiniqua's mom said I could stay with them if my family didn't want me. The best part of all was that I got to sleep with Shiniqua in her twin bed, just like we were real sisters.

Lisa Henderson

The next day

We woke to the sounds of Timothy having a little powwow in his room with his crew: Sean, Quincy, and Blackie. We knew their meeting was probably top secret, but that didn't stop us from making our way toward Timothy's room dressed in the long T-shirts which we wore as nightgowns—Shiniqua's showed off her hourglass shape while mine revealed nothing but the slight bumps of my A cups.

As we entered my crush's bedroom I saw an array of high-end jewelry spread across his bed. There were diamond earrings, rings, bracelets, and gold and platinum Rolex watches.

"Hey, Timothy," I said with lowered eyes.

Timothy frowned. "Get out!" he replied. The other members of his crew just stared at us.

We both ignored him and sat on his bed anyway.

"Didn't I say get out?"

Still ignoring him, we both looked around the room. A heavy, stainless steel safe was open, money was scattered in stacks across Timothy's bed, and there were a few guns on the dresser. No drugs were visible.

The other guys were packing up the rest of the money and guns and adding them to the duffel bags that were packed and stacked near the bedroom door. Timothy was draped in new jewels. He had on a platinum Rolex watch and a diamond and platinum chain adorned his neck. He was counting out thousands of dollars and handing over the stacks of money to Sean.

"I want something!" Shiniqua squealed as her eyes scanned the luxurious pieces. The thought of Shiniqua getting something made my stomach flop. Although she was my best friend, I couldn't stomach her getting something while I got nothing.

Timothy didn't hesitate to fulfill his sister's demand. "Yo, how much for these?" he asked, pointing to a pair of diamond studs that sparkled on the bed.

Sean picked up the earrings and read the label. "These cost four thousand. Give me two large."

"Nah, man. After all this shit I just bought, that's the best you can do?" Timothy looked insulted.

Sean looked to Quincy for support, but Quincy wasn't about to go against Timothy. "A'ight, you right," Sean conceded. "Give me twelve hundred and I'm good."

Timothy licked his thumb and began counting out hundred dollar bills.

"What about Lisa?" Shiniqua asked. She really was my best friend.

"Come on, man," Timothy retorted. He glanced up into my eyes that I knew were larger than saucers. My heart was palpitating and my hands began to fidget. I wanted something so badly I couldn't contain myself. "Lisa, you looking all thirsty and shit. A'ight, give her those hoops."

The earrings weren't anywhere near as glamorous as Shiniqua's diamond studs, but they sure beat a blank. They were gold hoops with diamond chips. I glanced at the price and they cost eleven hundred dollars. Timothy got them for four hundred dollars.

"You heard what happened to Shareef last night?" Shiniqua asked Timothy after Sean and his crew left.

"Yeah, and I heard your stupid ass wouldn't leave the scene of the crime," Timothy snapped. "What if 5-0 comes here to question you? That's why I gotta move my shit."

Shiniqua rolled her eyes. "Who gonna snitch and tell po-po that I was holding Shareef down until the ambulance came through?"

"Why the fuck were you holding that dude down anyway?"

I wondered if Shiniqua would be straight up with Timothy. Instead she said, "Somebody had to. I mean, everyone broke out. I couldn't just let him lie there alone."

Timothy's eyebrows creased with disapproval. "Yes the fuck you could have!"

"Well, I didn't. How 'bout that?" Her face was a mask of defiance.

"Don't make me smack your grown ass!" Timothy threatened. "And I will. Right in front of your company." Even though Timothy was all about his business, he adored his only baby sister.

Ignoring his threat, Shiniqua asked, "Did you hear anything from the hospital? Is he gonna make it?"

Timothy snorted. "Please. That nigga was DOA!"

Shiniqua froze. "He's dead?"

Timothy nodded. "Yup. He got bodied."

Slowly Shiniqua got up and left the room.

"Thank you!" Timothy half-joked with relief. When he realized that I was still there he said, "What the fuck you waiting for? Put some wings under your ass and bounce."

I didn't really hear him because I was fantasizing about him and me being together. I wanted him to throw me on his bed and kiss me.

I wanted his hands to feel my body and do whatever he wanted with me.

"Yo, Lisa, you deaf? I said leave. I got business to take care of."

Instead of hearing the warning in his voice, I decided to make small talk.

"So who would want to kill Shareef? I mean, he seemed like a nice enough guy."

A slight smile twitched around his lips. I loved his lips. "Well, nice guys get murked too."

"Well, I heard it was Little Paul and Havoc from Sumner."

He frowned again. "Really? They tryin' to put that on them?"

I shrugged and looked down at my hands. "Well, that's what I heard."

"What else you hear?" Suddenly he was interested in what I had to say. In fact, everyone in Timothy's crew was interested. They all stopped packing up and paid attention to me.

"Not much really . . ." I started off slowly. I knew once the information stopped, Timothy would kick me out, and I wanted to stay for as long as possible. "Everyone was saying they had beef, and it was time to settle the score. Didn't Little Paul used to go out with Jackie?"

"That little ugly bitch?" Timothy commented.

It was a mark of my relationship with Jackie that I didn't even come to her defense. "Yeah, her."

"Ain't that your sister?" one of the other guys asked.

"Yeah, but we ain't close," I shot back.

"Yeah, I think he used to fuck with her back in the day," Timothy stated. "Why? Is she relevant?"

"Well, the way I see it—"

"The way you see it?" They all laughed.

Ignoring the laughter, I said, "The way I see it, Shareef was seeing

Jackie. In fact, she was standing there too when he got murdered. And everyone is speculating that she could have set up Shareef to get murdered. Maybe she called Little Paul and told him where she was meeting Shareef. I mean, once he was shot, she never returned."

No one else really came to that conclusion, but as I spoke those words, it all made a lot of sense to me. I couldn't wait to share my analysis with Shiniqua.

"Yo, that's a good angle," Timothy said in approval. You could tell his mind was racing. "LL, I know you would love to sit up in my face all day, but I got shit to do. I gotta handle grown man's business. Now you don't gotta go home, but you do gotta get the fuck up outta here."

Firmly he grabbed me by my arm and tossed me out of his room.

"I live here now," I blurted out.

"Merry fucking Christmas," he replied and slammed his door in my face.

I stood outside the closed door, feeling good and stupid. First off, I hated when he called me LL. That stood for Little Lisa because he said I didn't have any chest and no ass. Even though I was fifteen, my body was little, just like a child's. And then he put me on blast, acknowledging that he knew that I had a crush on him. Finally, he told me to get the fuck out. He could have been more polite, even though he spoke to Shiniqua the same way. I decided not to stress over that today, though. I'd stress over that tomorrow and just enjoy the fact that today Timothy had paid more attention to me than he had during the entire five years I'd been living in Marcy.

Each day, as we got closer to the end of the school year, Shiniqua continued to look for Jackie to beat her ass. After I shared my theory with her about Jackie setting up Shareef, Shiniqua wanted to fight, but Jackie wasn't anywhere around. Once Little Paul and Havoc were gunned down by Shareef's brother, Rakeem, the block got hot. As a result, Shiniqua felt it was her duty to handle Jackie in a good old-fashioned street brawl, but Jackie had left Marcy immediately after the shooting and must have gone back to Queens, because the extensive Ship network couldn't locate her anywhere in Brooklyn.

Once in a while, I'd knock on my Nana's door to try to make up with my family, but they wouldn't let me in. My mother and Nana both walked past me as if we weren't related whenever they saw me on the streets. Only Uncle Billy had the nerve to smile or give me a quick wave when he thought Nana wasn't looking, and he would occasionally slip me a few dollars here and there before he became too strung out on crack. No member of my family tried to beat me up again, though, and I knew that had a lot to do with the family that was holding me down. For the first time in my life I felt loved and protected. For that I owed the Ships, especially Shiniqua.

Words could never express how grateful I was to the Ship family. For once in my life, I felt like I had a real family and they seemed to love me equally. Whatever Timothy bought Shiniqua, he bought me. When her mother made dinner, my plate was right there too. I kept waiting for them to say or show me that I was an outsider, but that day never came and I eventually relaxed and stopped waiting for it to come.

Lisa Henderson

As the years passed by in Marcy I began to feel more like I was born to run the streets of Brooklyn. The excitement and allure of danger around every corner was so unlike Queens, and I loved it. And I loved my new family.

Since graduation was approaching, Timothy took me and Shiniqua shopping for graduation dresses at Bloomingdales. It was at the last minute because Timothy kept waiting for the boosters to sell him something for us, but they kept coming with the wrong types of dresses like hoochie momma stuff, or the wrong sizes. So we piled into Timothy's Lexus and rode to 59th Street and Lexington.

Neither Shiniqua nor I was really impressed with the massive, expensive shopping center. When my father was around he took us to Roosevelt Field Mall on Long Island all the time, and that had high-end stores as well. And Shiniqua was used to expensive price tags dangling from her garments, since her whole family was in the drug game.

After rummaging through several racks, we both decided on off-white Gucci dresses. I wore a size two and Shiniqua was a size four.

I was still Little Lisa, even though I had breasts and hips now, albeit small ones. The dresses were conservative and Shiniqua wanted something more revealing, but Timothy wasn't having that.

"Your grown ass will get what I say to get!" he screamed. "Ungrateful little bitch!" He turned to me. "Lisa! You like your dress?"

"I sure do," I sang in a ringing tone. Even after living with the Ships for the past two years, I still got butterflies in my stomach whenever Timothy acknowledged my presence.

"I see someone has some sense. All Shiniqua wants to do is chase the little dumb niggas 'round the PJs that wanna get in her pants. Let me kick something to both y'all." He paused for emphasis. "Never chase anything you can attract!"

I thought about his message. Never chase anything you can attract? Was that why he kept overlooking me? All I needed to do was stop chasing him? Hmmm.

❋❋

The day before graduation, Shiniqua and I lined up our matching low-heeled Gucci shoes next to our dresses. Timothy had also bought us the matching purses. We looked like twins.

"Lisa, I think that when we get our hair done today you should get a perm, and let them cut you a cute bang. What do you think?"

I'd always wanted a perm, but my mother said I had to wait until I was eighteen. I always envied the girls with the wash and set hair and sexy bangs, and I couldn't wait to stop wearing my childish ponytail, or sometimes two ponytails if I wanted to look different. Despite Shiniqua's constant efforts to get me to do something with my thick, natural hair, I always thought about the immediate ass kicking I would get from my mother if I came home with a perm. And maybe, on some perverse level, I still held out hope that my mother would come around and love me like she loved John and Jackie. When I realized that none of that would be happening because I was no longer her daughter in her book, I started making my own decisions.

"I think that would be perfect," I agreed. "But I don't have any money." Timothy would give us pocket change, but I tended to spend mine on books, much to Shiniqua's dismay. I didn't have enough on me to get a virgin perm, plus a cut and style.

"Neither do I, silly." Shiniqua laughed. "We'll get it from my mom or Timothy. Don't worry, you'll be straight."

I bit my bottom lip. "Shiniqua, I can't keep taking money from your family. I feel like this is wrong." Shiniqua just shrugged off me comments as usual.

The Ships held me down and did for me like I was a blood relative, but I hated feeling like a charity case. I couldn't wait for the day when I had a job and could at least start to repay the kindness they'd shown me.

Later that day we went to the salon and even though Shiniqua pressed for something more dramatic, I settled on bangs that were feathered slightly to the side. The rest of my newly straightened hair hung past my shoulders in a dark, shiny sheet that was slightly bumped at the ends. With my skin tone, I looked like a Marcy Projects version of Pocahontas, or maybe even the late singer Aaliyah. I couldn't resist shaking my hair on the way back home, much to Shiniqua's amusement. Shiniqua went with a mass of spiral curls all over her head, also with bangs, and highlighted with streaks of cherry red. I loved the way I looked—more mature, like the other girls my age. A part of me wondered if Timothy would love my new look too.

The next morning was graduation. I got up half an hour early, put on one of Shiniqua's sweat suits, and ran to my old building at 606 Park

Avenue. I didn't knock on the door to apartment 7J, but I slid my four graduation passes under the door with a note. I'm sorry. Please come see me get my diploma. Lisa.

I fidgeted all through the graduation ceremony. Shiniqua and I weren't able to sit together because our last names were at different ends of the alphabet, but after we got our diplomas (at least the Ships clapped for me when my name was called) we walked around the auditorium, looking for loved ones. Parents were snapping pictures of their children giving the cheesiest grins they could muster while holding up their diplomas. When Shiniqua spotted her entourage, she tapped my arm and began waving her arms wildly. "Here we are! Here we are!" she yelled.

Soon flashbulbs were popping in our faces, making me dizzy. I tried to smile and be jovial, but I was sad. No one from my blood family came for me. I continued to look over my shoulder, squinting to try and catch a glimpse of a familiar Henderson face, but there were none. I had to face facts. My family, my new family, was the Ships, and had been for the past two years. I closed the door for good on my old life and turned my attention wholly toward the life I'd built with the Ships.

That night, Timothy took us to Red Lobster to celebrate. When we got back to the projects, the benches were abuzz with new gossip, or shall I say two-year old gossip. Not letting the past stay there, Jazzy, a girl from Marcy, just began running her mouth off about how on the day that Shareef was murdered, Little Paul and Havoc were in her apartment bagging up cocaine. She swore that they had been gunned down for the wrong reason, and now Rakeem was running around like a mad man, on a mission to find out who was really responsible for Shareef's death. He had already been questioned by the police for the two murders, and he vowed that he wasn't going down until he got revenge for his little brother.

The popcorn shrimp and garlic biscuits in my stomach churned with nervousness. I'd been the one shooting my mouth off to Timothy about a possible setup by Jackie, trying to impress him. What if I'd been wrong? Even though Jackie disappeared right after the shooting—which made her look even more suspect—and I wasn't the only one naming Little Paul and Havoc for Shareef's murder, I may have added fuel to the fire.

I bit my lip and stole a look at Timothy, who was getting the 411 from Jesse John, one of his crew members. I slowed my roll and hung back, trying to hear what was being said. Shiniqua had the same idea.

Soon Timothy realized that we were all still standing there, ear hustling. "Yo, let me walk my moms and them safely to the crib, and then we can talk some more," he told Jesse John.

"A'ight," Jesse said, and then he ushered us along.

Lisa Henderson

The summer of 2003 was a summer of many firsts. The first was my new hairdo, of course, and now I could pass for at least twenty-one. The second was getting in touch with my father.

It had just begun to get hot outside when Paris and Qwen, our rivals, came stomping through the projects wearing the new designer jellies. They were a remake of the $1.99 jellies we wore as kids, only now Paris was wearing a two-hundred-dollar pair from Marc Jacobs, and Qwen was sporting a one-hundred-seventy-five-dollar pair made by Fendi.

"Shiniqua, did you see them bitches, thinking they cute?" I asked.

"Who the fuck they think they are? Us?" Shiniqua grimaced.

"Don't know. Don't care. All I know is that I want me a pair of jellies too."

"Oh, best believe we gonna get a pair. Hand me my cell phone. I'm calling my brother!"

"You can't ask Timothy to buy me a pair too! I know he's tired of tricking on me. I'm not blood."

"Look, you're my sister. And this money is practically free anyway.

In case you haven't learned anything about the Ship family over the past seven years, the one thing you need to learn is that we're very close knit. We stick together. My mother would slap me into next week if I even thought about getting new gear and not making sure you could do the same."

I shook my head again, in awe at my good fortune. "My mom isn't like that at all. Her specialty is conquering by division."

"I know. That's why we kicked her ass!" Shiniqua laughed and I joined in, but I really didn't want to laugh. Although my mother was mean to me, I did miss her. I loved her. She was my mother, and I only wanted her to love me back.

"Well, when my father comes home, he'll want to repay your family for all they've done to help me."

Shiniqua raised her eyebrow, much like Timothy did. "Does your father know what's going on? Like the real story?"

"I'm sure he doesn't."

"Then you should tell him."

"How? I don't even know where he is. He left, telling us he was going back into active duty with the Marines."

"Well, I bet that's not true. I told you a long time ago he was probably in jail."

"Well, my Auntie Brenda did tell me that story about him going back to the Marines was a lie, but she wouldn't tell me the truth."

"See? I'm not the only one who thought that story was sheisty," Shiniqua said triumphantly. "Who knows, he may even still be in jail. Regardless, when we go back upstairs, I'll help you find him so you can write him and tell him everything that's going down. OK?"

"Yeah, OK. But how?"

She waved her hand in dismissal. "Girl, I know you were sheltered out there in your Queens bubble, but I figured you'd picked up a few things by staying with us." She shook her head and smiled, those deep dimples flashing. "As long as you know an inmate's first and last name, you can find him on the Internet. And even if he's not in jail, we may still get a hit on him."

Of course Timothy had upgraded Shiniqua's Dell computer and bought her a new Mac laptop for schoolwork, but she mostly surfed the Internet and sent instant messages and emails to boys all over the five boroughs. Whenever I used it, it was strictly for school, and even living around the Ships, I was still rather ignorant about the world of jails and prisons. Still, Shiniqua's words were music to my ears.

"Really?" I asked. "I can't wait!"

As promised, when we went upstairs Shiniqua got on the Internet and found my father—inmate Laurence Henderson, FCI, Federal Inmate #085-99999, Fort Dix, New Jersey. His release date was December 21, 2003. That was just over five months away! She printed out the information and I just stared at it in wonder and confusion. My father was alive, but he wasn't in the Marines. He was in jail. My daddy couldn't come for me because he was locked up, but why did he get locked up in the first place? Would he come looking for me when he got out? Did my mom know he was in jail? Should I write and tell him about me, Nana, John, and Jackie? So many questions popped through my mind that I ate dinner in a haze and went to sleep, still thinking.

The next day I wrote my father and when I got a reply, I sent him my graduation pictures and told him what happened between my mother and me. He wrote back with his sincere apologies for my mother's behavior, and his dismay that he was not there to take care of us like he wanted to be. Unfortunately, his words of strength and encouragement weren't enough. I'd needed him here. I'd needed him physically to pull me out of this ghetto and be my dad. But that was then, and this was now.

I wanted to visit him but since he was getting out soon, he asked that

I wait until his release. He didn't want me to see him in prison. I had to take what I could get, and his letters did help somewhat. At least they solved the mystery of his disappearance.

My father explained to me in his letters how he ended up in jail. He was a hard-working man who had made a huge mistake. One night, in a sports lounge in Queens, he'd gotten into an altercation with a man, and when the man reached for a gun, my father bashed him in the face with a bottle while they wrestled for the gun. The gun went off and shot the man in the stomach, and he almost died on the operating table at the hospital. That man happened to be an undercover police officer was watching the bar for any illegal activity (although there had been some high-stakes poker games in the back of the bar for years, the police never had enough evidence against the bar owner to charge him with anything). Bar patrons testified that the man never identified himself as a police officer and that my father was acting in self defense, but the jury still found my father guilty. He was sentenced to seven to ten years in prison for attempted murder.

My mother didn't want us to know about my father's crime, so she told us that he got sent back into active duty with the Marines. The house was sold to pay my father's lawyer's fees, and after the bank was repaid for the mortgage, there wasn't anything else for us to live on, which was why we ended up at Nana's.

Anyway, at least I was starting to build some type of relationship with my father through his letters. And I had his release to look forward to in the winter.

The third first for me of that summer was the loss of my virginity. Shiniqua was surprised when I admitted to her that I hadn't had sex yet. "What?" she asked incredulously. "You still ain't let nobody pop your cherry yet? As many dudes be hollering at you these days?"

After my hair makeover, Shiniqua bought me some new outfits as a graduation gift, compliments of the Ship network of boosters. With my new hair and clothes, and the revelation of my father's secret, my self-esteem increased. In the fall I would be starting as a freshman at CUNY, and with a scholarship too! I felt like a new person, and it showed. I suddenly received attention from guys who before had only given me brief hellos in passing. Suddenly I was in demand, but not by the person I wanted most.

I was tired of constantly being overlooked by Timothy, who was now running all of the blocks within a four-block radius. He sold heroin and crack, had a steady crew of fifteen men, including his brothers who were his lieutenants, and he was really balling. Even though he still claimed the Ship apartment as the place where he rested his head, he was gone a lot. Whenever I saw his black-on-black 2003 Mercedes S300 with the black-on-black spinners and super-dark tinted windows parked at the curb I would get excited, just like I used to when I was ten and saw him walking around Marcy.

One day I saw his car and ran upstairs to the apartment, hoping to see him. I straightened my hair and clothes, licked my lips, and unlocked the door to the apartment. Shiniqua's mom wasn't ever home. She was always out spending her son's money. She went to Broadway plays, the opera, the ballet, dinner at Mr. Chow's—she had an active social life. She always told me that you had to make the best out of life because you only got one. Since it was summer, the rest of the family was out enjoying the summer heat, especially Shiniqua, who had taken up with a twenty-five-year-old guy who lived on the other side of Marcy."

As I entered the apartment I heard grunting noises coming from down the hallway. While on my way to Timothy's bedroom, the noises got louder. I peeked through the partially open door of Timothy's room and saw Timothy's tight chocolate behind moving up and down as he rammed himself between the caramel-colored legs draped across his shoulders.

I hurriedly ran back out of the apartment and back downstairs to sit on the bench. I really wanted to sit in my room and sulk, but I didn't want to hear the sounds of Timothy giving that girl what I wished he'd give me.

Unbeknownst to me, someone else had other plans for me. His name was Ishmael. He was a new member in Timothy's crew, and at eighteen he was closer to my age than Timothy. He was a quiet individual and was known for wearing his iPod and listening to any one of Jay-Z's albums. Ishmael kept himself dressed in a fresh pair of kicks, crisp jeans, and a bright white T-shirt.

I sat on the bench in the July heat and began to dream about my future. I couldn't wait to get older and marry a rich husband and live like the rich and famous. I wanted to be like Kimora Lee Simmons, jet-setting around the world with fur coats and Louis Vuitton luggage. My daydreams were interrupted when someone stepped in front of me and blocked the sun. I looked up, and it was Ishmael.

"Hey, ma," he greeted. The ear buds to his iPod were jammed into his ears. The white cords made a nice contrast against his smooth chocolate skin.

"Hey, Ishmael."

"Is Timothy here?"

"Yeah, he's upstairs. But I wouldn't bother him right now."

"Why not?"

"'Cause he's got company."

My words must have come out sharper than I intended, because Ishmael smiled. He had nice teeth. "You jealous?"

I sucked my teeth. "Nigga, please. I ain't thinking about Timothy."

"Yeah, whatever." Ishmael continued to grin. He took his iPod ear-plugs out of his ear. "I gotta put this work in his room." He motioned toward a man-purse he was carrying.

"I just told you that Timothy got company."

"Girl, when you gon' learn that pussy comes secondary to paper?"

I shrugged. "Fine. Don't say I didn't warn you." If he wanted to get his head bitten off, that was his business.

"A'ight." He handed me his iPod. "Here, hold this for me. I'll be right back." As he walked off he tossed over his shoulder, "Oh, and why don't you listen to Jay-Z's album, The Blueprint 2. A song called 'Poppin' Tags.'"

I watched him walk off with a bowlegged strut, his freshly creased Pelle Pelle jeans only sagging slightly from his butt, just enough to show the red patterned waistband of his boxer shorts, which picked up the red stitching in his jeans. I put the ear buds in my ear, dialed to track "Poppin' Tags," and listened. Next, I scrolled down and found a song that wasn't by Jay-Z, but he did rap on the track. It was "Frontin'" by Pharrell. I listened to the song twice more and was listening to Vol. 2–Hard Knock Life when Ishmael returned.

"What you listening to now?" he asked. The man-purse hung empty over his shoulder.

"'Hard Knock Life.'"

"Instead of treating, you get tricked?" He winked.

"Instead of kisses, I get kicked."

An edge must have been in my voice because Ishmael looked at me and asked, "For real?"

I shrugged, removed the ear buds, and handed the iPod back to him. "Here."

He took it and just held it in his hand. "So what did you think of the song?"

"What song?"

"Poppin' Tags."

"It was OK. I remember when it came out."

"Just OK?"

There was an intensity in his voice that caught my attention. I looked in his eyes and was surprised to see that he was staring at me intently. I blushed and tried to ignore the butterflies in my stomach. I changed the subject. "So, did you handle what you had to handle with Timothy?"

"Yep." He patted the empty man-bag for emphasis.

"Was he mad?"

Ishmael smirked. "Naw. He was ready to talk business when I got up there."

"Oh." I didn't want to think any more about Timothy and the other business he'd been handling. "So what did y'all talk about?"

"Grown man's business."

"Grown?" I snorted. "Please. You're not much older than me!"

"Mentally I could be your daddy." He sat down next to me on the bench. "So where's your girl?"

"Shiniqua went to the movies with Jason."

"Jason from Marcy side?"

"Yeah, that's him."

"So what about you?"

"What?"

"Why you didn't go too? Don't he hang with Malik? Y'all could have double dated." He laughed.

"No, thanks. Besides, I got my eyes on someone else."

"Who?"

"What do you care? It's none of your business."

Ishmael held up his hands in a defensive gesture. "I'm just asking.

Maybe I could help you get with dude."

"I doubt that. Besides, he's not a young boy like you. He's a man."

"I'm eighteen. And, nah, just my age doesn't qualify me as a man, but my actions do!"

I rolled my eyes. "Why? 'Cause you sell your little drugs? That's what you think makes you a man? It doesn't." I tossed my hair. "And I don't want a worker. I want the boss."

Ishmael shook his head. "Well, that grown man will come with grown-man problems. I can guarantee that."

"Look, I don't want popcorn and peanut butter and jelly-eating niggas—"

"Word?"

"Word! Go get your father. Your father will buy me a car. You'll wanna ride in my car. Now do you see where I'm coming from?"

"Yeah, I do. You want a five-figure nigga that will come with six-figure issues. A dude that will treat you like a commodity, as if he owns you because he bought you a whip, and keeps your hair and nails done. Is that what you're looking for? Is that all you want out of life?"

"I can handle that," I boasted. Deep down, I wasn't so sure. Timothy was getting big in the drug game and even though I lived with the Ships, I was still pretty naïve about the drug game. "Sounds just about right to me."

"Nah. I don't believe you."

"You know what I've learned?" I asked.

"What?"

"When a person tells you who they really are, you should believe them."

We sat in silence for a minute, then he spoke again.

"So you're telling me that's who you really are?"

"Straight. No chaser."

"I still don't believe you."

"Suit yourself."

"Can I ask you something?"

"What?"

"Would you ever consider dating me?"

I was blown away and looked at Ishmael, my eyes widened in shock. I'd never looked at Ishmael in that way. I only had eyes for Timothy. I took a look at Ishmael now. I mean, I really looked at him. Nice, straight teeth, golden brown complexion that was a few shades darker from the summer sun, a low Caesar haircut with the deep waves, and full lips—a cute guy, by anyone's standard.

"I mean, I might not got all the money you're looking for in a boss," Ishmael continued, "and I'm still doing hand-to-hand transactions, but I got a plan. I'm not going to be doing this low-level stuff for long. I just need some startup money, and then I'm going to open up a Subway franchise over up on Broadway, right next to Woodhull Hospital. I'm going to make a killing!" His voice became excited. "I already got all the literature from off the Internet. The package outlines how much money I'll need and the way I figure, by the time I turn twenty, I'll have saved enough money to move forward with my dreams. I'm not going to end up a statistic. If Jay-Z can get out of Marcy, then I can get out too."

I was intrigued, and his excitement was infectious. I had to admit that the thought of being with someone who wasn't in the drug game—or anything else illegal—was appealing.

We sat on the bench outside and talked some more. I told him how I had aspirations of being a television journalist. I wanted to be a serious journalist like the greats—Dan Rather, Katie Couric, Peter Jennings. There weren't any black journalists who got as much critical acclaim as Barbara Walters other than Tavis Smiley, and I wanted to fill that void.

"You can be anything you want," Ishmael encouraged.

I laughed. "You sound like my father. He's always says that I can be anything I want as long as I keep up my grades and stay ambitious and determined."

"Your pops sounds smart. Where is he?"

I thought about whether I should confide in Ishmael. Even though our little chat was cute, and I'd seen him around, he was still a bit of a stranger.

"He's in the Marines," I finally answered.

"Fighting Bush's war? Why?"

"He's not in the war, but he loves his country. And in a few years, those are the types of questions I'll ask the right people."

"Well at least your pops is standing for something. I wish I could say that about mine."

As Ishmael confided in me about his dope fiend father, I felt a little bad that I was less than truthful with him. Hearing him open up to me made me see him in a different light.

After that first meeting, Ishmael made it a point to stop by at least three times a week to talk to me. A week later he came by again, to drop off some work for Timothy. This time I was alone in the apartment and Timothy wasn't home. Ishmael went into Timothy's room, secured the work, and came back. I was in my room reading a book I'd checked out from the library about breaking into journalism. Ishmael came in and plopped down on the bed next to me.

"Excuse you," I snapped.

"My bad, ma," Ishmael apologized. He took his ear buds out of his ear. "What you reading?"

I was a bit irritated by my solitude being interrupted, but the irritation couldn't mask how glad I was to see Ishmael. I showed him the cover of the book.

"Careers in Journalism," he read aloud. "That's good, ma. Plan your work and work your plan." He looked me up and down. I was dressed in a pair of black shorts and a pink spaghetti-strap top, my hair pulled back in a ponytail. "That's some sexy shit," he said, commenting on my outfit.

I blushed and ignored him, even though I felt moistness between my legs and my nipples got hard. Ishmael noticed and leaned in to kiss me, his tongue exploring my mouth. I didn't stop him. I felt his hand on my hip, slowly gliding up to cup my breast. When his rough thumb brushed across my hardened nipples, I arched my back at the sensation.

Ishmael carefully peeled the straps of my shirt from my shoulders to expose my breasts. He bent down and sucked one while I pressed his head into my chest, my hips writhing with the sensation. He repeated the action with the other breast. I didn't even notice that my shorts and panties were off until I felt one of Ishmael's fingers in my wet pussy. I moved against his finger and he pulled back from my breast to say, "Damn, ma, you wet as hell! I like that."

When he took off his clothes, I got a glimpse of his hardened dick standing out from a nest of thick, black hair and quickly shut my eyes. It looked so big. I hadn't seen a dick this up close and personal since I accidentally walked in on John in the bathroom one day, long before he left Marcy. Of course, I knew about the overall mechanics of sex. Shiniqua made sure to give me blow-by-blow recaps of sex with her boyfriends, and she answered any questions I had. And I read about it in books sometimes, but I'd never before let a boy feel my breasts, let alone suck my nipples. I'd hoped that Timothy would be the one to give me that pleasure, but I put thoughts of Timothy out of my head when Ishmael crawled on top of me and laid his body on top of mine. Timothy had his chance, and he blew it.

I heard the sound of plastic tearing, then I felt Ishmael fumble with something. I figured he was putting on a condom. I kept my eyes closed while Ishmael used one knee to push my legs apart, then he applied pressure with his dick. The harder he pushed at the entrance to my pussy, the tighter I closed my eyes. It felt like hours and then . . .

"Ouch!" I screamed. He finally broke my hymen and began to move in and out rapidly.

"It feel good . . . it feel good . . ." Ishmael chanted. Or was that a question? I had no idea what to do or say. One part of me wanted to enjoy the moment and the strange yet exciting sensations I felt despite the pain, but the other part felt guilty. Timothy was supposed to be my first. That had been my plan. What would he think if he found out about me and Ishmael?

"Oh shit, ma," Ishmael moaned as he sped up his thrusts. "Oh shit . . . oh fuck . . . damn, I'm about to cum!" He grunted, pulled my hair painfully, growled, and gave one final thrust that shot pain through my pelvis. His body shook for a few moments and then he collapsed on top of me in a sweaty heap. I tried to shift my body beneath his so that I could breathe. A few minutes later, he hopped up and pulled on his clothes. I pulled the sheets up over my naked waist and pulled my tank top back over my breasts. Ishmael sat back down on the bed and looked at me, then down at the sheet.

"I ain't know you was a virgin, ma," he said shyly. "You OK?"

"Yeah, I guess," I replied. My pussy stung from the rough thrusts, and my nipples were swollen, but overall I was OK.

"Did I hurt you?"

I was about to comment, but was interrupted by jangling keys hitting the lock. Ishmael and I both looked at each other in panic. I said a silent thanks to God that Ishmael was already dressed. When Timothy passed my door and looked in at us, my heart plummeted.

"What y'all doing in here?" he asked with a frown. He looked at me, then at Ishmael, then back at me.

"Umm, nothing. Just kicking it," I stammered.

"Word?" Timothy looked at me sternly. I got the sense that he wasn't fooled. To Ishmael he said, "You dropped off my shit?"

Ishmael jumped to his feet to show his boss respect. "Yeah. And I locked everything up."

"Well, bring your ass back here and help me count this paper then!" Timothy snapped. Ishmael didn't even excuse himself before running behind Timothy. I hurriedly pulled on my shorts and waited impatiently for Shiniqua to come home. I needed to tell someone what had finally happened.

"I feel so stupid," I said later that night.

Shiniqua shook her head. "Stupid for what? It's about time." She smiled.

"But I don't even know him!"

"Yes, you do. You see him all the time, and he's cute. A little too quiet for my taste, but at least he has money."

"What if it's a one-time only thing? And what if he tells the whole projects, and everyone calls me a ho?"

"Trust me, it ain't no one-time thing," she said confidently. "I don't know if he has a big mouth, but I doubt it. My brother don't hire people with loose lips. Shareef never told anyone about us . . ." Her voice drifted off with the memory, then she shook it off. "Anyway, Ishmael knows better than to do you dirty. You're a Ship now. He'd be a fool to play you, because if I didn't get in his ass, Timothy would."

I exhaled with relief at her words, only to suck the stress back in at the mention of Timothy's name. "You think Timothy knows what we did?"

Shiniqua laughed. "Girl, my brother ain't stupid. As much pussy as he done got, and right in this very house. Even if he suspects, he gonna act like he don't."

I didn't know how I felt about Timothy knowing. Of course, in all my fantasies, Timothy was the one who took my virginity. But in a way, I wanted him to know that someone in his crew didn't think I was a little girl. Shiniqua must have caught the vibe of my thoughts because she said, "Lisa, I know how you feel about my brother. I know you'd hoped that Timothy would be the one to pop your cherry, but trust me when I say that Ishmael was the better choice. Timothy has a lot going on right now and he wouldn't treat you as well as you deserve to be treated. Let Ishmael do his thing and enjoy the ride." She winked at the double meaning of her last words and I laughed. She joined in.

Suddenly Timothy walked in and ended all of our speculation when he said, "Let me tell y'all two knucklehead's one thing. Kisses are not promises. Don't think that just because a nigga gives you a nut and tells you how good you look, he's sticking around." He walked out just as suddenly as he had walked in, but not before giving me a pointed look.

"What was that all about?" I asked with a puzzled look on my face.

Shiniqua waved a hand in dismissal. "He's probably drunk. I don't know what the hell he was talkin' 'bout." We both giggled. "He's crazy, right?"

When Ishmael didn't come around for a couple weeks, you couldn't drag me out of the house. No matter where Shiniqua was going—the movies, the park, the pool, a jam—I didn't care. I stayed in the house, hoping that Ishmael would come by to drop off some work and then talk to me, like he did before. I didn't even care if he didn't have sex with me. I loved him. And I now thought about him each night instead of Timothy.

We were well into the month of July when I finally came outside. Shiniqua and I went to buy the quarter water ices from the icy lady when I spotted Ishmael. He was standing at headquarters with a few of his boys. We made eye contact before I turned my attention toward my strawberry icy.

"There goes your boyfriend," Shiniqua teased.

"Shhhh, be quiet," I hissed. "Do you want him to hear you?"

Shiniqua licked her grape icy. "OK. But what you gonna say?"

"I'm not going to say anything."

"But what if he says hi?"

"You think he's gonna say hi?"

"What's up, Lisa?" Ishmael greeted. I looked up and he had a large smile on his face. I turned and walked away quickly.

"Yo, Lisa, where you going?" he called out.

Fuck him! I sped up. I wasn't going to give him any of my time. Where had he been for the past few weeks?

I saw Shiniqua look at Ishmael, shake her head, and then she jogged to catch up with me. When we got upstairs, Shiniqua asked why I treated him that way.

"Because, Shiniqua," I explained, "he has sex with me once, takes my virginity, and then gets ghost! How is that supposed to make me feel?"

"It's like Timothy said, 'kisses aren't promises,'" Shiniqua replied.

"Well, if Ishmael wants me, then he better come get me, and I'm not going to make it easy for him! Timothy also said don't chase what I can attract!"

I could tell that Shiniqua was still confused, but she shrugged it off.

One week later, someone knocked on the door. I had just woken up from an afternoon nap, my hair was in bobby pins, and I had on an oversized T-shirt and a baggy pair of shorts.

I flung the door open without asking who it was. Standing there with flowers from the local bodega in one hand, and a bag of Chinese food in the other, was Ishmael.

"These are for you." He thrust the flowers at me. "May I come in?"

I took the flowers. "Timothy's not here."

"You know I'm not here for Tim. I came to see you."

"Why now?" I asked stubbornly.

He pushed himself inside, walked to the kitchen, and began making our plates of Chinese food. Finally he said, "Your first time shouldn't have went down like that. I know that being a virgin means a lot to girls, and I know you're not a ho." He paused, took a deep breath, and said, "I like you a lot and I wanna make you my girl."

I blinked slowly. I was still half asleep and the entire scene seemed surreal. "I told you that I like somebody else."

"Well he's gonna have to take a backseat, 'cause I'm not letting you go. Besides, I had you first. He's not gonna want you now, anyways."

I didn't know how to feel about that comment. "I don't want to do that again," I blurted out.

"If you don't want to, then we don't have to," Ishmael agreed. "But I will make you my girl. I don't want to sleep with you. I want to date you, which is something we should have done first."

I was still stunned.

"Will you go with me to the movies on Friday after I finish work?"

he asked.

That finally woke me up. Yippeeee! I wanted to scream. Instead I said, "That would be cool. What are we going to see?"

"*Spiderman 2.*"

After that, I sat down with my new man and we ate our Chinese food side by side.

When Ishmael wasn't working, which was often, we'd walk through the projects together, go to McDonald's, Chinese restaurants, the movies, but mostly we would have sex. I became more assertive in the sex department. I wanted to do it all the time, whereas Ishmael hardly ever pushed up. I decided to discuss my frustrations with Shiniqua.

I'd just gotten out of the shower and was putting baby powder all over my neck and chest when I began, "How often do you and Knowledge have sex?" I asked.

Knowledge was her new boyfriend from Sumner projects. Her boyfriends usually didn't last that long.

She wrinkled her forehead in thought as she stared at the ceiling. "Ummmm, I dunno. Why?"

"Because," I closed the bedroom door for privacy, "Ishmael and I only do it when I suggest it. Shouldn't it be the other way around?"

I watched as Shiniqua squeezed into her jeans. She was gaining a bit of weight.

"Did you talk to him about it? Maybe he's stressed out, trying to get that paper."

"Well if he is on a paper chase, he sure ain't giving me none!" I sulked.

Shiniqua stopped fumbling. "You mean he's not hitting you off?" Horror laced her voice.

I shook my head.

"Oh, no, that won't do!" Shiniqua angrily zipped up her jeans and pulled on an aqua blue and silver halter top. "He knows how the game is played. If he wanna be the boss, then he gotta pay the cost. You want me to tell Timothy to talk to him?"

I swallowed hard. And just like that, my crush for Timothy had resumed. "No!" I yelled. "I don't want everybody in my business."

"Well, then, handle your business," she coaxed. "School will be here before you know it. Ask him to take you school shopping. And not up on Broadway or Albee Square Mall either. Tell him to take you into the city. And don't forget to mention you'll need footwear too."

I thought about what Shiniqua was saying and I felt awkward, if not afraid. The only man that had ever bought me school clothes was my father. Although Timothy bought me clothes before, that was different. He did that because Shiniqua and I were as close as sisters, and he respected that.

Shiniqua wasn't ready to let the subject go. She continued, "And don't forget Marcy Day."

"What about Marcy Day?"

"Make sure you ask that nigga to buy you some gear for Marcy Day. You know how important that day is to us. We gotta stay fly and represent our hood."

I nodded.

Marcy Day took place once a year where all the tenants, surrounding projects, and outsiders all came out to celebrate. Everyone barbequed, did choreographed dances, and listened to the DJ play music into the wee hours of the night. It was so much fun and I couldn't wait.

I dressed in a pair of white shorts and a purple tank top while Shiniqua stepped into a pair of silver stilettos. I had no idea how she walked around the projects in such high heels all day, but I had to give it to her, she looked sexy. I also loved when she wore heels because it brought us closer in height. I stood 5'7" in my bare feet and always wore flat shoes, so her five-foot-two-inch frame in four-inch heels helped close the gap.

Of course, we went through our usual drama each day. I wanted to stay around the way in Marcy to sit around Ishmael, and she wanted to walk to Sumner and sit around Knowledge. Each day, we would compromise.

"I'll walk you to Sumner first, and then we can come back here," I stated.

"No, bitch, you think you slick." She laughed. "You know damn well ain't nobody outside this early. As soon as it gets popping outside, you're gonna want to come back on this side."

I laughed. "I will not! I promise, we can stay over there until at least nine o'clock."

She glanced down at the new Marc Jacobs watch that Knowledge had bought her. It was two in the afternoon. "OK. But tomorrow, we're staying late over in Sumner."

Fate had a funny way of revising your plans. When we came out of the building that day and began walking toward Flushing Avenue, we both spotted Ishmael, only he wasn't alone. He was standing with Toya and Kimber, both from Sumner. And from how close Toya and Ishmael were standing, they looked to be more than friends.

"I think your sex question has just been answered," Shiniqua stated.

"That bitch better get the fuck outta my man's face," I spewed. I walked toward Ishmael with a mean switch in my hips. My pressure had risen and anger was oozing out of my pores. I turned to my left to make sure Shiniqua was beside me, just in case shit jumped off.

Shiniqua whispered, "If that bitch swings on you, I'm whipping

Kimber's ass! Don't worry, I got your back."

I nodded my approval.

As we inched closer, I sized up Toya. Although she was shorter in height, probably around 5'4", she was thick. She was dark chocolate with the body of a video hoochie. She wore the Hawaiian silky full weave, dangling earrings, and the latest gear she could boost from the department stores. Instantly, I hated her.

As we approached, Ishmael took a few steps back and tried to put distance between him and Toya. This behavior didn't go unnoticed by Toya. She turned around to see who was coming. When she saw me, her face soured and her body language changed. She placed her hands on her hips and stepped forward.

"What's up, Ishmael?" I asked, and then glared at Toya.

"Yeah, Ishmael. What's up?" Toya questioned.

He ignored her. "What's up, baby girl," he answered me.

A surge of relief flowed through me. "Nothing," I replied. "Shiniqua and I are about to go get something to eat. Can I have some money?"

I was really showing out because I'd never asked him for money before, but Ishmael didn't hesitate to go inside his pocket and pull out a wad of cash. He peeled off five twenty-dollar bills and handed them to me. When I leaned over to kiss him, Toya went off.

"Oh, motherfucker, you gonna try to play me for this bitch?" she screamed.

"Who the fuck you calling a bitch, you ho!" I snapped back.

"You bitch! I'll break your fucking face!"

Ishmael jumped between us. "Toya, you better chill," he warned.

"Yeah, you fucking ugly-ass, monkey-looking trick!" I yelled. "Don't let the slim frame fool you! I will beat—"

Toya swung over Ishmael's head to hit me, but she only caught air. Before I could react, Ishmael hauled off and punched her dead in the face. Toya stumbled backward but caught her balance before she hit the ground. We were all stunned. I never knew that Ishmael would be the type of man to hit a woman, even if she did start wildin' with me.

Toya came up beefing. "You little-dick motherfucker! You gonna get yours! You gonna hit me for this skinny, toothpick-looking bitch?"

"Eat dick, tramp," I yelled.

Kimber grabbed her friend by the arm and began dragging her out of the projects, but Toya wouldn't go quietly. She continued to threaten me and Ishmael, so Shiniqua and I began popping shit too.

"We'll whip her ass if you don't get out of our project," Shiniqua yelled. After our screaming match was over and Toya and Kimber had disappeared from sight, I turned to Ishmael.

"So, you fucking her?" I asked point blank.

"That chick is crazy!" he said and looked toward the ground.

"You didn't answer my question!"

Ishmael looked back up at me. "Nah, ma, I ain't never touch her. She all on my dick. Kept coming through in tight jeans like I was gonna start liking her ugly ass, but I didn't."

Even though I still didn't quite believe him, I was glad to hear the words. "I can't believe you hit her!"

"She's lucky I didn't beat her ass! And I don't even hit girls, but when she tried to swing on you, I had to step in and defend my lady. Otherwise, I don't know what would have happened." He laughed.

"You got it twisted," Shiniqua jumped in to defend me. "Just because Lisa weighs a buck soakin' wet, she gets busy. Trust. I saw her go blow for blow with chicks twice her weight."

I looked at Ishmael and realized that he wasn't thoroughly convinced that I could handle mines in a street brawl, and that was why he hit Toya. There wasn't any way he was going to allow his girl to get beat down in her own projects by an outsider. I loved him even more for defending me.

We sat around Ishmael for less than an hour before Timothy scooped him up to go take care of business. We decided to go see Knowledge earlier than planned. As usual, Shiniqua was on point.

"Yo, I'm going upstairs first to take off these heels and put on my sneakers. I suggest you do the same."

"Why?" I asked.

She gave me an are-you-stupid look.

"You really are from Queens, aren't you?" She shook her head. "Let me give you a lesson 'bout the hood. This shit ain't over with you and Toya."

"But Ishmael is the one she should be mad with, and he also told her in her face that I'm his girl."

"Girl, you ain't learned nothing by living in Marcy all these years?" Shiniqua exhaled. "Just put on your sneakers and be prepared for anything as we walk through their hood."

I thought about what she was trying to tell me. Although I wasn't a punk, I thought that perhaps we shouldn't go into Sumner until the heat had died down with me and Toya. Truth be told, I didn't like Sumner. I never felt safe in there.

"Then if it could do down with me and Toya, why are we going on her territory? Shouldn't I just wait until she comes through here, and fight her?"

"Are you fucking kidding me? Everyone knows our blueprint. If we fall back from walking through Sumner, then we will be bait for everyone to test us."

What Shiniqua was saying made sense, although I still didn't have a good feeling about Toya. What if we fought and she won? Then I realized that I couldn't let that happen. If Toya wanted a fight, then that's what I'd give her. And under no circumstances was I coming out a loser.

As we made our way up Park Avenue past Tompkins toward Sumner, Shiniqua and I stopped at the local bodega across from Sumner to get a bag of potato chips and some Snapple's. When we came out, we saw a group of girls running our way. Toya was the ring leader. My heart began to flutter. I looked to Shiniqua for strength.

"Concentrate only on Toya. I don't care how many of them jump you, just continue to do damage to Toya. You hear me?"

"Most definitely!"

"I'ma stomp my foot in Kimber's ass!"

By now we were surrounded. No one said a word. We continued to walk toward Sumner with the gang scampering behind.

"I can't wait to see Knowledge," Shiniqua said.

"I'm sure your boo misses you," I replied, playing into the scenario.

"Knowledge don't give a fuck about you! You bum bitch!" someone yelled, and the crowd erupted in laughter.

Shiniqua stopped and turned to face the crowd. I knew it was about to go down. "No, Ishmael don't give a fuck about ya girl Toya, and Knowledge is on my shit!"

"Fuck you, Shiniqua! I don't got a problem with you! It's ya homegirl that I'm gonna fuck up!" Toya threatened.

"You feel froggy, then jump, bitch!" I stated, and it was on. The crowd opened up to give us room to fight. Toya began dancing around, hopping from one foot to the other like a pro fighter. She had the hand movements and all. I stood firm on my feet, hands cocked to block any blows. We both swung and connected. I charged into her and we began thumping. I was fiercely hitting her with upper left and right cuts while she kept going for my face and hair. When she had a firm grip on a handful of my hair, I followed with about six or seven quick body shots. Toya loosened her grip and I kicked her dead in her pussy. She screamed in agony, lost her footing, and fell to her knees, but not before she reached up and dug her fingernails into my face. I fell on top of her and bit into her fleshy cheek, almost ripping it off. Her screams were piercing.

You could hear Shiniqua's voice cheering me on, mixed in with my adversaries' shouts coaxing on Toya. Soon I felt fists beating into my back and head. Although I was in great pain, I continued to listen to Shiniqua and concentrated on whipping Toya's ass! I did everything in my power to do damage to the girl as I straddled her. My larger fists continually pounded into her eyes and mouth until she squirted blood. The pain from sneakers kicking me in my head and neck fueled my rage. I wanted Toya dead.

Soon a few neighborhood parents began breaking us up. As we were pulled apart, I got a look at Toya's face and it was fucked up. I had punched her right eye closed and her face was bloody and puffy. I ran to look at my face in a car mirror and was relieved when I saw that I looked OK. As everyone gathered themselves, I looked for Shiniqua and nearly fainted when I saw her.

Immediately I looked around, picked up a pipe, and went berserk. I swung wildly, trying to knock Toya's head off. She broke away and ran toward her building. When the others saw Knowledge running toward the scene, they began running as well. Everything was happening so fast. Just as Timothy, who'd gotten a call from Knowledge, came screeching up, I ran to Shiniqua.

"Shiniqua, your face!" I screamed. Her beautiful chocolate skin was furrowed with long, bleeding cuts. One of the girls in Toya's crew must have had a razor blade.

"Lisa, it's stinging! My face is stinging!" she cried. Her yellow shirt was soaked in blood. My back started stinging as well as if in sympathy.

Everyone started talking at once in a panic. Timothy calmed down the situation.

"Yo, Ishmael, take my car and drive my sister to Woodhull Hospital to get her face stitched up."

Shiniqua began to cry louder. She was almost hysterical. She kept yelling, "Oh God, my face . . . my face . . ."

"Tell them that only a plastic surgeon can work on my sister's face," Timothy instructed. "They sliced her with a razor. You understand me, Ishmael? Only a plastic surgeon. If I come there and a general doctor touched my sister's face, I'ma fuck somebody up!"

Timothy's brown eyes had turned black. He looked to me.

"Lisa, who the fuck cut my sister?"

"We were fighting Toya and Kimber. They jumped us. I don't know who pulled out a razor." I leaned down and placed my hands on my knees for support because I was so tired. That's when everyone realized I was bleeding from my back. Ishmael came over and lifted up my shirt.

"Yo, she got cut too! Lisa, get in the car. I gotta get y'all to the hospital."

As we climbed in, I overheard Timothy telling Knowledge to show him where Toya and Kimber lived.

When we got to the hospital, Ishmael told the triage nurse what Timothy instructed him to say. The nurse immediately took us in the back. They wrapped a special type of gauze around my back which stopped the bleeding until the plastic surgeon was called. I could either sit up or lay on my stomach. Shiniqua, on the other hand, was still hysterical when the nurse brought her in. They had to give her a sedative, then stop her face from bleeding with the same type of gauze until the plastic surgeon arrived.

As she lay on the hospital bed, I held her hand and couldn't stop crying. I felt awful. Her beautiful face would be ruined for life, and for what? Over a man who wasn't even her man? And was he really even mine? I was disgusted and angry with Ishmael. Had he been faithful, this never would have happened.

"Get the fuck away from her!" I screamed and startled everyone.

"Lisa, why you bugging out?" Ishmael asked as he moved to calm me down.

"This is all your fault!" I accused. "Those girls wanted to hurt us over you!"

The nurses and doctors came over and told me that I had to keep it down, and reminded me that we were in a hospital.

"I'm not being quiet until he leaves!"

They looked at Ishmael and then the doctor said, "Sir, you'll have to leave. These girls have been through enough."

Ishmael nodded. "Lisa, no matter what, I love you." He fidgeted for a moment with his jeans and cell phone, and then finally left. Once he was gone, I climbed into the small hospital bed with Shiniqua and hugged her as tightly as I could. After several hours we were awakened by the resident plastic surgeon, a Dr. Maddox. He was a short, balding Jewish man with kind eyes and soft hands.

"Hi, girls," he said. We both struggled to wake up and focus. When I looked around, Shiniqua's mother was sitting in the empty chair, her eyes bloodshot and puffy. "My name is Dr. Maddox and I'm going to be doing both of you girls' surgeries. I'm going to take Shiniqua first, and then I'll come back for you, Lisa."

Shiniqua began to cry again. Streaming tears flowed freely from her eyes and she gasped at the salty sting of the tears in the cuts on her face. Her mother grabbed her hand and whispered words of encouragement in her ear.

"Dr. Maddox, please do a good job on my best friend's face," I pleaded.

"I'll do my best," he assured me.

After they wheeled Shiniqua away, her mother said, "You know Timothy shot up that whole project looking for them girls. He even shot up Toya's door." She sighed deeply. "Lisa, it's bad right now for my son. He's gotta lay low for a while."

"For shooting a door?" I asked, perplexed.

"Toya's little brother was on the other side. He didn't make it." I closed my eyes and said a quick prayer for the little boy. "Her whole family is here and the cops have already been to my house, looking for Timothy. I done moved all his drugs and guns out of the house and he's going to stay with my sister in the Pink Houses Projects until all this dies down. At the moment, they don't got any eyewitnesses. Just hearsay."

"Toya's brother is dead?" I asked. I was dumbfounded.

"Look, they tried to kill my baby!" she snapped. "And you too!"

"Ms. S, I'm not judging. I'm just asking. It serves them right for fucking with us!" I stated what I felt she wanted to hear, although I was conflicted. On one hand, I did want revenge for what happened to Shiniqua, but I wasn't sure that the punishment fit the crime. Toya's brother didn't have anything to do with the situation. Then I realized that neither did Shiniqua. She was slashed to pieces over my beef. Fate was surely explaining to me in unequivocal measure how life could change in a nanosecond. The saying "Everything was all good just a week ago" was an understatement. How about, "Everything was all good ten minutes ago?" That's how quickly shit could escalate in the projects.

"Lisa, I know you're fairly new to how things are done around here, and you're a good girl. But if you're gonna survive out here in these streets, you gotta toughen up. I'm thirty-eight-years-old, and I've seen it all. We live old school out here—an eye for an eye. You stab my baby,

I'll shoot yours. You don't bring a knife to a gunfight, bottom line. I heard you whipped Toya's ass. That's what you were supposed to do." She paused as a tear ran down her face. She composed herself and continued. "Shiniqua will tell you that if she ever lost a fight around here, she'd have me to deal with. I told her at eight years old that if she ever came up in my household crying, talking about somebody whipped her, then not only would I whip her ass, but then I'd take her right back downstairs to fight that girl again while I stood there. And then I'd tell that girl to go and get her mother, because I'd whip her ass too!"

She wiped some more tears from her face. "In life, Lisa, besides your immediate family, you choose only one best friend to ride or die for. That's it. One. All other friends are expendable. Besides your best friend, you put yourself and your needs first. Get yours out of life, because you only get one."

I listened to Ms. S speak about the streets and something inside me connected. I was the one friend that Shiniqua chose to ride for. Timothy did what he had to do in the name of family to protect us. I started to understand their family values and loyalty. It was a little hard for me at first, because although it seemed that my family—growing up in a two-parent home—was more equipped to stand together, I didn't experience that loyalty until I stepped outside into a surrogate family.

After we were released from the hospital, it took about two weeks for Shiniqua's swelling to go down on her face and neither one of us went to Marcy Day. Things had changed drastically. With Timothy on the run in Pink Houses, Ishmael had to step up and handle Timothy's business. Sometimes Timothy would wake us up at three or four o'clock in the morning when he crept through to check up on us. We missed him so much, but it was best that he stayed away.

Things with Ishmael and me had also changed. We still continued to see each other, but my heart was no longer in it. I think he could sense that I was no longer feeling him the same way. We still had sex, but I no longer made love to him. I was just going through the motions. When it came time for shopping for college, he gave me two thousand dollars of his hard-earned money, hoping to turn the tide, but I just took the money as if it was owed to me.

It had been at least three weeks now since the incident, and Shiniqua still didn't want to go outside. I thought that my splitting my money with her would change her mind, but it didn't. When her mother overheard her turning me down, she flipped.

"You know I done let you sit up in here sulking for the past weeks 'cause I know you went through something traumatic. But those days are over. This girl done got some money, and she's willing to share it with you so you can have nice things for school." Shiniqua was going to take some classes at Kingsborough Community College. "I'm about to go down to Phyllis's house to play a game of spades and talk shit. When I get back, you better not be here! With or without cuts on your face, you're still the prettiest girl in this hood. You hear me?"

"Ma, I don't wanna—" Shiniqua whined.

"You heard what the fuck I said!" her mother roared, and Shiniqua got the message.

It took Shiniqua about an hour to decide on which outfit she would wear outside. Once she was dressed, she combed her hair toward her face to cover up as many scars as possible. Truly, her face didn't look great, but the doctor did a really good job, and I felt like it was healing nicely. Only time would tell how badly the scarring would be. Would I want to be scarred like her? No. But as she got dressed, I was still proud of her.

"My mother gets me so sick," she sulked. "But I feel her."

From that day forward there wasn't any more hiding in the house for her. She was almost back to normal. She even went outside sometimes without me, and once again she walked through Sumner to see Knowledge, alone. The only difference was that she kept a small .22 tucked nicely in her purse as an extra measure of protection. Her courage gave me courage.

My words at the hospital must have impacted Ishmael more than I thought, because he was at the apartment almost every day. Whatever we wanted—and whatever we didn't want—he got it. Clothes, ice cream, music, shows—Ishmael was a one-man Fulton Street Mall. It was like he had two jobs—holding down Timothy's business, and taking care of me and Shiniqua. Even though I knew his actions were from guilt, Shiniqua made it a point to thank him for every kindness, no matter how small. How she was able to forgive him, I didn't know, and I silently marveled at her strength. I don't know if I would have been as nice had I been in her shoes. In fact, I treated Ishmael worse than Shiniqua did.

"Ma, why you still mad at me?" Ishmael implored one day.

"Who said I was mad?" I flipped a page in my magazine.

"You don't hardly speak to me anymore, we never go out, and we ain't sexed in, like, forever."

"Why don't you call Toya to help you out?" I snapped.

Ishmael threw up his hands in frustration. "How many times do I gotta say I'm sorry, Lisa? I mean, damn! I ain't ask for Shiniqua to get slashed. I ain't tell Toya and her nutjob crew to be slashing people."

"If you had kept yourself to yourself, none of this would have happened."

"Fine, Lisa. If you want me to admit that I was wrong—again— then I'll admit it. I was wrong. I should have walked away from Toya from jump. I shouldn't have disrespected you. But I did, and it happened, and there's nothing we can do about it now."

"Yes, there is. Right now I can be there for Shiniqua while she heals from the scars those bitches put on her face." I turned my back to him to end the conversation.

"Well, what about us?" Ishmael asked.

"What about us?"

"You trying to break up or something? 'Cause you actin' like it's a chore just to be around me these days."

I was silent. I didn't know how to answer him without tapping into my own guilt. It was safer to put it all on him.

Ishmael shook his head and turned to leave. He put his hand on the doorknob and said, "You remember what I told you when you first became my girl? I'm not letting you go." He walked out the door, leaving me with plenty more to think about.

✳✳

By October things were going well. I was settling into my classes at Baruch College and Shiniqua was enjoying her classes at Kingsborough, but there was something that still didn't sit well with me. I still couldn't help but blame myself for my best friend getting slashed. That guilt alone was affecting my relationship with Ishmael. He knew it and I knew it. But he had to understand, I owed Shiniqua so much. She gave me friendship, she gave me a new family, and most importantly, she never blamed me for the Toya incident. When I mentioned it, she just said, "Charge it to the game!" Only I couldn't.

In the cold fall months, I began leaving right after school, dressed incognito, to infiltrate Sumner projects in hopes of seeking revenge. My first victim was Kimber. Her crew snitched her out and told the streets that she had pulled the blade from the inside of her cheek and took turns cutting Shiniqua, with Maria and Donna helping to open up my best friend's face.

After watching Kimber's routine for weeks, I hid behind a Dumpster on a day I didn't have class until she came stomping up the block on her way to the store. Her iPod was in her ears and she was oblivious to all around her. With a ski jacket and knitted cap over my face to disguise myself, I swung a metal pipe and knocked her to her knees. When she fell forward, I pulled out my razor and opened up her face from behind. Four to five slashes and I took off running down the block without looking back.

It took me longer to get to Maria and Donna, since they traveled almost everywhere together, but I got daring and used my pepper spray to get them both at the same time.

After I finished cutting Maria and Donna, I noticed my flesh was oozing blood from a deep cut that went down my thumb bone. I screamed in horror and bolted up the six flights of steps to our apartment. Quickly I opened the door and ran to Ms. Ship, who was in her bed taking a nap.

"I need help," I said, panicking.

Her eyes flew open in horror as she reacted to my tone. "What's happened? Is Shiniqua all right?" Quickly her eyes scanned my injury.

"Yes. She's OK, but I've done something awful."

"Who cut you?" Ms. S already had a washcloth pressed to my wound to stop the bleeding. She took it away and examined the cut. "You're going to need stitches. This is bad."

"Owww," I yelped as she poured peroxide over the wound. "It hurts!"

"Who did this to you, and where's Shiniqua?!" Her voice was level and stern.

"She should be at school, but I had some business to take care of."

"What kind of business?" she snapped. "With who?"

"With Maria and Donna from Sumner. Please don't be mad," I said in a rush, "but I cut them. It's bad."

Ms. Ship took a closer look at my blood-drenched ski jacket and assessed the situation quickly. "Don't tell me that you're the one who cut Kimber too?"

Rumors were running rampant around Marcy after Kimber's attack. Of course, everyone speculated that Timothy was back, terrorizing in the name of his sister. Kimber said she was attacked by four guys, only she didn't get a look at them because she was knocked out cold by a fist. The projects had begun to fear Shiniqua even more.

I looked down in shame. "Yes, ma'am," I replied.

She burst out laughing and gave me a big hug. "Girl, this project done brought the beast out of you! I always knew you had it in you, but this . . . this is what I'm talking about! You're a Ship now!"

"You're not mad?" I asked. Had this been my mother, I would be getting whipped and be on punishment.

"Mad for taking up for family? Never. It serves them bitches right! I hope you got them good too!"

"Yes, ma'am."

"And no more of that ma'am shit! I'm nobody's ma'am. I'm thirty-eight years young, so call me Ma, like my kids."

My eyes welled up with tears and I embraced her tightly around her waist. She had to pry my arms from around her and drag me to the hospital. We caught a cab over the Brooklyn Bridge to Beth Israel hospital in lower Manhattan. Ms. S said that she didn't want anyone suspecting that I was the one who cut those girls because I could face getting locked up. "You and Shiniqua have been through enough," she stated firmly.

When we got home that evening, Shiniqua was there. I was groggy from the pain medication the doctor prescribed for me on top of the local anesthesia for my thumb.

"What the hell happened to your hand?" Shiniqua asked, looking at my heavily bandaged thumb.

"I got into something," I said. "You heard anymore about who cut Kimber, Maria, and Donna?"

Shiniqua shook her head. "Nope. No one has a clue, except to think that my brother somehow has some super powers and got this done, even though he's laying low."

"I mean, them girls done did a bunch of folks sheisty, so who knows who got them?" I argued.

Shiniqua shook her head. Her hair fell across the faint scars on her face. She had healed nicely, and you had to get up close to her to even see the scars, but they were still there.

"It's my fault," she whispered.

"What?" I went and sat down next to her. I smoothed back her hair. "What do you mean, it's your fault?"

"This is my karma coming back on me, Lisa. This is what I gotta pay for, for fucking them girls up so many times during my fights."

"No, Shiniqua, this is not your karma. This was the work of some sick girls who didn't know how to let a nigga go gracefully, and then they wrote some checks their asses couldn't cash." I looked into her eyes. "So how is that your fault?"

She just shook her head again. "I just wish that people would stop saying that Timothy did it. He's out there laying low over the death of Toya's little brother, and that's enough. He wouldn't be stupid enough to catch a case over some razor cuts, even though I know that he would do it because he loves me."

"Well, I love you too, Shiniqua, and I'd do the same thing for you."

Shiniqua laughed. "No disrespect, Lisa, but you ain't built for that."

"How you figure?" I challenged.

"You just aren't," Shiniqua replied.

"That just goes to show what you know," I retorted smugly as I held up my bandaged thumb. Shiniqua raised her eyebrow, a la Timothy. When she realized what I was saying, her expression turned to shock, then admiration, then happiness and peace.

"You the one who got them bitches?" Shiniqua asked.

"Yup," I said proudly.

Shiniqua was still stunned. "I can see, kind of, you taking out Kimber, but Maria and Donna? Together?" Her face filled with admiration. "How did you do it?

I told her about my preparation and Shiniqua just nodded with approval. She listened then threw her arms around me in gratitude. Tears streaked her cheeks.

"Thank you, Lisa," she whispered. "I love you, girl. You like my sister, for real, a real ride or die chick."

"I love you back, Shiniqua," I said with tears streaking my voice.

Cutting those girls was a small repayment of the many kindnesses she'd done for me over the years. I could have been offended that Shiniqua didn't think I was tough enough to fight at her level, but I wasn't. Instead I proved myself with Kimber, Maria, and Donna, and the look on her face was priceless when I told her that it was me, alone. It was one of the highlights of my life.

Lisa Henderson

As winter's chill breezed through the projects, my relationship with Ishmael began to heat up. After months of handling Timothy's business, he was no longer selling hand-to-hand. Now he was supplying weight, which meant he was seeing money hand over fist. Rumor had it that he was fucking with the infamous BMF organization, which stood for Black Mafia Family. Ishmael wouldn't confirm or deny this to me. Whenever I asked, he simply told me to mind my own business and that he was a man behind anything he did and for me not to worry.

No longer was I satisfied with four chicken wings and shrimp fried rice from the Chinese restaurant. Ishmael would take me over the bridge to high-end eateries such as Chin-Chin or Tao, where our bills would be well over two or three hundred dollars. My small project closet was bursting with garments from Donna Karan, Yves Saint Laurent, and Gucci. My footwear was no longer Air Force Ones but Manolo Blahniks and Jimmy Choos.

The money was so good, and I was so spoiled, that Ishmael stopped talking about saving up enough money to buy a Subway franchise and go legit. He had enough money now to buy ten franchises, but he seemed to enjoy the hustle of slinging weight and the prestige of being Timothy's second in command. Even Timothy's brothers deferred to Ishmael.

On this particular day I was excited to come home with my first semester report card. Ishmael had promised that if I got all As, he would buy me a mink coat. It was a bit of a challenge since I was taking a biology class that was much harder than I'd anticipated, but I think he wanted to make gift giving more fun for himself as the giver.

The night before, I couldn't sleep. There were only three other girls my age in the projects that had a mink coat. First there was the local booster, Cocoa, who was fifteen years old. The older boosters liked her because she was fearless and under sixteen. When she got knocked, they usually just gave her a slap on the wrist and she was free to go.

The second girl was Missy. Technically, she shouldn't get any props because her mink coat was a hand-me-down from her mother. The coat looked dry and lackluster from years of neglect but still, it was a mink.

And finally, there was Shiniqua. She had just gotten her coat last month for her nineteenth birthday. It was a gift from Knowledge. Shiniqua squealed up and down when she got her coat, but she wouldn't even try it on. She simply stroked it and vowed not to wear her coat until I got one. She was my sister, for real.

That was when I put my plan into motion with Ishmael, although it wasn't hard for him to figure it out. He knew that once Shiniqua got a mink that I'd want one too. The report-card game was just a way for me to get it without making Ishmael seem too whipped.

As soon as I got upstairs, I called Ishmael.

"Hey, baby," I sang. "Guess who aced all my classes?"

"Who?" he asked, playing along.

"Me! I got all As and now I want my coat."

"You even got an A in that biology class? You was having some trouble with that for a minute."

"Yup," I said proudly. "I knocked it out the box, including the lab." I switched the phone to my other ear. "So when can I get my coat?"

"Geez, slow down, ma! I think I'm slowly turning you into a spoiled bitch!"

The smile died on my face. "Huh?"

"You heard me," Ishmael retorted. "It's like the only time you call with excitement in your voice is when you want something." He paused for emphasis, and then continued. "The only time I get my dick sucked is after I buy you some bullshit outfit, or some Jimmy Choos."

His harsh words threw me off balance. I didn't know why he was bringing all this up now. My eyes began to fill with tears. "That's not true . . ." I started to say, then I realized that it was.

Ishmael snorted. He knew he'd made his point. "Look, I gotta go. I'll call you later."

"Wait!"

"What?" he snapped with irritation.

"Are you coming over later to give me the money for my coat?"

Click. He hung up in my ear.

After doing my homework, I made a few phone calls to a bunch of phony bitches that had been blowing up my phone all day. Of course, it was mostly my fault. I had been bragging all day about getting the money for my mink coat, and everyone was calling to check up on it. Naturally I lied and told them what they didn't want to hear.

"Yeah, he just left here and gave me ten thousand dollars for my coat. I'm going to buy it this weekend. . . . Sure, you can come too."

I couldn't think about how I would answer the questions when my coat never surfaced. I'd think about that tomorrow. Today I couldn't wait for Shiniqua to come back from Knowledge's house. I needed her to school me on what the fuck had happened with Ishmael, and what I apparently did wrong.

Shiniqua looked really cute. She had on a winter-white ski jacket with white UGG boots and a pair of tight jeans. No longer feeling self-conscious about her scars, her hair was pulled back into a tight ponytail and she had on white fox earmuffs. Her cheeks were rosy from the frighteningly frigid weather.

"Wait. Hold up," I said. "Freeze frame, bitch. You look so cute!"

She laughed. "Yeah, my man liked it too."

"I bet he did. Ho," I teased.

Shiniqua walked into our room and began to take off her clothes. Once she was settled and changed into more comfortable at-home attire, I asked for her advice.

"Hey, girlie, we need to talk."

Brushing her hair, she replied, "About what?"

"Well, you know Ishmael was supposed to give me the money—"

"Oh yeah," she interjected. "What happened? Did he give it to you?"

"Nope!"

"No?" She spun around, brush in hand, and stared at me. "Why not?"

"You tell me, because I can't get an answer from him. I called him right after school and told him I aced my grades, and he gets all mad, saying that I'm turning into a spoiled bitch and he should kill me!"

"What? Are you serious?" She frowned. "What did you say to him?"

"I didn't know what to say. I was bugging out from his behavior, and then he hung up on me!"

"Get the fuck out of here!" she exclaimed. I now had her full attention. "I know you called back and cursed his ass out!"

I shook my head.

"Now had that been me hanging up on you, you would have went berserk!" she observed. "But let's think this through. He knew you would get all As."

"Exactly. So what's the problem?"

"There ain't one. He wanted to make a problem, 'cause that's what men do. He wanted you to give him a reason to prolong buying you that coat, and in the meantime, you'll be kissing his ass and all types of shit. You feel me?"

I thought for a moment. "True."

"Look, call him back and ask him again what time he's coming over to give you the money. When he tries to pull you into arguing with him, don't fall for it. Just keep being nice. Either you think like a nigga or get hurt like a bitch."

I nodded. "What if he doesn't pick up when I call?"

"Then call again. He'll play himself if he doesn't pick up all night. It's still early. It's only seven o'clock."

I flipped open my cell phone, and to my surprise, Ishmael picked up.

"Hey, I just wanted to know if you're still coming over?" My voice was smooth as silk and level.

"I don't know. I got shit to do."

"Well, let me know. Ms. S. made spare ribs for dinner, and I could save you a plate."

"You know I don't eat pork," he snapped.

"What's your problem? You're carrying me like a new bitch? I know what you eat and don't!" I flipped. I couldn't help it. He'd gotten underneath my skin with his bullshit tantrums. Shiniqua shook her head at my comment, but I didn't care.

"A'ight, make me a plate. I'll be there in an hour."

After we hung up, I exhaled.

"What did he say?" Shiniqua was enthusiastic.

"He said he'll be here in an hour to bring me my dough. He'd better had said that, or I was cutting his ass off, for real."

"You weren't gonna do shit, punk!" Shiniqua laughed. "You should have seen your face when he screamed on you. You looked like a deer blinded by headlights!"

I rolled my eyes.

Dinner came and went, but Ishmael never showed. I was furious and fearful. What did this mean? Was it over? Had he found another girlfriend?

"Don't worry," Shiniqua soothed. "You can share my coat."

"How's that gonna look? We're not crabs. People will know we're sharing one coat. They're not dummies." I sulked.

"That's true. So I'll get in touch with Timothy and tell him that he's gotta buy you a coat too."

"You know he's not gonna do it. Ever since Ishmael and I made it clear that we were together, Timothy said he's no longer responsible for me. Besides, he's not my man. Ishmael is."

"But Timothy is tripping. He still buys me shit, and Knowledge buys me shit too."

"Well, you have the best of both worlds, and Timothy is your blood brother. But honestly, let's not make this about Timothy. He's not the bad guy. Ishmael is. I hate when a person promises something and don't keep their word! That's tired."

I continually called Ishmael's cell phone until I fell asleep around midnight. In a delirious, dreamy haze, I felt something silky between my fingertips. As I tried to lift my heavy eyes open, they were snapped back shut when Ishmael blew into them with his hot breath. Suddenly I was wide awake.

"What are—oh my gosh!" I squealed. "You bought it! You bought it!" My smile was wider than a football field. Immediately I leapt from the bed and tried on my luxurious coat. This was one of the best days of my life. At that moment, I was reminded of my childhood fantasies. I wanted wealth. I wanted to live the life of the rich and famous.

"Of course I bought it." He smiled as he admired me admiring my coat.

"But how did you know what to get me?"

"I know what you like," he bragged.

Ms. S and Shiniqua both were up to help share my moment. You would have thought that Ishmael had just proposed marriage or something, because they both had wet eyes and concrete smiles of approval.

"I'm hungry as a motherfucker!" Ishmael stated after he'd gotten bored watching me model.

"Watch your mouth!" I scolded and did a head nod toward Ms. S.

"Oh, my bad," Ishmael said in embarrassment. "Pardon me, Ms. S."

"Boy, please." Ms. S waved a hand to dismiss his apology. "You ain't said nothing I ain't heard before. Lisa, go in there and fix him a plate of food. There's a new bottle of Pepsi y'all can open up, but make sure you close the bottle tight when you're done. I don't like me no flat soda. And make sure you clean up the kitchen when you're done. I don't want to wake up in the morning to a table full of roaches and a sink full of dishes."

"I will," I replied. I looked to Shiniqua to see if she was gonna come and join us, but she climbed into bed.

After Ishmael ate his dinner, he sneakily motioned for me to come with him into the living room. When he put his index finger over his plump lips, I knew what he wanted to do. He sat on the sofa and unzipped his jeans. He gave me a nasty look and said, "Come thank daddy for your coat."

I removed my panties from under my nightgown and straddled him. As he gently eased inside me he began to whisper how good my pussy was. All I could think about was my coat. The mere excitement had me wetter than Niagara Falls. As Ishmael made promises to love me forever, I thought about the next gift I'd crack for—a car.

Lisa Henderson

This was the night of all nights! Shiniqua and I had decided to go out on a double date with Ishmael and Knowledge. We were going to the Sunrise Cineplex movie theater in Queens, and then shooting over to City Island in the Bronx for a seafood dinner.

We both wore form-fitting sweater dresses by Anne Klein. I wore knee-high boots with a flat heel by Marc Jacobs and Shiniqua wore her favorite pair of Christian Louboutin stilettos. Our hair was long and flowing. The only difference was that Shiniqua had recently dyed her black hair a chestnut brown. The color brought out the gold undertones of her skin. To make our outfits complete, we both donned our most prized possessions. I adored my full-length, jet-black mink coat with bishop sleeves, while Shiniqua had the mahogany three-quarter length swing coat.

"My girls look fly," Ms. S commented as we were about to walk out the door. "Are they downstairs?"

"Yeah, Knowledge called and said to meet him and Ishmael at the cut on Park Avenue," Shiniqua replied.

"OK, be careful," she stated. "And have fun." We both kissed Ms. S before leaving for our dates.

As we walked through the projects, all eyes were on us. Little kids came running up to us asking stupid questions. Mothers were giving us looks of approval as we passed by. And haters were doing what they do as they sat on the bench, as if it wasn't thirty degrees outside.

Two sound systems boomed. Knowledge was an old-school lover so I was sure that vintage Run-DMC cut, "Run's House," was blaring from his 2000 black Yukon. And since I knew Ishmael pegged himself as a lover, "I Don't Wanna" by Aaliyah was definitely coming from his ride. What I didn't know was that Ishmael had traded in his modest Honda for a stunning, black 2004 Mercedes S430. I nearly peed myself when I saw it, but I remained calm. The thought crossed my mind that Ishmael was no longer trying to be like Timothy. He was trying to be Timothy. That took me through a few emotions all at once—jealousy, envy, resentment, anger, and bewilderment. Where the fuck was my ride?

Ishmael and Knowledge were posted up outside of their vehicles, politicking with a small group of guys who were obviously riding dick.

"Lisa, you see that shit?" Shiniqua asked.

"Uh-hunh," I replied.

"Did you know about the car?"

"Not at all."

When Ishmael spotted me, he rudely pushed a few strangers out of his way and ran to embrace me. My sour mood faded instantly.

"Don't my baby look hot!" he bragged. I heard a few ohhhs and ah-hhs. "What's up, Shiniqua?"

"How're you?"

"I'm good. You're looking good too."

Knowledge came forward to sweep up Shiniqua and shower her with compliments, especially after Ishmael had made such a show. Soon we were all in a circle, chatting in the cold. None of us had much of anything to say that we couldn't have said at dinner or the movies, but each one of us had the same idea—stay just long enough for as many people in the projects to see and admire us. The one person I didn't expect to see, though, saw me.

"Lisa? Is that you?" The familiar voice resonated through our chatter and cut the thick air like a knife. I spun around.

"Mommy?" It sounded almost like a question.

My mother's eyes scanned up and down my mink coat and then self-consciously she adjusted her wool frock. Even though we lived in the same housing project, I hadn't seen her since that day almost two years ago.

"Don't you look gorgeous? So grown up," she commented as she came and gave me a warm embrace. The crowd was dead silent. They all knew what had happened years ago, when my mother tried to beat me down in the courtyard in front of everybody over some stolen groceries. "Who are your friends?"

I hesitated. She knew who Shiniqua was. "Well this is Shiniqua, the girl I've been living with since you kicked me out."

She gave a faint smile in Shiniqua's direction but her eyes remained glued on the icy platinum chains around Ishmael's and Knowledges's necks.

"And this is Knowledge, Shiniqua's boyfriend." Knowledge gave her a head nod. Finally I said, "This is my boyfriend, Ishmael."

"Nice to finally meet you," he replied. To my amazement, my mother extended her hand and shook his vigorously.

"Likewise. So, Lisa, why don't you come over and bring your new boyfriend for dinner? I'm sure your family would love to meet him."

My family? She wasn't claiming me as family when she tried to beat me like a dog with an extension cord. Did she really think that she could waltz back into my life just like that after years of exile? I hesitated. The Ships were my family now, but I did miss my mommy.

"Ummm, OK, I'll do that." I turned to Ishmael. "You ready?"

"Yeah, let's bounce."

※※

Ishmael and I had just finished making love in a local motel on Atlantic Avenue. We were lying around watching cable when Ishmael made his announcement.

"Listen," Ishmael began, "I'm going to start giving you an allowance each week."

"An allowance? I'm sayin', I ain't a child!" I snapped.

Ishmael frowned. "What did I tell you about speaking like that? Saying 'ain't' and shit."

"You say it!"

"Well, you ain't me!" he teased. "And I don't want my lady speaking like a thug."

"Yes, sir!" I said, and did a one-hand salute.

"Yeah, so back to what I was saying. I'm going to give you two hundred dollars a week—"

I sucked my teeth. "Is that on top of the pocket money you already give me?"

"Nah. That's it. You gotta learn how to budget money."

Budget? I hadn't ever heard that word pass Ishmael's lips. "But I get more than that from you now," I sulked.

"Lisa, I'm not a Rockefeller. I got big dreams for us, and we gotta start preparing now. I want to own a chain of my own businesses, remember? And you're going to be a journalist. How do you think I'm going to pay for your college if we keep blowing through money like it's water?"

"I get financial aid, remember?"

"Yeah, but you still need extra stuff."

He stood, naked, and went to pee. When he walked back, fully exposed, I felt really adult. I loved looking at his naked body.

"OK, so two hundred for me a week. What, exactly, is that supposed to cover? I got to buy lunch for school, my Metrocard for the train, and what about clothes? Am I supposed to use that little bit of money for my clothes too?"

"Didn't I buy you more clothes than you can wear?"

"So I don't get any more clothes?"

"Lisa, stop acting like a spoiled bitch! You never used to carry me like that when you was broke and had just graduated from high school, so I don't know why you letting this little bit of paper go to your head." He stood and pulled on a pair of sweatpants and a T-shirt. "You ain't going to school for no fashion show. You're at a CUNY college, not FIT. So act like it. Wear what you got and concentrate on your grades." He picked up the remote control and started flipping channels.

I walked over and snuggled up next to him on the couch. "Are you still going to pay me every time I get straight As on my report card?"

Ishmael sucked his teeth and pushed me away. He climbed into bed, turning his back to me, and turned out the light. I sat there in the darkness, confused about what I'd done wrong.

Lisa Henderson

When I didn't move as quickly as my mother might have wanted, she came looking for me.

"Lisa, your mother's here. I'll get rid of her if you want," Ms. S stated as she stood at the doorway of the bedroom.

"She's here?" I asked, perplexed.

"Yeah. I made her wait in the hallway. She's lucky I didn't cuss her ass out! I been taking care of her daughter for years, and she didn't have the decency to send over a few dollars for food, shelter, or nothing. What she want now, after all this time done passed?"

"I don't know, but I'm gonna find out."

I walked toward the front door with trepidation. Why now? kept going through my head.

"Hey," I said.

Her grin was massive and inviting.

"I thought you were going to come over for dinner?"

"Actually, I didn't think I was welcome."

"Not welcome?" she repeated incredulously.

"Yes. You heard me. Not welcome. As in, I've knocked on your door in the past and you wouldn't let me in."

"When did you come by?" Her eyes were wide and innocent.

"Don't pretend as if you didn't hear me begging and pleading to be allowed back home."

"I don't have any idea what you're talking about. Just the other day I asked Jackie where were you? You know Jackie's returned back from Queens. She should be getting her associate's degree soon."

"Jackie? And what about my graduation? Huh? How could you have missed that?" I snapped.

"Lisa, I didn't come here to talk about the past," she stated, dismissing my issues. "I came here to tell you that we're family. I'm your mother and I want you back home."

"My home is here," I replied defiantly. "Look, I got homework to do."

"Of course. You always were a smart girl."

"See you around," I said and slammed the door in her face.

That night, I couldn't sleep. As angry and sullen as I felt about our relationship, if my mother was trying to embrace me, then I should at least allow her to do that. I missed my family. Still, my pride wouldn't allow me to go knock on their door. What if she changed her mind and didn't open it?

In the morning, I was quieter than usual. Shiniqua immediately noticed.

"What's wrong?"

"Did your mother tell you that Julie came by?"

"Yeah. So?"

"So she's trying to be friends again."

"Lisa, she's not your friend. She's your mother. Tell her to try that."

It wasn't a secret that Ms. S and Shiniqua couldn't stand my mother. Especially after they had to wipe away all my tears and fill me with praise to mend my broken heart. But this wasn't their decision. It was mine.

As the weeks passed, my mother and I rebuilt our relationship and it was better than ever. I was now the favorite daughter and Jackie had to take a backseat. Although I chose to continue living with Shiniqua, I visited my family regularly. And most times, I brought Ishmael with me.

"So, what time is your boyfriend coming?" my mother asked one day. "I don't want his food to get cold."

"Ma, Ishmael can put it in the microwave. We don't got to wait for him."

It was only her and me. John had reenlisted in the service to escape the projects, Jackie refused to be around me, and Nana was locked up in her room.

"Your father never had to microwave his food. It was always piping hot."

"Well Ishmael and I aren't married and even if we were, I doubt I'd be slaving over him. He's the man and should cater to me."

She stared at me with contempt. Those same sneaky eyes were back, the same eyes that made my skin crawl.

"You always think you're so much better than everybody—"

"No," I interrupted. "I didn't mean it to come out like that," I explained. My heart began to flutter with fear. "Look, you've prepared a nice dinner. But if you'd prefer to wait for Ishmael, we can do that. Just let me call him and find out how long he'll be."

I flipped out my phone and called Ishmael, hoping to get a pause from fighting with my mom. After he assured me that he'd be there within a half hour, which in his time meant one hour, my mother and I went to sit in the living room. My mother began to tell me about this banquet event that she was invited to by her girlfriend from our old neighborhood in Queens.

"Really? That sounds nice. When is it?"

"November first."

"On your birthday?"

"Yes, but I don't think I'm going."

"What? But why? You should go and have a good time."

"Well, I want to, but . . . I really don't have anything to wear. And even if I did find me a proper dress, I don't have a coat."

"Well do you want me to help you pick out something to wear in your closet while we wait for Ishmael?"

"Lisa, there isn't anything in that old closet."

"Nonsense. You've got to have something in there. Daddy used to buy you nice things."

"How long ago was that?" she snapped. "I haven't had anything new in years!"

Her anger resurfaced and I didn't know what I'd done to trigger it. "Well, maybe I could help you buy something to wear. I have some money from Ishmael that I could give you."

"That would be nice." Her smile resurfaced. "Do you think you could give it to me now? I want to go shopping tomorrow."

"S-s-sure," I sputtered. "Where are you going shopping?"

"Where do you go?" Again her tone was condescending.

"It depends. But mostly Shiniqua and I shop at Bloomingdale's on 59th Stree—"

"I know where Bloomingdale's is. I've been shopping there since before you were born."

It took every ounce of my restraint not to flip the fuck out on her. She was really testing me.

"So when's Daddy coming home?" I asked, trying to change the subject.

"I have more things to worry about than your sorry-ass father." She held out her hand. "You said you were giving me money."

We both stared fiercely into each other's eyes. I broke first, reached for my bag, and fumbled in my wallet. I knew I had close to six hundred dollars in there, but I didn't want to give it all to her. Nor did I know how much she was expecting. Her greedy eyes peered into my wallet and she observed my hesitation.

"I hope you have at least one thousand dollars in there. I want to get something really nice. You know how those Queens women are. They've already been talking about how we got kicked out. If I walk up in there in rags, I'll never be able to show my face again."

"I'll give you all that I have," I stated, and then peeled out all my money and shoved it into her palm.

"Well, how much is this?"

"It should be six hundred."

She licked her thumb and began counting the twenty-dollar bills quicker than a bank teller. She sighed. "It's only $564 here. When do you think you could get me the rest?"

"What rest?" My voice flared up. "This is all I got. You can either take it or leave it."

Her attitude quickly changed.

"Lisa, I know that we've never been close. I just want to apologize for treating you so poorly all your life. I've never shown you the love that I've shown your brother and sister. You're my daughter and I love you, and I know I've made mistakes. But please don't hold them against me. Can we please just move forward and forget about the past? We're family, and we're all we got."

Her heartfelt apology was unexpected. Yet I was grateful. In all these years, she'd never acknowledged that she treated me differently until now. Unfortunately, no one was around to witness this apology.

"Mommy, you don't have to apologize. I know you love me," I replied, and then we embraced. As we wrapped our arms around each other, I wanted to hold on forever, but my mother had other plans. She pulled back.

"Thank you again for this money. I'll go buy something really nice."

"Great!"

"Now you've solved one problem, but I still got another one. My coat. I don't own a decent coat, nor does your sister. What can I do for a coat? The only nice coat is your mink, and I don't want to wear that."

Is that a question? I wondered.

"Well, I got other coats that you could borrow," I offered.

"Other mink coats?"

"No. Regular wool coats. And one shearling."

"I'm not walking in there in a wool coat while everyone else will be in furs."

"I don't think so at all. Since when do Queens women know how to dress? You'll be fine in one of my other coats. I think a nice wool coat with a two-piece skirt suit will be appropriate for a banquet."

"Since when do you have the perfect etiquette? In my day, I was wearing tailored blazers and custom-made shoes. I know what is and is not appropriate! And a mink coat is what they're expecting me to wear!"

"But you just said that you didn't want to wear my mink."

"And I didn't hear you offer it, either."

"Well, if you want to wear it I'm sure that would be OK," I began, "but let me ask Ishmael first."

"Never mind. Forget it. If it's going to be all this damn drama over a little funky coat, then I'd rather not go. Besides, I shouldn't have to wear my daughter's coat. I should have my own."

Ishmael never did show up to have dinner that night. Finally, she wrapped up my plate of food and sent me on my way. When I walked in and saw Shiniqua and Ms. S sitting on the sofa sharing a pint of ice cream, I decided that I really wanted to work on my relationship with my mother.

My opportunity to do just that would come when Party, the best booster in our projects, came around selling a stolen mink jacket. She wanted twenty-five hundred. I thought that was fair, since it was brand new. I rushed upstairs and got my stash. I'd managed to put away close to four thousand dollars and I was about to take more than half and spend it on my mother. I thought this was a step in the right direction, but Shiniqua felt differently.

"Why are you doing this for her? Don't you realize she's just using you?"

"Shiniqua, this isn't your business."

"How you gonna say that, after all we've been through?"

"Because she's my mother!"

"And I'm your sister!"

"You're not my blood sister!" I retorted, and she stepped back as if I had slapped her face. If I wasn't so focused on doing this good deed for my mother, I would have realized that I'd just hurt her feelings.

"OK, that's true. I felt that you were my sister, but obviously you feel differently."

"Look, it's not that serious."

"Not that serious? I've sacrificed everything for you. And what about my mother? She's treated you like her own child. If anybody deserves that gift, it should be my mother!"

"Why are you acting jealous? You get money from Knowledge. Buy your mother a fucking coat. Stop being a hater!"

"A hater? Are you kidding me? You're a bum-ass bony bitch, sweetie. Didn't you get the memo? There's nothing much to hate!"

I flung my long hair in her direction and stood my ground. "At least when I look in the mirror I don't see Freddie Kruger!"

Shiniqua charged me fiercely with wild angry fists. Her anger was momentous as I blocked her blows. I began swinging back and we fell on my bed, her heavy weight on top of me. I reached up and dug my thumbs in her eyes to temporarily blind her. I needed to get her up off me or I was surely going to lose this fight.

She let go of me for a moment and grabbed her eyes. I took this chance to weasel out from under her dead weight. Thinking quickly, I picked up one of her Manolo Blahnik heels and began to beat her upside her head and face with one hand while punching her with the other.

"You thought you could beat my ass, bitch!" I taunted as I wailed on her. Soon we were in another physical embrace going punch for punch, slap for slap until I felt a stronger force pull us apart. Ms. S had come running into the room to separate us. We were both breathing heavily. I scanned the room for another weapon because I didn't know if they were going to jump me. I wasn't thinking straight and neither was Shiniqua because when I looked up, she was pointing a gun in my face.

"I dare you, bitch! Go ahead and pick somethin' else up! I fucking dare you!"

"Shiniqua, put that fucking gun down before I whip your ass!" Ms. S threatened. "I promise you that you don't want none of me!"

I was still popping shit because I knew she wasn't going to shoot shit. "Please, you punk bitch! You should have shot those bitches that cut your face!"

"I got cut for you! This is how you repay me!"

Ms. S roared, "ENOUGH!" I could see the hurt in her eyes. "Lisa, go take a walk for a little while until you cool off. Call Ishmael and tell him to come get you. Shiniqua, you leave too. I don't want to see either one of you until you got some sense in your heads."

Lisa Henderson

I could not believe Shiniqua and I had a fight! She truly had a gangster mentality by pulling out a gun on me. I thought we were better than that. Our altercation barely fazed her mother. It made me wonder how common this type of behavior was in their family. After I walked to the store to clear my head, I came right back. I grabbed an overnight bag, my mother's mink coat, and anything that I thought was irreplaceable just in case Shiniqua tried to spite me and destroy my things. After I put on my mink coat, I proceeded to leave.

"You moving out?" Ms. S asked with concern.

"I need a few days to myself," I hissed. "I'll be back next week." But I never planned on coming back. I called Ishmael. "Where are you?" I asked.

"I'm handling my business. What's up, baby?"

"Shiniqua and I just had a fight."

"Why y'all do that?" His voice was monotone and unenthused. His calm demeanor infuriated me.

I screamed, "That fucking bitch is crazy! She pulled out a gun on me!"

He panicked. "Word? You all right?"

"Hell no I'm not all right. I just had a gun in my face by that ghetto rug-rat! I need you to come get me!"

"OK, I'll be there in an hour. Where will you be?"

"I need you to get here sooner than that!" I snapped.

He countered, "I'm all the way in the Bronx, handling business. I'll get there when I can."

"I don't want to wait in this place! I'm so sick of living like this. These walls are closing in on me. I need to get out of here. Can I get in a cab and come meet you? I got money."

"Nah, not up here. It's too dangerous for my lady. Listen, just chill there for a little while. I promise, I'll be there before you know it. Just sit tight and wait on me."

"I'm going to my mother's. Come get me from there."

Walking through the projects while struggling with my heavy bag, all I kept thinking about was how Ishmael had to get me out of here. He surely had enough money to get us our own apartment. We were too fly to be sneak fucking on people's sofas and in seedy motels. I deserved better. Now all I had to do was get him to give me some money to go to a real estate agent, so we could locate an apartment. I realized that I didn't want to live in Brooklyn or Queens. I wanted a nice apartment in the SoHo area of Manhattan, away from all of the riffraff, drama, and jealousy. I wanted to finish college so that I could begin my successful career as a TV journalist.

When I knocked on the door to my family's apartment I heard, "Who?" It was Jackie. She looked through the peephole and then retreated. I knocked again and again until finally my mother opened the door.

Her smile was wide. "Lisa, honey, what are you doing here without calling first?"

"I'm in a situation. Shiniqua and I just had a fight and she pulled a gun on me!"

I expected a gasp, or maybe she would clutch imaginary pearls before grabbing me into a tight embrace. Instead I got, "That sweet girl did what?"

"Yes, she sure did." Any second you can invite me in, I thought.

"Well, I'll go over there tomorrow and speak to her mother about it. You girls are so close, I would hate for this situation to come between you."

I was flabbergasted. This was the same girl who had beat my mother in front of the whole projects.

"Where's Ishmael?" she asked.

I realized that the ten inches of open doorway wasn't going to open up wide enough to allow me passage unless I said the magic words. "I bought you something for your birthday."

"Oh, my gosh!" She beamed. "Come in."

I walked straight into the living room, dropped my bag, and then slid off my coat and tossed it on the sofa. I walked past my mom and went to see my family, deliberately ignoring her gift.

"What's up, Jackie?" I asked. She was watching the small color television and eating a bag of potato chips on her bed. She rolled her eyes and ignored me.

"So it's like that?"

Still nothing.

I left and knocked on my Nana's door before opening it.

"Hey, Nana." Her room was filled with cigarette smoke and she was listening to her favorite gospel radio station. Her hair was in a soft Afro and she was wearing a housecoat and slippers.

"Is that you, chile?"

"Depends on what chile you looking for," I stated. I hated that she never called any of us by our names. I found that disrespectful.

Ignoring my comment, she said, "You got five dollars?"

"Umm, sure." I reached into my jeans and slid off a twenty. I knew I didn't have anything smaller and was too smart to pull out my stash to double check. She took the money and stuffed it into her bra. At that moment I knew that she had no other use for me.

I walked back into the living room while counting the roaches crawling up and down the walls. I wondered briefly if it would make any difference if I stopped to kill them. Then I realized that there were about ten thousand more where they came from. Why exert my energy?

My mother had impolitely gone through my bag and found the mink jacket. Her face was sour.

"Is that for me?" she asked.

I paused before answering. Why did she possess the know-how to piss me off within a nanosecond?

"Yes, that's your birthday gift to wear to your function. Do you like it?"

Although when I purchased the coat I had envisioned giving it to her in a different manner—professionally wrapped with a card—life had a way of remixing your plans. My voice was less than enthusiastic and hedging on the verge of sullen.

She tried it on and began complaining immediately. "This isn't even my size. Look"—she held her arms out for emphasis—"these sleeves are too long."

"You can turn up the cuff on your sleeve to adjust it."

"Do you have to turn up your cuffs?" she spewed. "And this is a jacket. I'm too old to be wearing a jacket. No one my age wears jackets. That's for you young kids. How am I supposed to get caught wearing a jacket when my own daughter has a full-length mink? I'm sorry, I can't wear this!"

"Are you kidding me?"

She glared. "Tell your boyfriend to take it back. Who does he think I am that he can buy me this little funky jacket? Tell him your mother said—"

"He didn't even buy that for you! I did!" I roared. "Why would he buy you a coat? Who are you?"

Jackie and Nana came running out of their rooms. Nana yelled, "What's going on in here, now? Y'all better not be up in here fighting!"

"Ma, it's nothing. Go back in your room. You too, Jackie," my mother said firmly. Jackie couldn't go without saying her piece.

"Lisa always starting some shit. I don't know why you let her ass back in, anyway!"

Before I could respond, my mother yelled, "You better watch your mouth before I put my fist in it!"

I was flabbergasted.

In all my years, I'd never heard my mother take up for me. Ever. Jackie was just as shocked, but she wasn't stupid. She observed the new mink draped from our mother's body.

"Oh now you're kissing Lisa's ass 'cause she can buy you shit? You're so pathetic!"

"Keep talking," my mother threatened.

Jackie went into her room and slammed the door. Nana followed.

"I've created a monster." She laughed, nervously. I didn't. I walked off into the kitchen and then decided I needed to clear my head. I turned to leave.

"You leaving?"

"Yeah. Ishmael is coming to get me. I'll come get my things in the morning."

"Oh, it's no rush. Tell him I said hello."

I slammed the door.

For two weeks Ishmael and I stayed with some of his friends, in motels, and at his mother's place until she caught us having sex and kicked me out. Like, what did she think we were doing? To me, all she wanted was an excuse to get rid of me. I had been going to real estate agents in the city, but they were so intimidating. None of them believed that I was twenty-one, and they kept asking for a lot of paperwork— W-2s, pay stubs, letters of recommendation, and finally a credit check. I didn't have bad credit, but what I had was no credit. Not to mention, Ishmael felt that the rent was too expensive. He preferred to go to Queens. We sat in his Mercedes in front of the projects, arguing.

"They want damn near three grand for a small, one-bedroom apartment. That's house money."

"Well, until we get a house, then that's rent money!" I challenged.

"Nah, it don't go like that. You still young—"

"Don't give me that 'I'm young' bullshit. You always use that excuse when you want to win an argument over money. I'm not too young to fuck you. I bet that!"

"Here we go!" he replied and threw his hands up in surrender.

"No, I'm serious. I know what I want out of life and how I want to live. It will be better for my career if we live in the city. That's where all the television stations are, and I could easily go there and intern to get my foot in the door and not have to worry about traveling at all times of the night on the train. Did you hear me? Train . . . I don't own a car!"

"Lisa, everything with time. You want me to jump out the window and spend all my dough on you in one lump sum. I'm telling you that I'm going to always give you what you need, but first I gotta lay down the right foundation so that we don't get the nice things you want and then six months down the line, the repo guy comes to take away our house and cars. I'm telling you, I've seen it happen. You too. If your pops would have handled his business correctly, you and your family wouldn't be in this situation."

My eyes popped open in shock. He had used the information I finally told him in trust against me.

"How dare you judge my father!" I roared. "You don't know shit about our situation!"

"I know what you told me," he snapped smugly. "And I'm saying it won't be me. Bottom line."

"You're sitting up here all high and mighty like your shit don't stink, when you're living in the projects and driving an eighty-thousand-dollar car! You can't even afford to put a decent roof over our heads! At least my father did that!"

He shook his head, still determined to win our argument.

"First things first. For your information, this car was a business investment. It's a lease. No money down. Not only is it building up my credit—something you don't have—but it's in my company's name—something else you don't have. And be clear. It's not that I can't put a roof over my head. I just choose not to at this moment."

His words slapped me in my face and I was momentarily speechless.

"Look, I can't tolerate this ignorant conversation," I said. "Walk me up to my mother's house!"

"You good. Besides, I ain't going up there anymore. I'm tired of your mother begging me for money."

"What?" I asked incredulously.

"You heard me," he snapped. He was truly feeling himself this afternoon. He was definitely in rare form. "I don't know why you gave her my cell number. She's always calling, begging me for money. Sometimes I send my little man up there to give her a couple of dollars, but I ain't fucking her. I'm fucking her daughter. She act like she's your pimp!"

I was speechless. Ishmael continued, "I must have given her at least two grand!"

My skin began to crawl. At this point I started to hate my life, my family, my friends, and my man. And the worst part of it all was that I couldn't do anything about it. I didn't have a job, nor did I have enough money to tell them all to kiss my ass.

I couldn't let Ishmael get away with speaking to me so condescendingly, though. Now that Timothy was gone, he had really started to believe his own hype.

"Two grand? And? That's what the fuck you're supposed to do! You running around here like you're a baller! As long as I'm your girl, my mother gets VIP treatment. Timothy always knew how to take care of all the chickens in the hen house. You should have been taking notes on how to be a real man. Now if my mother wants something, you send one of your flunkies to get it for her!"

He chuckled.

"So you and your moms are chickenheads? Is that the lesson of the day?"

"You heard what the fuck I said!" I repeated, holding firmly to my stance. Of course, I didn't mean any of it.

"You know what? You're right. My bad," he stated, and gave me a peck on my forehead. "Get upstairs safely. I got to make a run and I'm already late." He unlocked his doors.

My breathing was still erratic and I wasn't ready to go. I felt stupid.

"Ishma—"

"Don't worry. I'ma call you later. But I got to go."

Reluctantly I got out of his car and went upstairs. I was furious, but I knew better than to argue with my mother about Ishmael's accusations. She could easily kick me out and I had nowhere else to go. Shiniqua hadn't called me, and I surely wasn't calling her first!

When I entered my family's apartment after being gone for two weeks, you'd think at least one of them would be happy to see me. But once they all asked for money and I turned them all down, their true colors came out.

I asked my mother, "How was your function?"

"I don't want to talk about that now," she replied dismissively.

"Well, did you at least go?" My pressure was up!

"Yeah, she went," Nana answered after my mother chose to ignore the question. "She looked like a movie star."

"Ma, that's enough," my mother snapped.

I waited a few hours before I called Ishmael. I took notice that he hadn't called me since we had our argument earlier. When he let me go to voicemail, my stomach got squeamish, but I left a cheery message anyway asking that he call when he had a moment. Then I went to look for my overnight bag so that I could take a shower and sleep off the day's aggravation. I was sleeping on the hard cot in the living room again.

"What's wrong with you?" My uncle Billy asked.

"Nothing," I snapped.

"You seem like you want to be left alone. If you give me twenty dollars, I'll leave and you can have the living room all to yourself."

"Damn, aren't you tired of being a rock star?"

"Excuse me?"

"Yeah, excuse you! You need to lay off that fucking crack. You look and smell awful. And if you steal any of my shit for that crack, Ishmael will kill you!" I threatened.

He shook his head. "Lisa, I always felt sorry for you because my sister treated you like shit. Out of everybody in this house, I was the only one who treated you like family. Before there was a Ishmael, if I had it, I would give you a couple dollars. Now I realize that the reason my sister hates you is because you are her. You're a mean, selfish bitch who only cares about herself. And the older you get, the more you look just as ugly as she does!"

"I look nothing like her!"

"Take a long look in the mirror!"

I sucked my teeth. "You look like doo doo on a stick so you shouldn't be talking."

"You are so annoying I don't know how people can stand you…"

As everyone practically stood on an assembly line for the shower that night, I asked my mother for my bag.

"I don't know where you left it. I ain't seen that bag. Check the hallway closet."

Just as she stated, I found my bag buried in the back of the closet. As I pulled it out, I could immediately see someone had rummaged through it. I had two shirts and one pair of expensive jeans missing. I knew the only person who'd take my shit and wear it was Jackie. But I didn't want to argue. Not tonight. I'd deal with that issue tomorrow.

After I showered and made my way down the hallway on the cold, concrete floor, Uncle Billy said, "Did you look in the mirror!"

I just rolled my eyes and tried to ignore him as he prepared to go back outside.

In the morning, Nana announced that her only son was arrested again for armed robbery. And with his record, he wouldn't be coming home anytime soon. Secretly, I was overjoyed. Guess who would have the living room all to herself?

Lisa Henderson

The next morning, which was a Saturday, I woke up breaking. You could hear my mouth yelling and screaming throughout the small apartment. I was miserable because Ishmael hadn't called me back last night and when I called him, his phone went straight to voicemail. I went and accused Jackie of stealing my clothes and she denied knowing anything about my garments until I found my jeans hidden in her closet and my dirty shirts stuffed in the bottom of the hamper in the bathroom. As I went to complain to my mother, it dawned on me that I hadn't seen my mink coat.

She began fussing at Jackie for wearing my things without permission when I interrupted her.

"And where is my coat?" I began to panic. "I haven't seen my coat since I came back. It's not in the hallway closet or Jackie's closet!"

"Didn't you wear that coat out of here?" my mother asked.

"No, I didn't."

"Lisa, I can't keep track of everything that goes on in this here apartment!"

"How can you not notice my coat gone missing? I see you still got your coat!" I accused.

"Your coat wasn't my responsibility. Maybe your uncle took it and sold it."

The thought horrified me.

"What?! Nana!" I yelled. She came running out of her room. "Mommy said Uncle Billy stole my mink coat!"

"I never said that!" my mother retracted.

"Julie, don't you go putting that on your brother. Your brother may be a thief, but he ain't never stolen nuthin' in all my years from his family!" Nana spat. "I'm too old for all this arguing. Y'all better find that girl's coat that fella done bought her."

"We haven't seen it since she left!"

"Look, I'm not gonna say it twice. Find that gal's coat 'fore she get on the phone with her boyfriend and they come and shoot up my door. Don't think I'm too old to know what goes on in these projects!"

"Oh, so, Lisa, being that you misplaced your coat, you're gonna get your gangster boyfriend to kill us?" Jackie asked sarcastically.

"I never said that!" I screamed.

"Chile, when the last time you saw your coat?" Nana questioned.

"Two weeks ago. The day that I left."

"Well, your mother done seen it after that. You let her wear it to her function. So, Julie, you better remember what you did with that coat! 'Cause if I have to, I will put my foot straight up your ass until you remember! You keep messing around with these Marcy boys if you want. They don't play. This ain't Cambria Heights!"

"Why would you wear my coat, when I bought you your own?!" I screamed.

"I told you that I wasn't wearing no baby mink to my function!"

I couldn't believe her audacity. I felt like I was in another world.

"Where's my coat!" I demanded. My voice had elevated to a high, unrecognizable pitch.

"I said, I don't know!"

I began searching through the house like a crazed woman. A half hour later I came up empty handed. I went into the living room and called Ishmael, who I knew was deliberately ignoring my calls. I left a frantic message telling him what happened. I knew that there wasn't any way we'd broken up. He said that he wasn't ever letting me go. He just needed a break from me and my smart mouth.

After that, I collapsed on the sofa and bawled my eyes out. I cried and cried for what seemed like hours.

"Chile, is this here yours?" I heard Nana ask me.

I looked up. Nana was holding my coat in her hands. I sighed in relief. "Where was it?"

"Somebody stashed it in the back of my closet! They know that I never look back there!"

"Well, thank you for looking today," I said. My voice was strained and cracked. "It was a cruel thing for someone to do."

I took my coat from my Nana and was horrified at what I saw. Someone had gotten paint on the back of my coat. My eyes welled up with tears of defeat. Nana's old eyes hadn't spotted the vandalism until I pointed it out. Needless to say, my mother explained that as she was leaving the banquet, there was a sign that read "Wet Paint", only she didn't see it, and she had inadvertently gotten paint on "her" coat, and she didn't even notice until it was too late. Yes, she said "her" coat. I just shrugged my shoulders and gave up.

I couldn't worry about that today. I'd have to worry about that tomorrow. Ishmael would just have to buy me another coat. Unfortunately for me, he was still angry over our childish argument. But I knew he wasn't angry enough to breakup with me. He wasn't that stupid. Besides, I had that recall pussy.

Didn't I?

Lisa Henderson

Over the next few weeks, I realized that it was over between Ishmael and me. Was I brokenhearted? Of course. Was I going to swallow my pride and continue calling him? Or beg for him to come back? Never. With the remaining money that I had saved up, I bought my Nana a new living room set with a pullout sofa bed. I also bought myself a forty-six-inch Sony television and a closet with a lock to store all my clothes and to keep Jackie and Julie out of them.

Now that Ishmael and I were through and the gravy train had stopped, my mother and I were at odds again. She didn't hesitate to tell me that I was the daughter who wasn't going to amount to shit. It didn't matter. I learned that if I wanted my life to be smoother, then I needed to grease my Nana's palms. My mother didn't hold any weight. This wasn't even her apartment. And Nana's needs were nickel-and-dime stuff. Once I bought her the living room set, some beer, and cigarettes, that was enough to keep the feisty old lady on my side.

To get pocket money, I pawned my bracelet that Ishmael bought me. I got nine hundred dollars for it. That was the only piece I knew I could let go without anyone noticing. People in the PJs looked for my earrings and chain, and I still had an image to keep. I made sure

I always came out looking fly, even if my clothes were things they'd seen me in already. I knew how to put them together differently, and I couldn't let Shiniqua out-dress me.

Soon the whole projects knew about me and Ishmael, so I pretended to have a new dude from Lafayette Gardens. I was sure that Ishmael was seeing Toya, but I didn't have any proof. I wanted desperately to speak to Shiniqua, but I kept my guard up and so did she.

2004

The spring weather blew in and I welcomed the warmth. Funny how time flew by. It seemed like yesterday when I was just graduating from high school. As I switched down Park Avenue I couldn't help but notice that I was being followed by an old car. I glanced back to make sure and the driver continued to coast along. I tried to get a look to see how many people were in the car, but I couldn't see past the illegally tinted windows.

Slowly I slid my hand in my back pocket and inched out my razor. The cold blade was my new best friend. After I'd cut Kimber, Donna, and Maria, I couldn't walk around Marcy without some sort of protection.

"Ayo, Lisa . . ." the driver called out.

A familiar voice drifted from the lowered window. I peeked inside. It sounded like . . .

"Get in!" the driver said.

It was! It was Timothy! I exhaled from relief and climbed into the front seat. Timothy sped off almost immediately.

"What are you doing around here?" I exclaimed and gave him a kiss on the cheek.

"I'm always creeping around here. Fuck these police!" Timothy stated.

"But they're still looking for you. They continually put up your posters, even after we tear them down."

He smiled. "You tear down my Wanted posters?"

"You know I do."

He chuckled. "Where you on your way to?"

"I was going to the store."

"OK." He looked over at me, his eyes raking me from head to toe. "Damn, you done grown up nicely. Last time I saw you, you were a little girl. Now you walking with the mean switch in your hips. Jeans so tight they look painted on!"

I blushed. "Whatever, Timothy. I'm eighteen. I can't be a little girl forever." I paused, then said, "Not that it mattered to Ishmael."

"What didn't matter to Ishmael?"

"That I was getting older and having a more mature outlook on life." I sighed. "Anyway, it doesn't matter. Ishmael and I broke up. That shady bastard didn't even have the nerve to tell me to my face! He just stopped calling. I haven't heard from him in months!"

Timothy looked confused. "You didn't know . . ." His voice trailed off and he suddenly turned his attention back to the road.

"Know what?"

"Nothing." He shook his head. "That nigga was stupid to let you go. If you were mines, I'd never play you like that."

"You wasn't trying to make me yours, remember? Don't hate because Ishmael knew a good thing when he saw it and scooped me up."

"Ishmael only scooped you 'cause I let him scoop you," Timothy shot back.

"Whatever, Timothy. You wasn't feeling me because I was young and ain't have no shape."

"Yeah, you were young, and you ain't have no shape, but that didn't mean I wasn't feeling you."

I turned and stared at Timothy in surprise. He'd been checking for me all along? All those years when I fantasized about being with him, he'd been thinking of me too? I wondered if Shiniqua knew and if she did, why she didn't tell me.

I needed a replacement for Ishmael, and Timothy was the perfect revenge. Then again, Ishmael was actually a replacement for Timothy, if I was honest with myself. Regardless, I still had feelings for Timothy, and he could be my way out of Marcy.

"Well, then, make me yours," I said coyly.

Timothy threw his head back and laughed. "Whoa! I see that Little Lisa has grown up!"

Timothy took me back to his apartment in the Park Slope section of Brooklyn. He was renting the first floor of a brownstone. It was at least twelve hundred square feet and decked out with lavish amenities—plush carpet, huge television, fully stocked bar, hardwood floors, and a buttery soft leather living room set. Being on the run from a murder rap had done him good. One look at his setup, and I knew I wasn't leaving.

I looked around with wide eyes and said, "This is a really nice place, Timothy."

"Thank you. Make yourself at home."

"How did—" I stopped myself. How he afforded this place was none of my business, and Timothy didn't like people digging in his business.

"How did I what?"

"Afford to live like this?" I asked, letting my curiosity get the better of me.

"I wasn't one of these dumb niggas out here on the blocks, tricking their money on stupid shit like hoes and clothes," Timothy stated. "I knew to stack my paper for a rainy day. When it rained, I pulled on my rubber boots. Ya feel me?" He went into the kitchen. "Don't nobody know about this house, not even my moms or Shiniqua."

I sat down on the leather sofa. It was like sitting on a stack of cotton candy. Timothy bustled about at the bar. "You want something to drink?"

I wasn't a big drinker, but I wasn't about to clown myself in Timothy's eyes. "Yeah. Let me get a Henny."

Timothy raised his eyebrow, which I'd always found sexy, and made my drink. He brought it over to me and clinked my glass with his own, which was also full of Hennessy. "Here's to LL growing up," he toasted.

I took a sip of the drink and tried not to choke. Timothy sipped on his and watched me over the rim of his glass. "So what do you want from me, Lisa?"

I looked down into the brown liquid in my glass. "I . . ." I took a deep breath, tried to ignore Timothy's stare, and said, "I don't understand what you mean. Aren't we just chilling? I haven't asked you for anything."

"You haven't asked me for anything, yet. Don't you think I know your skinny ass by now?" he asked, then chuckled.

I was furious. "Stop calling me that!"

"What?"

"Skinny!"

"Girl please…that's a good thing. You're sexy-slim like a bicycle rim."

I grinned, "I'm sexy?"

"You know it."

We both laughed.

I relaxed and then began. "Well, I really don't have any place to go."

"I thought you was staying at your mom's?" he asked.

"I, uh . . ." How could I tell him that I no longer wanted to live in the projects? That I felt I deserved better? I wanted to live a ghetto fabulous life, and I was tired of being broke and giving my pussy away for a couple of trinkets that could get snatched away at the blink of an eye. "I'm too old to be living under my mother's roof. I want more for myself."

"Yeah, I feel that," Timothy agreed. "Ain't nothing like having your own spot." He stretched his arm across the back of the couch and massaged the back of my neck. "So you like my place?"

"It's a'ight," I said nonchalantly.

Timothy laughed. "Just a'ight?" He looked around in appreciation. "Yeah, I did good for a brother straight out of Marcy."

The neck massage felt good and, combined with the Hennessy, made me relax. Timothy moved closer until I could smell his Acqua di Gio cologne. I looked up and his full lips were right there within kissing distance.

"You told me to make you mines, right?" Timothy asked.

I nodded. I was too scared to speak, worried that my words would ruin my long-time fantasy of being with Timothy.

Timothy guided my head down to his crotch. "Show me how much you want it."

I pulled down the band of his sweatpants and removed his dick from his boxers. Timothy wasn't that long, but he was thick. I twirled my tongue around the head of his dick experimentally, then up and down his shaft. Timothy pressed my head down farther and I took him into my mouth and began to suck.

"Ooh, shit . . . that's right, girl . . . shit . . . watch the teeth . . . yeah, Lisa . . . suck my dick, girl . . ."

I sucked and licked until Timothy finally came in my mouth. He held my head so that I had no choice but to swallow his cum. When he let me up, I wiped my mouth and took a sip of watery Hennessy to clear the taste of cum out of my mouth. Timothy had his head thrown back on the back of the sofa, eyes closed. He opened one eye and looked at me.

"Yep. Little Lisa has definitely grown up."

We went upstairs to his bedroom where he proceeded to fuck me six ways from Sunday—doggy style, on the wall, on the floor.

In the weeks that followed, Timothy made sure that I never forgot that he was fucking me. He would always ask me, "Whose pussy is this? Whose is it?" In exchange for giving myself to him, I got to live in Timothy's plush brownstone. He gave me money to shop and run his errands for him, since he was careful about being seen on the streets. He still had enemies out there who wouldn't hesitate to snitch and have him thrown in jail for the murder charge.

Everything was butter for the first month, then Timothy started introducing me to his particular sexual kinks. He had a thing for porn, and he also liked threesomes. One night I sat at home, waiting for him to come back when he finally made it home—with company. The girl, Cherry, was a stripper at the club he'd visited that night. He took her upstairs and told me to follow. When I finally got upstairs after recovering from the shock, Cherry was on her knees in front of a now-naked Timothy, sucking his dick. Timothy looked at me and said, "Get naked and get over here."

That was my first threesome and, unfortunately, not my last. When I complained after the first one, Timothy said in a cruel voice, "You don't like it, then there's the door. But remember that you'll also be giving up the clothes, the cash, the food, and all the other shit that goes with me." He eyed me up and down. "I pay the cost to be the boss, LL, and anyone who doesn't go along with my program gets fired."

I lasted for three months.

I wish I could say that Timothy was everything I'd ever wanted in a man, but he wasn't. He treated me disrespectfully, and not at all like the lady Ishmael had once shown me I was. The old Timothy, who used to treat me as well as he treated Shiniqua, was gone. In his place was this cold, callous, womanizing man who deliberately set up shop under the noses of the cops who wanted to put him away for murder, just to prove a point. I had to continually tell myself that he wasn't Ishmael. I guess that old saying was true: be careful what you wish for, because you just might get it. Maybe this was why Ishmael, and even Shiniqua, had warned me against Timothy.

The final straw in our relationship was when during one of Timothy's random threesomes he turned me over doggy style and spread my ass cheeks. Suddenly I felt a burning pain in my asshole. "Owww!" I screamed.

But Timothy barked, "Shut the fuck up with all that screaming! You gon' take this dick however I give it to you." The other participant, Charla, lay back against the headboard and massaged her clit and titties while Timothy continued to ass-rape me. The tears that streaked down my cheeks had no effect on either her or Timothy.

Once Timothy was done and finally asleep after fucking both of us, I crept out of bed, packed the few items of clothing and toiletries I had, put Timothy's house key on the table, and took the G train back to Marcy.

I reached my Nana's house at three o'clock in the morning. I banged on the door for almost an hour before Nana opened the door. I'd left my key back at Timothy's. Nana didn't say a word. She just opened the door and went back to bed. I'd been gone for three months.

That morning Nana woke me up, only I didn't want to get up. Again,

I was miserable.

"Chile, get up and take this here note!" she demanded. "And where have you been? Next time you do some foolishness like that, you could at least call. I was worried."

I looked at my Nana's face and I could tell that she meant her words. She did look worried. I peered down at the note and it was Ishmael's handwriting, and new telephone number.

"Where did you get this?"

"That fellow came here a couple weeks after you went missing. He said he got locked up in California and he didn't have anyone's telephone number. He said for you to call him."

"What was he doing in California?"

"Do I look like the psychic hotline? Call him!" Nana snapped.

I leapt from the sofa and called Ishmael. My heart was pounding so fast that I thought it would jump out of my chest.

He answered immediately.

"What's up, ma!" His voice was filled with happiness.

"I can't believe this is really you!" I squealed. "What happened? I thought you left me for good. Why were you in California? I thought you hated—"

"Where are you?"

"At my Nana's."

"I'll be there in five minutes. Come downstairs."

I rushed and took a three-minute shower, washed my hair, and flew downstairs in a sweat suit. Unlike usual when it came to Ishmael, this time his five minutes meant exactly that. I jumped in the front seat and he hugged me so tightly that I couldn't breathe. He looked so cute and smelled so good.

"Lisa, I've missed the hell outta you, girl! Where've you been? I've been going crazy!"

"Where've I been? Look who's talking!"

He shook his head. "I got jammed up two days after our argument. I flew to California because they were having a franchise seminar at the Los Angeles Convention Center. I went with this kid named Corey. He's straight corporate."

"Corey?"

"You've never met him. So I'm out there and bam! We get pulled over for speeding. He was driving, but he wasn't drinking. I was a little tipsy, but I wasn't fucked up. So my man breathes in the Breathalyzer and he passes. Then the cop asked me to breathe. I'm like, 'Nah. I'm not even driving. What type of shit is this? Y'all on some setup shit.' If I failed, they could have put it on my man and did some crooked shit and charged him with a DUI. So I started beefing with the cop and he cold spit in my face, like a real hock of spit. I floored him and we started brawling. When I got down to the precinct, like, five cops whipped my ass. Ma, I'm telling you, they beat my ass!"

"Oh, my gosh!" I couldn't believe he'd gone through all of this. "They could have killed you!"

"I know . . ." He shook his head. "My hands couldn't touch my paper, since I was three thousand miles away from home. I was fucked up, and I couldn't make bail."

"Why didn't you call me?" Anger had surfaced because he left me in the dark all these months thinking he'd left me.

"I didn't know anyone's number by memory. You know how that go. You have so many numbers in your cell that you don't commit any to memory. The only number I knew was my mom's, and I didn't want to tell her that I was locked up. I just called her and told her I was away on business. I couldn't worry my moms."

"Why didn't you write?" I was still looking for reasons to be mad with him.

"I did write you! I sent about five letters. When you didn't respond, I knew you didn't get them. I knew in my heart that you wouldn't leave me and step out on me over that bullshit argument we had. I prayed to God that you'd wait for me."

I looked down, shamefully, and said nothing.

"I know you ain't give my coochie away!" He touched my pussy and I jumped.

"Of course I didn't!"

"So what are you doing? I got a surprise for you."

"Nothing."

"Then let's bounce."

I thought for a second. "Wait. Let me run upstairs and tell Nana where I'm going."

"Yeah, that would be nice. And when you get back you better tell me where you've been for three months!"

When I ran upstairs, Nana handed me six letters, all addressed to me. By the time they'd reached here, I was already laid up with Timothy. Again, life kept dictating my story for me. And I didn't like it one bit.

As we drove to my surprise, I sat back and listened to Ishmael sing Teddy Pendergrass's "When Somebody Loves You Back." After the serenade, he cut down the radio and asked, "So, where you been?"

"Huh?"

"Where did you stay all these months? Your grandmother was frantic and Shiniqua said she didn't know."

"Fuck that bitch!" I said, trying to buy some time.

"OK. Fuck Shiniqua. Now answer my question."

"I went back to Queens with my old best friend Tracy from the neighborhood. Her parents let me stay there until I couldn't give them any money for food or rent. They started complaining about their heating bill, light bill, phone bill, then finally they said I had to go. That was yesterday, and here I am."

Geez, I didn't know where that lie came from, but it sounded good. In fact, it sounded great.

"Well, you don't have to ever worry about getting kicked out of someone's crib again. I got us something I think you'll like!"

Ishmael pulled up in front of a new building on 47th Street in Manhattan. There was a doorman and an underground parking garage.

"What are you doing?" I asked.

"I'm taking you home," he announced proudly. "It seems you were right. While I was locked up for that short while, there was this real estate guru in there for fraud. He broke down to me that property in Manhattan is an investment that most black people aren't hip to. White men played this game. They bought apartments and flipped them every two to five years at a huge profit. As long as I can maintain this apartment for a couple years, my money will make money. I was so focused on owning a business that I never looked at real estate."

"Are you saying that you live here?"

We were inside a massive lobby. I could see a gym off to my far right and numerous people were exercising. I felt a little out of place with my sweat suit and damp hair until the concierge said, "Good evening, Mr. Lawrence."

"Good evening, Bob."

We rode the glass elevator up to the twelfth floor. Ishmael opened the door to the apartment and finally said, "No, I'm saying we live here."

He escorted me into an-all white decorated apartment with stainless steel appliances in the kitchen, granite countertops, and marble floors. There was a small breakfast nook with two bar chairs and a gas fireplace in the living room. The bedroom was a nice size with one walk-in closet. But what was most amazing was the panoramic view. You could see the whole city.

I took off my sneakers and walked around in awe. He did it. He really did it! He had bought me my Manhattan apartment.

He noticed that I was in intense thought and said, "This is only the beginning. I'm going to make you proud of me one day."

I wrapped my arms around his neck. "I'm already proud of you today!"

Ishmael ordered Thai food from a local restaurant and we crawled up into our king-sized bed and watched movies, but not before I told him all the things I wanted to buy for the apartment to make it more feminine. He just grinned. When he wanted to make love, I pulled away and claimed fatigue. I felt dirty from Timothy, and I needed a few days to cleanse. I felt Ishmael at least deserved that. I fell into a peaceful sleep, wrapped tightly in his arms.

In the morning Ishmael made plans to go back and get all my clothes from Nana's house.

"You don't want me to go with you?" I asked.

"Nah, I'll pick up everything. I gotta make a few moves and then I'll be back. I want you to get comfortable in here." He kissed me, and then said, "Come join me in the shower."

Again I made up an excuse, only this time he looked at me oddly, as if he wasn't buying my story. But he said nothing.

As he was showering, my cell phone began to ring. The number on the caller ID was private.

"Hello?" I answered.

"Where the fuck are you?"

"What?"

"Yo, don't play with me! You heard what the fuck I said!"

I whispered, "None of your business. And you better not ever, ever call my phone again!"

"Oh, you with that nigga?"

"Fuck you," I said and hung up. Then fear took over. What if Timothy told Ishmael about us? What would I say? What could I say? Should I tell him first? I was panic stricken and almost started to hyperventilate. I wished I could call Shiniqua for advice.

Not sure what to do, I shook off my fears, hopped out of bed, and jumped into the shower with a surprised Ishmael. We made love in the shower and then again in our bed. When he left the apartment he had a huge grin plastered on his face.

Ishmael called a couple times throughout the day to check up on me and tell me how much he missed me and loved me. After I gave him a dozen kisses through the phone, I decided to explore my new neighborhood. The weather was wonderful and the scenery was so trendy. If I walked north, I would run into 42nd Street, a tourist gold mine. If I walked east, I would be in the trendy Village.

I stayed out for hours, and then I realized that I forgot to ask Ishmael to leave me some money. I was broke and couldn't buy anything to eat, so I had to go back to our apartment.

As hours passed and Ishmael still hadn't returned home, I began to feel an awkward feeling in my stomach. When I called and the phone went to voicemail, I really began to worry. I hope nothing awful happened to him, I thought. Being out in the streets, anything could happen to your man. By midnight I was frantic. I called his phone a million times, and then I called Nana.

"Did Ishmael come there today to get my clothes?"

"He sure didn't."

"Well, did he call?"

"Yup. And had me up waiting, like a fool, for all types of hours."

"I hope nothing happened to him," I replied.

"Chile, you too young to be worrying!" she snapped. "Ain't nothin' happened to that fella. He'll be home soon. And don't be getting on his nerves when he walk through the door with stupid questions. You hear me?"

"Well he better not be with a chick, after I've been in here worrying all night!"

"Who's paying the bills?"

"Ma'am?"

"You heard me! Who's paying the bills? He is, right?"

"That doesn't mean anything!"

"It means everything! Keep your mouth shut about nonsense and focus on your schooling and keeping him happy. Nothing else matters. Ishmael is a good man. I can feel such things. Don't mess that up."

Nana's words gave me little comfort, especially since I was now thinking that Ishmael was up in a warm bed in between some bitch's legs. Although I couldn't sleep, my eyes finally closed around four o'clock in the morning.

The strong nudge was meant to wake me. My eyes struggled to open and there stood Ishmael. He was towering over me with his hands dug deeply into his oversized jean pockets. Instantly, I wasn't angry. I wanted him to crawl in bed and make love to me.

"Get up," he whispered. I could smell the alcohol oozing out of his pores.

"Where have you been? I've be so worried. I thought something bad happened."

"Get dressed."

"OK," I said, excitedly. "Where are we going?"

"You're going home."

"Huh? What are you talking about? Are we moving?" I asked

dumbly. Only I knew what he meant. I was stalling for time.

"Nah, we're not moving. You are. You're going back home. I need my space."

"What are you talking about? Why are you doing this?" I asked the questions, only I didn't want to hear the answers. I knew that Timothy had gotten to him.

"Look, Lisa, I'm tired and I want to get in my bed. But you gotta go. Now!" When I resisted, he grabbed me from off the bed and began to pull me toward the front door. "Either you're gonna get dressed and walk out of here, or you're gonna resist and get tossed out of here. It's your choice. And I want you to look in my eyes to see that I'm not playing with your ass!"

I did look in his eyes and I saw his pain. He was too much of a man to physically hurt me. And in too much pain to repeat what he knew was true. At that moment I wondered if I should tell him the truth, tell him why I ended up in Timothy's bed.

"Can we talk about what happened?" I asked, and then pleaded, "Ishmael, please! I love you. I don't want it to end like this."

He tossed three hundred dollars in my face. "When I get out of the shower, you better be gone."

Lisa Henderson

Back on Park Avenue. In Brooklyn. It took me a few days to stop crying constantly. Now I only cried sporadically. To ease my pain, I thought of how I would get Timothy back for ruining my relationship with Ishmael. For ruining my life. I dialed 1-800-555-TIPS.

"Police hotline. Are you calling in to give a tip?"

"Yes. I have information about a murder."

"City and state in which the murder occurred?"

"Brooklyn, New York."

"Do you wish to remain anonymous?"

"Of course."

"If there's a reward, would you accept it?"

I thought for a moment. That could get complicated. Even though I could use the money, if this ever came out, my life would definitely be in danger. "No, ma'am. I don't want any reward money."

"Very well. Tell me what you know."

I snitched on Timothy and gave his current address in Park Slope. Two days later, he made the front page of the Daily News, and the New York Post. He was also featured on the eleven o'clock news on practically every channel. The projects were abuzz with drama and gossip. I took much pleasure out of seeing him being dragged out of his palatial apartment in handcuffs. I prayed he spent the rest of his life in jail. At this point I was like, "fuck the world!"

Timothy wasn't in jail for more than a few months when rumors began to circulate about his involvement in another murder that had occurred three years prior—of the murder of a nineteen-year-old kid named Shareef. My mind was blown when I heard that. Shareef worked for Timothy at the time, so of course no one would ever suspect Shareef's boss in the killing. I also remembered the rumors that Little Paul and Havoc were killed for the wrong reason, that they didn't murder Shareef on some alleged beef. Timothy had been playing everyone all along.

I was shell-shocked. Everything in me wanted to call Shiniqua, but I wondered how much she knew. If she knew that her brother had the man she'd been in love with killed, would she have bucked up against him? Or did she keep quiet, due to Timothy's violent streak? As a matter of fact, was Shiniqua the reason that Timothy killed Shareef? Shareef had been talking about Shiniqua after he popped her cherry, and word may have gotten back to Timothy. And to add insult to injury, Shareef had started messing with Jackie shortly thereafter. I couldn't ask Shiniqua, though. We weren't close anymore, and I wasn't considered family. Even if she knew the truth, Shiniqua wasn't going to snitch on her brother for no one. I wished I could call Ishmael.

I was sitting on the couch one day, watching the stories, when Nana came in looking upset.

"I don't know how to say this, but Shiniqua was just shot," she said abruptly. "They said she's hurt badly. I think you should run to the hospital to see her."

"Shot? What do you mean shot?"

"Mrs. Blakely just called and told me the bad news. I don't know any answers. Just get to the hospital if you want to say goodbye to your friend."

I rushed out of the house and ran a gauntlet of nosey neighbors who'd already heard the news and were trying to get more details. Good or bad, news spread quickly in the projects. I hopped in a cab and threw the driver an extra twenty dollars to drive like a bat out of hell and get me to the hospital quickly. I called Knowledge, who was on his way to the hospital too.

"What happened, Knowledge?" I asked. "How did she get shot? Who shot her? Where was she?"

"She was walking to my building. I heard they shot her up bad," Knowledge said and his voice cracked. I could tell that he was holding back tears.

"Who? Why Shiniqua? What the fuck is going on?" I screamed.

"I don't know. I don't know," he repeated. "But I bet this is her brother's beef!"

Timothy may have been behind bars, but he was still poisoning people's lives. "Where did she get shot? Is it bad?"

"She took two to the back, one to the thigh, and one grazed her ribcage. It's bad. But she's a fighter, you know. She's gonna make it," he said, trying to convince himself.

We all arrived at the hospital within minutes of each other. The lobby was full and it was just nearing nine o'clock in the morning. Shiniqua had already been rushed into surgery. Ms. S. rushed over to a nurse. "Where is the doctor? I need to speak to a doctor about my baby!"

The nurse looked at Ms. S like she'd lost her mind. "What is your child's name, ma'am?"

"Shiniqua. Shiniqua Ship. She was shot and . . ." Her voice faltered.

"I got a call, and they said she was shot bad." She began to cry.

The nurse punched some keys on her computer. "She's in surgery as we speak. I'll page Dr. Mosimov. He was the attending on duty when your daughter was brought in." She called the doctor's name over the loudspeaker, then turned back toward us. "Have a seat and someone will come and get you when he comes back."

We all sat down on the hard plastic chairs and waited for news.

"Who would want to hurt her?" Ms. S asked aloud. "She's just a baby!"

I shook my head. Shiniqua randomly getting shot in the Sumner projects just didn't make sense. I wondered if Knowledge was right, and the shooting was in retaliation for something that Timothy had done. Once again, all roads led back to Timothy.

As we waited impatiently, Ms. S led us in prayer. "Father God so merciful, please watch over Shiniqua while she's in surgery, from the top of her head to the bottom of her feet. Cover her in the blood of Jesus Christ. God, please guide her doctors' hands, keep them steady and precise. Let my daughter know that we are all here, praying for her, and will all be here when she pulls through. In the name of Jesus we pray. Amen."

"Amen," we all said.

Then I saw him. Ishmael came in with his same swagger, searching for Ms. S. He had completely taken over Timothy's business since he got locked up. When Ishmael found Ms. S, he bolted right to her. My eyes were fixed on him hungrily, but he ignored me. My best friend was on an operating table, fighting for her life, but all I could see and think about was Ishmael. He embraced Ms. S and murmured words of encouragement in her ear.

A doctor in rumpled green scrubs and a surgical cap with a surgical mask hanging around his neck, walked up to our little group. A nurse, similarly dressed, was right behind him.

"Mrs. Ship?" he asked.

Ms. S. stepped up. "Ms. Ship. I'm Shiniqua's mother. Is she OK? When can I see her?"

The doctor's eyes were sad. "I'm sorry, ma'am, but she's gone. She had massive internal bleeding from the type of bullets used, and we did all we could for her. She lost too much blood. I'm so sorry."

Ms. S collapsed into a wailing heap on the floor. "NOOOOOOOOOOOOOOOOO! Not my baby! Not my Shiniqua! Why?" She sobbed. "Why they want to do this to my baby? She ain't never hurt nobody like that." Ishmael got on the floor beside her and cradled her in his arms. Knowledge just stood and stared at the retreating form of the doctor as tears ran down his face. Ishmael's eyes met mine over the top of Ms. S's head and mirrored my pain.

Shiniqua. My best friend, my sister, my ride-or-die homie. Gone. Dead. Just like that. No warning, no time to say goodbye, no time to apologize, no time to tell her how much I loved her and was grateful for the day she came into my life.

I closed my eyes and tried to tell myself that Shiniqua was back at the Ship apartment in Marcy, asleep in her twin bed. When I got back, she'd wake up, take her silk scarf off her head, and shake her wrapped hair into her face to hide the faint razor scars. Then she'd get dressed in her favorite outfit of tight jeans, a Baby Phat shirt, and stilettos, and we'd go shopping. Or she'd go meet up with Knowledge. Or we'd just kick it while she schooled me on men and clothes. Or we'd go outside and sit on the bench to watch the goings-on of Marcy.

Yeah, that was just what we'd do when I got back to the apartment.

Lisa Henderson

After Shiniqua was buried, I knew I'd never be the same. The way my heart hurt, I knew I'd never recover from her murder. They let Timothy out of jail to attend the funeral, and he looked haunted. Whatever mental issues he had, I got the feeling that Shiniqua's death pushed him over the edge. She was his baby sister, his favorite, the one person he'd do anything for, and he'd adored her. Ms. S had to be sedated during the service, and Ishmael was there to support her, literally and figuratively.

Ms. S asked me to come back and stay with her permanently, but I declined. She'd practically made a shrine of Shiniqua's image in her apartment. She'd blown up numerous pictures and pulled out her baby shoes and clothes, all her awards, and every card Shiniqua had ever given to her. It was hard enough coming around to see Ms. S and glancing in the room I had shared with Shiniqua, seeing her clothes and makeup scattered around the room like she'd just left and would be coming back soon.

I constantly felt Shiniqua's presence so strongly that I began smoking weed. It was all I could do to try to fall asleep and not expect her to be there when I woke up. Plus, with Ishmael out of my life, I took it as a sign that it was time to leave Marcy—and Brooklyn—for good this time.

Lisa Henderson

QUEENS - *2005: 19-years-old*

Happier times came when my father finally came home after a delay in his release, and rescued us from the Marcy Projects. A few of his friends gave him a big welcome home party and gifted him with envelopes that were filled with money. Just as he'd promised, he moved us into a four-bedroom, three-bathroom home that made us all proud. No longer was I sleeping on the couch. I had my own room, bed, and privacy. This move couldn't have come at a better time for me. I was completely done with Marcy.

My brother John had come home for good from the military and was now working full time for UPS. The house was full, but each of us had our own space. Unfortunately, the short-lived "happy" times my mother and I shared were long gone. I was no longer the breadwinner with the drug-dealing boyfriend. Her husband was home and she was once again the head bitch in charge.

One day, a couple months after the move, Julie was moving her mouth at me, but as usual she wasn't saying anything I wanted to hear. I rolled my eyes, wondering how long I would have to stand there and take in the nonsense she was kicking. I realized that I hated being nineteen, just as much as I hated eighteen. And just like most women my age, I couldn't wait to get the fuck outta Dodge!

My mother and I just couldn't coexist under the same roof. Let her tell my story and I was a complete fuck up. My mouth was too disrespectful and I was a pathological liar with the tales I told on her. Anyone within earshot would get to hear her rip into me. I was a menace. The devil's spawn. A problem child. In all my years I'd never heard her utter one kind word about me.

"If I have to tell you one more time to stop having on ten things at one time in your room in my house, you're gonna get the fuck out!" Julie screamed. "I will take that goddamn iPod, your cell phone, your laptop, all your shit and throw it the fuck out! This ain't the projects. We pay for utilities around here!"

"Who are you talking to like that?" I replied. "I'm not some child!" I heard her the first time she said it and eight times later I was still hearing her. And why was she screaming?

"Don't get smart with me!" she screamed. "You don't pay one bill in this motherfucker!"

Truly I didn't. But neither did she. And neither did my two siblings. But the only person who consistently got blamed for shit was me. If Julie had it her way, I would be to blame for September 11, the looming recession, George Bush getting elected twice, and the rising gas prices. I could do no right in her eyes.

"And neither do you!"

"Don't get cute, honey! This house has my name on the deed. My husband—"

"My father!"

"Let me explain something to you. The wife holds all the cards. NO ONE comes before me. Not his mother, his father, his siblings, or his kids. You understand me? What I say goes under this here roof. If you don't like it, you can take your ass back to Brooklyn with the thugs!"

"Were they thugs when you had your hand out begging?"

"What?"

"Yeah, how quickly we forget who put food in your mouth and clothes on your back. My thug!"

Julie made a lemon-sucking face. "You lie, just like your father!"

"I tell no tales!" I huffed.

"Shut up!" she barked. "As a matter of fact—"

She never finished her sentence. She ran upstairs to my room and began grabbing my cell phone, my iPod, clothes, shoes, and any and all the things she felt I needed. I watched in anger, but said nothing. After she gathered up all my things, she wrapped them in my bed sheet and pushed past me.

"You're acting childish!" I screamed.

She swung back around and slapped me. My head flung back, hit the wall, and I blacked out.

When I came to my hands were wrapped tightly around her neck and my sister and brother were pulling me off her. When I wouldn't let go, Jackie and John began to jump me. I fought them both off as best as I could, but I was no match for three sets of fists.

I took my ass whipping like a grown woman and then went and locked myself in my room and waited for my father to come home. Outside my door, I could hear the story Julie began spinning.

"You see what I've been telling y'all? You two are my witnesses when your father comes home. That girl is crazy and miserable and I cannot handle her one more day! She is getting the fuck out of my house!"

"How dare she put her hands on you!" Jackie screamed. "That little bitch has no respect!"

"What happened?" John inquired.

"I asked her nicely to unplug some of this junk and you know Lisa, she gave me attitude and said she wasn't doing shit. When I tried to unplug a few things, she went berserk and slapped me!"

I buried my head in my pillow and cried. I was exhausted from Julie's antics. I was fed up with Julie's lies.

I knew my father was home when I heard Julie's deep, baritone voice booming throughout the house. "Lisa attacked me in here today and Jackie and John are my witnesses. I'm telling you, Laurence, I'm afraid of her. She might try to kill me one day."

"Don't you think you're overreacting?"

"You're taking her side again, aren't you?"

"I'm not taking anybody's side until I have both sides of the story! Where is she?"

"You got all the sides you should need. Didn't I just tell you that Jackie and John witnessed the abuse?"

"Lisa?" my father yelled. "Lisa? Come down, baby girl."

I hopped off my bed and did a slow trollop down the stairs. I looked at Julie and she was glaring at me. Why did my own mother hate me so much? I wondered.

"Lisa, what happened in here tonight?"

I hesitated for a moment. "Everything she said was true. I did everything she said."

"See, didn't I tell you? What did I tell you? Now what are you going to do to her? She needs to get out of here and go back to Brooklyn, where she can behave like an animal!"

"Julie, knock it off."

"Knock it off?" She gasped. "You think only white kids kill their parents? She took all those biology and chemistry classes. What if she poisons my food!"

"Well, I suggest you be very careful about what you eat around here," I threatened.

My father was spent. I knew he was annoyed that in all these years, Julie and I had never mended our differences. Instead, they had festered. Now Daddy was older and more weary, and he often told Julie and I that he really didn't want to keep refereeing our arguments and fights.

My father came to my room shortly thereafter and asked, "Now what really happened, because you know I wasn't believing one word your mother said."

I shook my head. "I'm so tired of this, Daddy. Each day I'm a target in this house. All my life I've been battling with her and it's draining all the good in me. I swear, I can feel it going."

"Look at me," my father said. He took his hand and raised my chin. "Don't ever let anyone—mother, or father, or anyone else—ever steal your joy of life. Life is too precious."

I began to cry. "You don't know how it is when you're not around. She's constantly riding my back. Like, why does she hate me? I keep trying to be her daughter, but she doesn't want me, no matter how hard I try to prove myself with her."

"Sometimes, people have their own issues that they need to sort out. No matter what you do, she'll never love you as much as she loves Jackie and John. Let me tell you something that parents won't ever admit. We don't always love our children equally. That's a myth. I know your mother doesn't love you the way she loves John and Jackie, but that's where I come in. I try to give you enough love to make up for her lack thereof. Lisa, you're a smart girl. I'm not saying Julie doesn't love you. I'm just saying she doesn't love you as much as the others. Can you handle that?"

I shrugged my shoulders. "I'll have to. But I still want to know why.

What did I do, or what can I do?"

"Whatever you do won't ever be enough. Haven't you realized that yet? I know sometimes I talk to you as if you're made of steel, but I know you can handle it. You see how you let her win her childish battle downstairs?"

"Yes."

"I know you did that to gain points."

"Not points, Daddy. Her love."

"You won't. You could personally serve her breakfast in bed each morning and she'll complain that the toast is burnt. You dig me?"

"I guess."

"But more importantly, I cannot leave you here feeling down about your relationship with your mother without letting you know the role I played in her feelings toward you. Your mother and I were very young when we hooked up. As you know, I've never met my father, thus you've never met your grandfather. I promised myself that I would always be around for my children. When your mother got pregnant, I married her. I didn't necessarily want to get married, but I felt that if I wanted to play like a man, then I better be a man. Things went well and then your mother got pregnant again with Jackie. I was delighted when she had a little girl. We had the perfect family, or so your mother thought.

"When Jackie arrived, I thought I knew how to successfully keep a few mistresses and also maintain my household. But I was sloppy with my affairs and I hurt your mother deeply. The fights between your mother and I grew into all-out brawls.

"This went on for years, and then she came up pregnant for the third time. She threatened to have an abortion, and I begged her not to. At this point she realized the power she held over me. She realized that I really wanted my third child, and that I wasn't the type of man who believed in abortion. Day in and day out your mother walked around, making demands as you grew inside her belly. I made her a promise that I knew I couldn't keep, at least not for long, anyway. I told her that if she had my third child, I'd stop cheating and become a real family man, not just the man who paid all the bills. I promised her that our third child would bring us closer together. I stopped cheating and began coming home right after work just in time for dinner.

"But when Julie reached her second trimester and medically she wasn't allowed to abort my child, I fell right back into my womanizing ways—"

"Daddy!" I hissed.

"I know, Lisa. It was wrong, but I had this young, sexy woman who was also a professional ballet dancer. . . . she was fine. . . ." He looked off into space, as if he were reliving the moments between them, and then he continued. "The last few months of your mother's pregnancy with you were difficult. She'd ballooned to an unhealthy weight, her stomach stretched so wide I thought you'd pop out. You did a number on her body. And to make it just a tiny bit worse, you came out looking just like me. Inside the delivery room I didn't think I could love anyone any more than I loved you. As soon as I laid eyes on you I knew you'd be Daddy's little girl."

I hugged my father. "I love you, Daddy."

He squeezed me so tightly that I almost couldn't breathe. "So you see, this is partly my fault."

"Are you kidding me? If it weren't for you, I wouldn't be here. At least I have a life and can have my own family and love my own children. Julie didn't want to afford me that luxury. And having love from one parent is better than not having love from either parent. Julie needs to get over her issues. I'm glad you shared this story with me. It really helped my heart."

"Now all you have to do is graduate from college with your journalism degree, get married to a man that I approve of, and then have me a few grandbabies." He smiled.

"In that order?"

"It better be in that order!" We both chuckled and I felt optimistic about my future. With my father by my side, I didn't care who was against me.

Lisa Henderson

2006

She was going to flip.

My mother.

Because although she told my father that he was not to buy me a car to get around in, he did. We lived in Queens, which meant we were in a two-fare zone and it was virtually impossible to get around without a vehicle.

My father and I snuck out the house early one Saturday morning and drove to Northern Boulevard, where there was a host of used car dealers. I tried to get a new car, but my father said I was pushing it, which was true. Plus my driving wasn't that great, and he didn't want me practicing in a high-end car. But he said if I was responsible with my first car, then he'd buy me a new car once I graduated from college.

My father had plans for me to get a reliable car such as a Honda or a Toyota, but I had other plans. After we perused the reliable cars, I made my feelings known.

"Look, Daddy, I like these Hondas and shit—"

"Girl, watch your mouth." He laughed and gave me an amused look.

"I suppose you call yourself 'keeping it real' with me."

"Yeah, Daddy. Like, we got a great relationship. I can tell you anything and I feel so comfortable with you. I want you to know your daughter. I want you to know who I really am. I use profanity with my friends. Why can't I use it with you?"

"Because I'm your father. Not your friend. If your mother were here, she would have slapped your face."

"Let's not go there. I was having a good day," I said and we both laughed. "But like I was saying. I like Hondas. I really do, but they're just not for me. I'm damn near six feet tall—"

"What? You're five seven."

"What about when I wear heels?"

"Well, you got a point there."

"Gee, thanks, punk!" I playfully stated. "So I guess what I'm getting at is that I want a Jeep. Something to compliment my height and show off my personality."

"And this Jeep will do all of that?"

"If you buy it for me, it will. You don't understand how it is for me, being so tall."

"Well, don't go that far. You're hardly a giant. You just feel tall because you're taller than your mother and sister."

"I've always been taller than most women so if I climb out of a small car, people will clown me."

"I dig you," my dad said.

As we drove toward the other dealerships, I wondered how to crack on my dad for apartment money. It was time for me to move on. I couldn't take one more day living with my mother. I decided to be straight up.

"You know I'll be twenty soon, and I'm doing really great in college. And as soon as I graduate, I'll get a job and be able to take care of myself. But not only do I need a car, I also need a roof over my head. If I'm able to find a small apartment, can you cover the rent? I promise, I'll pay you back as soon as I get a job. I promise." I pouted and gave him slight smirk.

"Don't give me that puppy dog look. You got me wrapped around your little finger, don't you?"

"I do?" I laughed.

"Girl, please. Look, money isn't tight, but it's not exactly flowing. This car is going to set me back and I don't know if I can also handle covering your monthly rent and expenses. I know it's hard, living with your mother, but you don't have much longer. I know we always planned for you to go to school full time and not work but if you could get a part-time job, then I might be able to supplement your rent."

"OK, I feel you. Maybe I can get a job at Green Acres Mall."

"You can do anything you put your mind to if you want it bad enough. Lisa," he began.

"Yes?"

"Your mother told me about the guy you were seeing in Brooklyn. Ishmael. And what he did for an occupation. I'm glad that part of your life is over and you're concentrating on school. I hope that when you fall in love it's with a respectable guy, and not a drug runner. I hate to say this, but Ishmael is going to either end up dead or in jail, and you deserve better than that. I tell you this from experience. I had many friends who took that same path. You dig me?"

"I dig you."

Since returning from prison, my father often talked about his days growing up in Brooklyn, but he never said anything about being in the drug game. I wondered, briefly, if those "friends" he just spoke about was really himself. After hooking up with Ishmael, I began to wonder how, at such a young age, my father had so much money and so much style. There were whispers inside our family, but no one ever came out and said he did illegal things to take care of his family. And no one could ever explain how, at twenty-one years old, he was able to move his pregnant wife out of Brooklyn and buy her a nice brick house in Queens to raise his children. I needed to get the details from my dad someday soon. Apparently, there was more to his past than I knew.

After we arrived at the next dealership, I decided on a blue Jeep Cherokee with chrome rims and trim. When the purchase was complete I followed him back to our house to show off my ride. Julie went berserk as soon as she saw it.

"You just had to go and do it, didn't you?" she screamed.

"Go back in the house and stop making a spectacle out of yourself."

"If you buy her another fucking thing—"

"She deserves it! That's the bottom line."

"I'm tired of hearing about her grades. What about punishing her for selling those drugs for that boy in Marcy?"

"What?!" My father and I said in unison. That was news to me. And evidently my father too, because Julie was silenced by a slap. And then my father dragged her into our house and beat the fire out of her in the middle of our foyer.

"Don't . . . you . . . ever . . . let . . . me . . . catch . . . you . . . saying . . . that . . . ever . . . again!" As each blow landed, Julie screamed for mercy and tried unsuccessfully to cover her face. The anger and outrage pouring from my father was a side of him I'd never seen before. I was frozen with fear. Although Julie and I had our differences, I felt sorry for her as my father pounded on her face and back. But my sympathy was tempered when my father spoke these words.

"You want to have the cops run up in here and drag your daughter to jail over your stupid-ass mouth and accusations? I've been to jail, and it's no place for anyone. You'd rather have your daughter caged up than to see her shine? You're so jealous that she's everything you wish you could have been at her age. Instead, at nineteen you were a dropout and already pregnant." My father snarled. "Yeah, don't think I don't know what this is all about!"

"You're going to jail, Larry!" my mother threatened. "I'm calling the cops. You're not going to keep putting your hands on me!"

"Bitch, call the cops! I dare you! And the second I get out, I'ma go upside your head again!"

I wanted to tell my dad to slap her again, but I didn't. Instead I ran upstairs and quickly changed my casual clothes into something more sexy. When I came back downstairs my father was in the family room, drinking, and Julie had retreated up to her room.

I whispered in his ear, "If Julie gets you locked up, call me and I'll come bail you out."

He was drunk by now. "She ain't gonna do shit. Get out of here and go have fun." He then patted me on my head and I left them alone to sort out their adult issues. My father was right. Being an adult was difficult.

Lisa Henderson

Our household—after my father whipped my mother's ass—I guess could be described as the quiet before the storm. As Julie tiptoed throughout the house, I reveled in her misery. Had I been less self-centered, and more intuitive, I would have peeped that there was something rotten in Denmark. Instead, I was too busy running the streets to see the forest from the trees.

I have to admit that college wasn't enough to keep my mind off of Ishmael, Shiniqua, and Brooklyn. I wished desperately that I could go back and change a few things. Perhaps, had I kept my mouth shut about Little Paul and Havoc, Rakeem would have dealt with Timothy while he was on the streets and not taken his revenge out on Shiniqua. And had I just kept my grown ass still, I would have been around when Ishmael sent those letters from jail and we'd still be together. I had so much in my past that I regret, yet I couldn't think about all that now. I'd have to think about my mistakes tomorrow.

One thing was for certain: I was grateful that the cold weather had broken and it was officially spring. In two months my semester would be over, but I had decided to enroll in two summer sessions. I wanted to graduate earlier than planned. I had shit to do. My lifestyle of being rich and famous was almost at my fingertips. I knew in my gut that I would be successful. I needed to prove those who doubted me wrong. Deep down inside, I knew I needed to be more successful than Jackie to spite Julie. And I also wanted to do it to prove Ishmael wrong. They all thought I wasn't going anywhere in life. But I knew better.

My cell phone rang and I decided not to answer it. I was sure that it was Tracy without even looking at the number. Lately, she had been harassing me to do a threesome with her and her boyfriend, Rob. At first I couldn't understand how she could ask me to do such a thing. Why would she want me to join in with the man she hoped to marry? Then, slowly, I began to see how Rob manipulated her. I knew that the invitation came from Rob and not Tracy and she was only complying to keep her man satisfied. I wish Ishmael would have tried to play me and ask that I allow Shiniqua join in. I would have cut him off immediately. But Tracy was weaker than a newborn baby.

"Lisa!" I heard my name and spun around. I searched for anyone familiar and then my eyes rested on Tracy. Parked in front of my school were Tracy, Rob, and a new, gleaming silver Range Rover.

"Hey girlie," I stated, and then, "Whaddup, Rob? What ya'll doing here?"

"We came to get you!" Tracy squealed. "Rob bought a new jeep and he wanted to show it off. Let's all hang out and get some drinks. You free?"

"Let's breeze."

We weren't in his jeep for five minutes before I heard, "Next we're gonna have my man, Ishmael from Marcy projects up here to let you people know how he went from the block to the boardroom. Back after we pay some bills on Hot 97."

My jaw fell open. A light bead of sweat formed on my forehead and under my armpits. As Ishmael came on the radio and told about how within one year he opened up a string of franchises and was slowly buying up real estate in Manhattan, Albany, Syracuse, and Rochester New York. He was so articulate and confident. The interview was meant to inspire young men and women who found themselves in his same situation, but instead it did the opposite for me. Sadly, I didn't want him to be successful if we weren't together. Yes, sadly, I guess I was a hater.

After several drinks, Tracy, Rob, and I had sex. We all sat in silence as Rob drove me home. I had no idea why they were so quiet. But I was quiet because I couldn't stop thinking about how Rob's dick felt as it slid inside me. The way he caressed my thighs and looked me directly in my eyes as he was cumming. For some reason I felt a connection toward him. I knew I didn't have a right to feel this way but at that moment, intoxicated, and missing my ex—I couldn't really help myself.

"Lisa, which exit do I use for your house? Linden Boulevard or do I take the Cross Bronx Expressway?"

"Get off on Linden, go to 225th Avenue and make a left. My house is in the middle of the block on your right-hand side."

"I can show him from there," Tracy chimed in.

Who asked you anything? I wanted to say, but said nothing.

I closed my eyes again so that I could relive Rob. His strong hands, thick dick, long tongue—

"Lisa, oh God, isn't that your house? The police are there!" Tracy yelled.

My eyes shot open to hear a blaring siren and see blue and red lights flashing. Several police cars were in front of my house and the police were stopping all cars from proceeding down the block. All I could think of was that my mother had called the cops on my father. Again. I rolled my eyes.

"You know Julie can't live without making me or my father's lives miserable," I replied. "Your mother would actually call the cops on you?" Rob asked as he inched toward the police barricade.

"For sure. You don't know my mother. She hates me. Tell him, Tracy. Tracy is the only person that believes that my mother has it in for me."

Tracy agreed. "Her mother is crazy. She's so jealous of Lisa you wouldn't believe it."

"I do find that hard to believe," Rob said in disbelief as he rolled down his window for the officer.

I piped up.

"Officer, I live there at that house. My name is Lisa Henderson." As I gave up my name I wondered if this could somehow be about something I did. There was an awful lot of police on the scene for this to be about domestic abuse.

"Sir, please pull over your car on the right-hand side."

The police officer then walked over to the group of cops who were guarding the barricade and they moved it to the side to give us entry.

At that moment I knew this wasn't about me. The second clue was the blaring ambulance that had just arrived on the scene.

"Lisa, I don't think this is about you," Tracy assessed.

"Ya think?" I snapped sarcastically.

This time the police officer approached my window.

"Ma'am, your house is being closed off because it's now officially a crime scene."

"What?" I panicked. "My father! Where's my father?"

"Your parents were both hurt severely—"

I flung open the door and tried to bolt down to my house, but I was stopped by the policeman. At this point I was crying hysterically and he gave me a firm embrace and began to rock me in his arms.

"You can see them at the hospital. Do you hear me? They're being taken to Jamaica Hospital. Can your friends drive you there? If not, I can get a policeman to escort you."

"Is he dead?" I mumbled.

"Ma'am?"

"My father. Is he dead?"

"No, ma'am. Both of your parents are alive. Again, you can see them at the hospital."

I let go of the police officer and stepped back to take in the scene. There were four police cars, two ambulances, an unmarked police car, and now a van was pulling up with the word Forensics written on the side.

What the fuck happened here? I wondered.

I stood stone still in a daze. Nosey neighbors were trying to inch over to me to see if I had any news on the situation. One in particular kept trying to get my attention by flailing her arms. Purposely I ignored her. I turned to Tracy who was standing outside the car being comforted by Rob. Wasn't this my crisis? Why was he comforting her?

I ran into his arms and wrapped my arms tightly around his waist, startling him and pushing Tracy out of the way.

"How could this happen?" I screamed. "Who would want to do this to my family?"

Slowly he began to rub my back as I clung to his broad chest and cried real tears for my father. I didn't have a clue what was going on or how badly he was hurt, but from the onset things didn't look good. Tracy inched over and began rubbing my back. She pulled me from Rob and forced me to hug her.

"It's gonna be all right," she soothed. "We gotta take you to the hospital so you can find out more. Don't cry, OK? I love you."

I nodded my head to acknowledge her.

"I don't mean to be a bother, but do you think you could take me to the hospital?" I asked Rob.

"Of course I will. Don't worry, I'm sure your parents will be fine. Get in."

My long legs were put to use as I beat Tracy to the car door, making it to the front seat first. As we sped down the Queens tree lined streets, I said a silent prayer for my father. What on earth could be going on?

Lisa Henderson

As Rob pulled up to the busy entrance to the emergency room, I noticed two familiar figures. Jackie and John were just arriving. For a split second I felt guilty that I hadn't thought to call either one of them. Then I realized they hadn't bothered to call me either. They must have pulled up to the scene just as I did.

We all ran to each other, flustered.

My father taught me it was always best to keep your mouth shut and listen, and that way you'd find out more information than if you had asked any questions. I listened to Jackie and John both announce how Julie had called them in a panic telling them that she and my father were assaulted by intruders, and for the both of them to meet her at the hospital. I was the only one who wasn't blessed with a courtesy call.

"She called you both?" I asked.

They both nodded their heads.

"Well I never got a call," I stated

"Then how did you get here?" Jackie snapped.

"I had to roll up on the crime scene and nearly have a heart attack!" I snapped back. "Why didn't she call me too?"

No one cared. It was never about me. As long as they were in the loop, my situation was null and void as far as they were concerned.

We entered the hospital with Rob, Tracy, John's current fuck-buddy, Samantha, and Jackie's fiancé, Neil, trailing behind.

At the emergency trauma window, John took charge. "Our parents, Mr. and Mrs. Henderson, were both injured. Have they arrived?"

The receptionist lazily typed the names into her computer and shook her head yes. Her nonchalant attitude had me stressed. "Where are they?" I asked. "I want to see my father."

John glared at me. "We want to see our parents, ma'am."

"Yes, of course. Well Mr. Henderson has been rushed into emergency surgery, but your mother is in triage waiting for a few tests to be run."

When she said my father was in surgery, tears streamed down my cheeks uncontrollably. I got choked up and was unable to speak as a lump had risen in my throat.

"Is our father going to be OK? Was he shot or something?" John asked. You could visibly see the stress surfacing from his body to his face.

"I don't have any answers at the moment. But you can go in to see your mother. Two at a time."

"Well she has a set of three children. So we'll be seeing her three at a time," I replied.

After a brief staring confrontation between me and the receptionist, she allowed us all to go see Julie. The emergency room was noisy as RNs, LPNs, doctors, and surgeons all scattered around in the small setting. I heard agonizing cries of pain as loved ones passed on, and conversations of joy as families realized that their loved ones would live to see another day. The hospital stench permeated throughout the open space and my stomach got queasy. I turned around for the support of

Tracy and realized that she wasn't allowed in with me.

What would I see when I saw Julie? I had no idea what type of injuries my parents had sustained. And what about my father? Why was he in surgery?

We finally reached a thin curtain behind which Julie lay. John pulled back the curtain and I saw her husky body, draped in a hospital gown with a white bandage wrapped tightly around her head. Her face didn't have any visible scars, nor did her arms. Her eyes were puffy from crying and she appeared to be weak. She stretched her arms out wide and her two golden children ran to embrace her. They all began to sob, and I couldn't help but feel contempt for the three musketeers.

"What happened to you and Daddy?" I asked.

Ignoring my question, she continued to weep. Finally she let go of John and Jackie and proceeded to compose herself.

"Mommy, what happened? I was so worried driving here," Jackie said.

Shaking her head, she began to tell her story.

"I don't know. Your father and I were inside the family room watching television. We both looked up and there were a couple of intruders. Before I knew it your father and I were being beaten to death!"

Once again she began crying. And once again her two clones began to cry as well.

"What did the intruders want and how did they get in?" I asked.

"Lisa, I don't know!" she snapped. "It all happened so fast."

"Well they must have asked for something—money, jewelry, something. And why is Daddy in surgery?"

"Lisa, what is wrong with you? Didn't she just say she didn't know? She's been through a lot. Do you not see the huge bandage on her head?" Jackie asked in Julie's defense.

I spun around. "I need a doctor over here immediately!"

The whole nurses station looked up and a female doctor came rushing over. "Is everything all right?" she asked.

"No, it's not. My father was admitted and I don't know if he's dead or alive! I need help. His name is Laurence Henderson!"

"OK, yes, he's in surgery with Dr. Carole."

"Again, what happened to him?"

As I was making a fuss, three detectives came over. They looked the part—middle-aged, white, and wearing long trench coats.

They all introduced themselves, flipped out a few notepads, and the one named Detective Moss began the questions.

"Mrs. Henderson, can you tell me what happened in your home tonight?"

She cleared her throat.

"Well as I was telling my daughter, I don't know. My husband and I were in our family room watching television and we both looked up to see three intruders."

"Can you identify those individuals?"

"Well, it all happened so fast."

"Why don't you give it a shot?" Detective Moss persisted. "Anything you might remember? Race? Height? Any identifiable scars? Things like that."

"Well they were . . . white—"

"White?" Detective Moss interjected. He raised his eyebrow as he jotted down notes.

"I . . . ummm . . . I mean, they had white skin, but they were Hispanic."

"How would you know that?"

"Their accents."

"So they were all Hispanic?"

"Yes, sir."

"How tall were they?"

"I don't know."

"So you said that you and your husband were watching television in the family room. I assume you were sitting down. Am I correct? You were sitting down when they entered the room?"

"Yes, sir."

"OK, well we've been inside your home, so as far as height, would you say that they reached the ceiling fan? Or just above the light switch? Or maybe halfway to the wall painting? I'm just trying to give you options here."

"I said I don't know," my mother replied.

"Detective, she's been through a lot tonight," John said. "Can't this wait?"

"Well, this is preliminary. It's good to at least get a description of the perps when the visual is fresh inside the victim's mind. Mrs. Henderson, were any of them my height? Or the height of any of the other detectives standing here?"

"I think . . . well . . . they were his height." Julie pointed to Detective O'Leary, who stood about six feet tall.

"Really?" Again the skepticism was back in Detective Moss's voice. "They all were the same height?"

"Yes."

"OK. What about facial hair, any scars, hair color?"

"They were wearing masks. I couldn't see anything."

"Why didn't you say that from the beginning?" Detective O'Leary asked.

"Because I just said it now."

Did I just hear a hint of sarcasm from Julie's fragile mouth? Something wasn't right, and from the line of questioning, I wasn't the only one in the room feeling this way.

"Julie, we don't need you trying to be a smart ass!" I said. "You need to tell them what you know. My father is in—"

"You better watch your fucking mouth!" Julie roared and sat straight up in her hospital bed. "Or I will leap from outta this—"

"Mommy, calm down," John soothed and pushed her back into her hospital bed.

"Lisa, look what you've done!" Jackie shouted and we both started arguing. As our argument escalated, none of the detectives did anything. Finally some nurses came running over, but the third officer, Detective Pitt, held them at bay.

"I don't give a fuck," I roared. "You don't even know what happened to your father, and Julie is sitting here doing shows!"

"Do you not see the fucking bandage wrapped around her head? For all you know, she could have a concussion!"

"She don't have no damn concussion! You would think that bump on her head would have knocked some sense into her. Instead, she's behaving like an illiterate fool!"

"Lisa, if the police weren't here I'd knock the shit outta you!" John threatened. "You only showing out 'cause they're here!"

"Touch me! Touch me! I dare you! Bitch!" I jumped up in John's face, but Detective Moss finally intervened and held me back.

"Don't touch her." Julie reached out toward John's hand, which he had balled up in a fist. "That's what she wants you to do. She ain't even worth it."

And then she looked at me, knowing I was hanging on to her every word, and she gave me the evil eye, that stare filled with hate that she reserved only for me.

Finally the detectives took control of the situation and began to break down what they knew about my father's condition.

"Well, Mrs. Henderson, I'm sure you'll be glad to know that your husband has survived his injuries," Detective Moss said. "We spoke with his doctor, and under normal circumstances any normal human being would be dead—"

"Oh, my gosh! Daddy," I yelped as my body trembled from fear.

"He sustained traumatic brain injuries because of the numerous blows to his head and back, but it seems he'll survive, although they don't think he'll make a full recovery. His spinal cord was injured and his brain is swollen from the blows to his head. He may not be able to walk again. The intruders really worked him over."

Detective Moss looked at Julie for her reaction. It took her a few moments before she began rubbing her eyes and making funny noises. Was she supposed to be crying?

"Where are his doctors?" Jackie asked. "Shouldn't his doctors be here giving us this news? We have questions."

"Yes, I'll go get them," Detective O'Leary said. "We asked that they let us break the news to the family."

"Well, we appreciate your bedside manner," John stated sarcastically.

I was numb. I said nothing. I did nothing. My father was paralyzed.

It was hours before my father was admitted to a room and I was able to see him. Miraculously, Julie was discharged after only a few hours in emergency. Turned out that the huge bandage on her head wasn't covering up a wound from a blunt object cracking her skull. All she had was a small gash, maybe one inch in length. She tried her best to get the hospital to keep her, but she was tossed out. Jackie and John had gone back to our house with Julie and promised to return later. They were told that they could only use the upstairs of the house until the forensic team was done with the crime scene.

I listened carefully as the detectives promised Julie they'd be in touch. Before exiting, I ran to Detective Moss and asked him if I could get his card too. He gave me a sly smile and pushed his card into the palm of my hand.

"Come see me tomorrow. OK?"

I nodded.

Nothing could have ever prepared me for the horror I saw when I finally entered my father's hospital room. He'd been taken to ICU for observation. The haunting sound of the monitor beeping, the tubes conspicuously dangling from his body, and his almost unrecognizable, swollen face was too much for me. I collapsed on his chest and began to sob.

"Daddy, what happened to youuuuu," I cried. "Who did this? Who …"

Crazy thoughts began to go in and out of my head, thoughts of finding out who did this and then murdering them myself. I would shoot each Hispanic guy in the face and watch their brains explode. So much hatred was running through my veins, it fooled me into thinking I was a killer.

After several moments of tears, I had an epiphany. I stood and looked down at my father. Then my brain rewound back to Julie. The difference in injuries was like night and day. My father looked dead and Julie could have gotten her injury by bumping into a door.

I couldn't wait to speak to the detectives. I knew she had done this. Somehow, some way she was behind this. But why?

Lisa Henderson

My father had been home from the hospital for months, and the investigation regarding his assault had come to a standstill. His insurance company had only covered minimal rehabilitation. I thought that he needed to be inside a facility twenty-four hours a day with a physical therapist helping him to get back his strength in his legs and body. But the insurance company didn't care that he needed physical and cognitive rehabilitation. Instead, it denied his claim, citing that his condition was permanent, and no further efforts would be helpful.

I didn't believe that. I wouldn't believe it. Miracles happened every day. My father was a good man. He certainly deserved one. Besides, I didn't trust Julie. I could only imagine what she did to him when no one was around. I'd begun noticing her giving my father the same evil eye she gave me. And he also had a look in his eyes that I could understand. It was a plea for help. His once vibrant eyes were now filled with hurt, pain, and most importantly, fear.

Each morning, when Julie went down to prepare herself breakfast before I went to school, I went into their room to check on my father. I usually washed his face and changed his bedpan. If I didn't do this, Julie would probably have him sitting in shit all day. When I first began doing this I could see that my father was embarrassed that I was seeing him that way, his manhood exposed in this compromising position. But I told him that I loved him and I did this because I loved him. Soon I could tell that he was grateful.

"Hey, Daddy," I said and kissed him on his cheek. His eyes popped open and I could swear he smiled. "Did you sleep well last night?"

I was already in the bathroom preparing a soapy washcloth and basin of fresh water. I turned to clean his face and noticed that his left eye was slightly bruised. It was puffy and almost bloodshot. I gasped.

"What happened to your face?" I asked and he looked down. "Did Julie do this? Blink once for yes."

I waited impatiently and my father just continued to stare.

"OK, if she didn't do this, then blink twice."

Again I waited, but as I looked into my father's eyes, I already knew the answer. My father understood perfectly what I had asked, and I knew he could have answered the questions. The only reason he didn't was because he was afraid. Tears began to stream down my cheeks as I watched them slide down his. My heart broke. Out of anger I wanted to charge downstairs and kick Julie's ass, but I knew I couldn't. I couldn't put my father in any danger.

"Don't be afraid, Daddy. I won't mention this." I leaned down and kissed his lips. "I love you and I promise I'm going to get you out of here one day. I'm going to get up the money to get you proper help. You hear me? Blink once for yes."

He blinked.

In school I could hardly concentrate. I had to think of a plan to help my father. His life was in danger each day he lived with Julie. She had already tried to have him murdered. There was no telling what she'd do next. I thought of an idea, but I needed a favor from Tracy to make it work. I left class and called her.

"Hey," I said.

"Lisa, I don't want you to call me anymore!"

"What?! What are you talking about?"

"Rob told me how you asked could you two swing an episode without me!" she yelled. Her voice quivered with anger. I was furious at that cockroach Rob! He was a liar! In fact, he called me and asked those very words. And although I was tempted, I refused him and this is how he chose to seek revenge. Obviously he couldn't take rejection. I knew I should have immediately told Tracy, only I didn't want to hurt her.

"He's lying and you know it!"

"I don't know shit but my name! How can you betray me like this?"

"Look, Tracy, don't let a man come in between our friendship. Last week Rob called and asked could we hook up, and I emphatically told him no!"

"Why would he lie?"

"Because he's a liar?" I replied sarcastically. "And this is your fault! Your stupid ass is the one who allowed her man in another woman's bed. If I was a grimy bitch, I could have fucked him and you wouldn't have known shit!"

"He would never fuck you again!"

"Tracy don't make me take your man . . . please don't push me!" I threatened. Click.

Obviously she couldn't take the pressure. I still had a dilemma. I needed a video camera. I couldn't take any more bullshit. I ran to the mall and charged one. My father was more important than a bill.

It took me weeks to have the opportunity to plant the video camera. After the first bruise showed up on my father, Julie was like a hawk. I had to wait until it went away and she began to trust me being around him before she began to fall back into routine.

Finally, my opportunity to plant the camera came when my brother John announced he was moving out. Apparently he had gotten some girl pregnant and he was moving in with her and her parents. He didn't want to marry her, so I guess this was the next best thing. Julie announced she would be moving my father's "smelly ass" out of her room. John's room was the closest to my room, and I only had to make sure everyone was asleep before I made my move.

That very night I went to check up on my father and plant the camera. I found a great spot on John's old armoire next to his trophies. I camouflaged the lens with all of John's junk. As I stood back and surveyed my work, I couldn't see the camera at all. Now all I had to do every morning was push play, and then review the tape when I got home from school.

I tiptoed over to my father, gave him a kiss, and gently massaged his face. He felt my presence and woke up. His eyes smiled as they focused on me.

"Sorry to wake you, Daddy. Do you know I love you?"

He blinked once for yes.

"Do you want me to get you out of here?"

He blinked once. My heart broke.

"You believe me when I say that I will, right?"

He blinked once.

I stayed up all night giving him a sponge bath and exercising his legs by moving them back and forth. Then I pulled up a chair and began to read his favorite book, In Search of Satisfaction. When he drifted into a peaceful sleep, I was satisfied.

On day one I got a hit. I snuck the camera into the basement and began to watch the events unfold. I fast-forwarded most of the tape. It took hours before Julie came into focus. At this point my heart palpitated. I listened carefully.

"You a lucky motherfucker that I have a heart to feed your slimy ass!" she shouted as she came into view of the camera. She was still dressed in her nightgown with rollers in her hair and a silk scarf on her head. The clock on the screen read one thirty, and she was just feeding my father. She had a tray in her hand that she plopped down on his chest.

"Open your mouth, dog!" she yelled. "Eat this here food, just like the dog you are!" She began to forcefully push the spoon in his mouth.

"Don't cry now!" she mocked. "Is that supposed to make me feel sympathy for you? Huh? How many nights did you leave me in here to take care of your kids while your ass was fucking everything that moved? Huh?" Her hand came all the way back and I heard the smack, but couldn't see it. Her body had blocked the view.

"Now I gotta spend the rest of my life taking care of your trifling ass! Why am I being punished? What about that red bitch down the block? Oh, yeah, you didn't think I knew about you fucking that young girl, Anita!" I heard another slap. The shock that my father was sleeping with Nasty Nita almost stopped my heart. If Julie knew he was sleeping with Nita, this could be the motive that the police needed. I continued to listen.

"Yeah, you always did like them redbones. That's why you always treated that little bitch Lisa like she was some sort of princess! She walks around here like she somebody. Mark my words, that bitch will never amount to nothing! You hear me? Nothing!" Smack.

She said a few words that I couldn't make out because she was puffing on her cigarette. But when she said, "And just to let you know, I got a young stud on his way over to fuck me in our bed, in your house, and

I'm going to be sure to moan real loud so you can hear me! Now I gotta go and freshen up. You can feed yourself. Oh, I forgot, you can't. I guess you'll starve!"

And then the tape ran out.

Tears streamed down my cheeks. I sat there trembling for hours before I called Detective Moss.

"Detective, listen, I just found out some disturbing news about my mother. It could help with the case."

"Really? What have you found out?"

"My father was having an affair with one of our neighbors. A young woman."

"How young? And watch what you say, because I would hate to lock up a quadriplegic for statutory rape."

"She's twenty. Her name is Anita Morales."

"OK, how does that help the case?"

"Doesn't that give Julie motive for wanting him dead?"

"Well that information does raise questions, but we'll need more than that. For instance, if we had that coupled with the fact that she would benefit financially, then I'd say you struck gold. But your father didn't have a substantial life insurance policy. It was worth only ten grand. And I can't convince the district attorney to prosecute with such little evidence. I need more."

"She beats him!"

"Have you seen this? And if she does, that doesn't contribute to the assault case with the other assailants involved. That would be a whole different case, and we'd need evidence."

"Well, I'm gathering evidence."

"Can you get an admission? Maybe if you could get her to give you the name of who she might have used to try to kill your father; anything along those lines would help."

"Why can't you put surveillance on our house? Who knows what she does during the day while we're not here? Or tap our phone?"

"We'd need a warrant for all those things and with the evidence that we have, no judge would sign off on it, even if I got the DA on my side."

"Well, I was saving this information for last. She's having an affair and she has the man inside our house, fucking him while my father is in the other room."

"That information isn't really relevant unless the affair was happening before your father's injuries. It could give her motive. Do you have a name? Perhaps he could have been the one who attacked your father. I'll go talk to him and ask him his whereabouts on the night in question."

"I don't have a name . . . yet."

He exhaled. "Lisa, my hands are still tied. There isn't anything more I can do."

"No one cares!" I yelled.

"I care. I'm still working on this. I never close a case unless I've solved it."

"OK, detective. I'll gather more evidence and get back with you."

"Lisa?"

"Yes?"

"Be careful."

"I will."

I needed more evidence. I needed to find another location in the room, a better angle to catch all the abuse. And I also needed to get Julie to slip up and either admit guilt or name her accomplices.

The next day was Saturday and I couldn't sleep in late. I decided to be proactive with my father's case. When I went in to check on him I noticed more bruises, only they weren't on his face. He was black and blue all over his chest, stomach, and arms. Thinking quickly, I ran to my room, grabbed the digital video camera, and began taping him. When I heard a noise, I quickly thrust the camera into my brother's drawer.

Seconds later Julie burst in. She was startled by my presence and looked to my father. I tried to fix his clothes as quickly as possible, but she could still tell that his buttons were undone. I looked down to my father and his eyes were as large as saucers. I looked at the drawer and it was slightly open. I knew that if I closed it, she'd get suspicious. Against my better judgment, I left it slightly ajar.

"What are you doing in here?" Julie demanded.

"What does it look like?" I snapped back. "I'm visiting my father."

"Well, get out. I gotta bathe him and prepare his breakfast."

"I'll bathe him this morning."

"I said I'll do it!" she snapped and practically shoved me out the room, locking the door. I didn't put up a fight for the sake of my father. But I wanted to beat the life out of Julie. All my hatred was boiling over and I wanted to commit a homicide up in there. But what about my daddy? Who would take care of him if I was gone?

After getting dressed I knocked on each neighbor's door and asked them questions about the night our home was invaded. Most didn't have any information. Their only goal for talking to me was to illicit information from me, but I wasn't giving up any.

Then it dawned on me. Why didn't I go talk to Nasty Nita? It was a long shot, but she might have some information.

I trotted down the block to her house and was glad to see her car was in the driveway. Her parents had remodeled their basement and that was where she lived. I walked around to the side of the house, and their ugly pit bull was barking his head off. He was chained to the gate and aggressively trying to charge at me, only to be pulled back by the chain. I knew if he got loose, I'd be his breakfast. I quickly rang the bell.

"Who is it?" she yelled.

"Lisa."

Again she yelled, "Who?"

I refused to respond. Soon she got the hint, walked her lazy ass to the door, and flung it open. She was startled to see me. She stepped back and used the door to put distance between herself and me. It dawned on me that she was afraid. I was known in my neighborhood for being a terror (thanks to Julie) and perhaps she thought I was coming to fight her.

"Hey, Anita."

"Hi." She smiled forcefully.

"Listen, I need your help."

"Sure. Anything," she eagerly replied.

"I just got the 411 that you were fucking my father." I couldn't resist giving it to her raw.

"Who told you that lie?"

"My question is, did you ever get wind that my mother knew about the affair? Did my father ever mention to you that he had to break it off because my mother might have suspected something? This is really important to me."

She thought for a moment and I guess decided to answer truthfully.

"We had been messing around for months, but we were discreet. We'd usually go to the Galaxy Motel up on the parkway and we never entered together. But one day we got careless. Neither one of us had time to drive to the motel and since your mother wasn't home, I snuck over through the back door."

"You're so stupid!" I yelled.

"I'm so sorry, Lisa. I tried to talk your father out of it, but he said it would be OK."

I thought for a moment. It wasn't only her fault. She shouldn't take the brunt of the blame. Two adults had made the decision.

"No, I'm sorry. It's not only your fault. It's just that I feel helpless about my father."

"Yeah, it's a sad situation. But what do I have to do with what happened?"

"Do you think Julie saw you enter or leave? Like, did you see her see you? If so, this information could be useful."

"No. She didn't see me leave or enter. I'm sure of that. I was very careful. But the next day I did realize that I had lost my nameplate pendant. I called and told your father, but he never found it inside your home. We both thought that I might have lost it on the street."

So that was how Julie knew. Finding the nameplate of a woman who was also your neighbor inside your home, or possibly even in your bedroom, was definitely a motive.

"Lisa!" Anita yelled. I had drifted off into my own world. "What does this have to do with what happened to Larry? Wasn't he a victim of a home invasion?"

I didn't want to give away my theory. Her big mouth would tell the whole block.

"It was just for informational purposes. Listen, where were you on that night my father was injured?"

"Well, for the most part, I got an alibi. I was at work, and my boss can verify that."

"Stop being paranoid. This isn't about you. Did you see anyone suspicious on the block? Someone you didn't know?"

"Nope. The police asked me that question when they went door to door."

"So I guess it's safe to say you didn't see three Hispanic guys that you didn't know?"

"Nope. Everyone I saw I knew, right down to your uncle Billy."

"What? Did you just say you saw my mother's brother Billy?"

"Sure did. I almost didn't recognize him. I had circled the block trying to find a parking spot because my parents had company, and they took my parking space. I had to park around the corner on 226th Street and as I exited my car, I bumped straight into Billy. He and his friend were in a rush because when I tried to chat, he totally blew me off."

My heart was racing. Why hadn't I thought about my lowlife uncle Billy? Because he was supposed to be in jail, in someone's prison, but apparently not! I couldn't wait to get this information to Detective Moss. That, coupled with my tape, should be enough to lock up Julie's ass for good! I thanked Nita and dashed down the block to get the video camera.

As I approached my house something looked very wrong. I saw a few neighborhood people scurrying away with their arms full. Then I looked at the lawn and realized that the lawn was littered with all of my belongings—jeans, coats, panties, and books were all strewn on the lawn. She had found the video camera. Immediately, I was enraged. Visions of what I was gonna do to her when I got inside flickered in my head.

I stuck my key and turned the lock. That part went smoothly, but as I tried to push the door open, it wouldn't move. I tried again. Nothing. Julie had pushed something in front of the door to restrict my passage. I began kicking on the door and screaming like a maniac. I got lost in my own fury and didn't even realize that she had called the police on me. It wasn't until I was dragged away, kicking and screaming obscenities, and tossed in a holding cell that I was told I was being arrested because my mother said I had become irate and pulled a knife on her.

The next series of events were unbelievable. How could my life change its course in a nanosecond? How could I end up in someone's stinking jail? This wasn't the life my father had planned for me.

From Central Booking, my first call was to Ms. S—only her telephone was disconnected. Next, I called Jackie. I was hysterically crying from the treatment and horrible conditions of the jail.

"Jackie, let me tell you what Julie did to me."

She didn't have any patience or tolerance for my situation.

"She already told me, Lisa. You were upset with her because she wanted to bathe and feed her husband, and you went crazy because you're a control freak and pulled a kni—"

"What? She's lying! I wasn't even there! I was canvassing the neighbor—"

"Stop it! Stop telling your tales! We're all tired of your drama! No one is gonna believe your lies. You're in jail where you belong! I hope they fucking beat the shit out of you in there! You think you're so tough, pulling out a knife on your own mother! After all she's been through?"

At that moment I became very calm. I saw my future and reflected on my past. Why did I continue to fight an uphill battle? Nothing I said would ever be believed. Julie had made sure of that. All my life she had managed to put a wedge between me and my siblings, as if their being on her side validated her. She needed to win, and she had. Once again, I was being portrayed as the villain, and being accused of something I didn't do. My innocent pleas would fall on deaf ears.

Julie was good at manipulation, but something inside of me broke for Jackie at that moment. As much love as I could have had for a sister now turned to hate. She meant nothing to me. They meant nothing to me. They were as good as dead. They believed in Julie because they wanted to. No matter how I tried to tell my story, they ignored me, and that was inexcusable from family.

I listened as she said words like, "Don't come back around. . . . John will beat you up. . . . You need help. . . . troublemaker . . ."

"Why don't you ever believe me!" I yelled.

"Maybe because you're always lying!"

"Have I ever lied to you? Or John? I know I can be a bit fucked up, but I've done nothing but love you! And John! Why are you always treating me this way!"

"Because you're always disrespecting our mother!"

"She disrespects me!"

"She's your mother!"

"So that means she has free reign to treat me like shit?"

"In what world? This is your version. You always want someone to feel sorry for you. Poor, poor Lisa! Give me a break!"

"Give you a break? Why? I wasn't ever given one. All I ever wanted was to be loved equally. Was that so bad? Was that too much to ask for?"

"Parents will always have a favorite! That's the way life is. No one says shit when Daddy caters to you. I didn't hear you screaming for equal rights when he was buying you a car, or taking you on massive shopping sprees!"

"That's different!"

"Of course it is. It's different because you're on the receiving end."

"No, it's different because he bought you a car too. And took you on shopping sprees too. He visually shows me love because he knows I don't get it from Julie. And besides, he doesn't hate you!"

"You sound so stupid right now!"

"Hey, since you have already made up your mind without hearing my side of the story, and you've just stated that John has already sided with you and Julie, how 'bout everyone just write me out the family's history? You are now dead to me."

"That's the best thing I've ever heard come from your mouth." Click.

Since I had nothing to lose, and only freedom to gain, I called Tracy.

"Tracy, look, I'm sorry for everything, but I need your help."

"Who is this?"

"Lisa. I'm in jail and I need—" Click.

I thought about calling Nana, but I didn't for two reasons. The first was I didn't know if my mother had gotten to her and if she would take Julie's side. But the second most important reason was she was broke and didn't own a car. How could she help? My last resort was Ishmael, only his number was no longer in service.

I was portrayed as a menace to the judge and my bail was set at five thousand dollars. I had no one else to call. I sat on Rikers Island for thirteen days before I went back before the judge and I was let go on my own recognizance. I had another court date given to me, one month away. I walked out with not a dime in my pocket and only the clothes on my back.

The moment I was released from jail, I wondered about my future. How would this arrest affect my career as a news anchor? How could I report about criminals when I was one? I told myself that I couldn't worry about that now. I'd worry about that tomorrow, or the day thereafter. Right now, I needed a place to sleep.

The fresh air felt like a hot shower; it was that invigorating. I stood on the steps of the Queens courthouse, broke, hands dug deeply into my empty pockets. I surveyed a few bystanders until I found one that seemed approachable.

"Ma'am, would you mind allowing me to use your cell phone to make an important call?"

"Sorry, my anytime minutes don't start until seven."

"I'll only be a moment. The call is really . . ."

She didn't stay to hear my plea.

"Bitch!" I yelled after her.

"You were just inside the courtroom, right?" a man asked from behind me. I turned to see a correctional officer in uniform.

"Yeah, and?"

"And nothing." He shrugged his shoulders and kept it moving. I ran behind him.

"I'm sorry. I was just in there. I thought you'd be a dick, like the rest of the officers."

"I have my moments," he said and smiled.

"You know, this world is fucked up. How can they kick people out of court and not make sure they can get home safely?"

"This is New York! And you're an adult. If you do a grownup crime, you'll do grownup time. We ain't got time to hold your hand throughout the criminal system. You know your ass was dead wrong, trying to stab your momma!"

I looked into his eyes to see if he was joking. He was.

"On my life, I didn't do it!"

He gave me a long stare. "You sure? 'Cause you skinny girls always got something to prove. I've seen it all my life. You gotta prove you're tough, so you pick up a weapon to help fight your battles."

"Geez, what ever happened to innocent until proven guilty?"

"That shit only works in theory. You're guilty and you'll have to prove yourself innocent because if you don't, you're gonna see the inside of our correctional facility for longer than a couple weeks."

I didn't want that to happen. I had already learned my lesson. No more fighting with Julie, because I wasn't a match for her treachery. No matter how hard I tried to hate her, I could never hate her as much as I realized she hated me. I would go back inside her house and abide by all her rules until I was stable enough to take my father out of there and properly take care of him. Whatever lesson she wanted me to learn, I had learned that and more. She was the head nigga in charge, and there wasn't anything I could do—for now.

"Do you think I could use your cell phone? I promise not to run up your minutes."

"Sure. Take your time. Are you calling your parents?"

"Yes, I'm going to call my mom."

"Good luck with that. Do you want some advice?"

I didn't, but I said, "Of course."

"Apologize and stay humble. You only get one mom."

I called Julie and she picked up. "Mommy?" Click. My heart plunged. I called back, but she didn't even bother to acknowledge my call. Finally I left a long message on the machine. I was desperate.

"I'm sorry about everything and I've learned my lesson. They just released me from jail and I don't have anywhere to go. I'm hoping that when I get there, you'll let me in. I promise not to be mean to you, and I promise that I won't say a word about Daddy."

I welled up with tears and hung up. I walked back over to the correctional officer and gave him back his phone.

"Thank you."

"What did she say?"

"She wouldn't talk to me."

"Wow, it's that bad, huh?"

"More than you'll ever know."

"Where are you going?"

"Home. Hopefully she'll let me in."

"Where do you live? Do you need a ride?"

I looked at the clean-shaven older man with the speckles of gray hair and nice mannerisms, and I decided to trust him.

"I live in Cambria Heights, off 225th Avenue."

"Oh, OK. I know that area. Follow me." When I hesitated for a moment, he continued. "And although you can trust me because I got a daughter your age, you better not be jumping in strange cars with strange men in the future. You hear me?"

"Yes, sir."

"Save the sir for your father. My name is Michael. And you're Lisa, correct?"

"Yes."

I followed my new friend to a black Yukon truck inside the parking garage and got in. When he cut on the engine, Jay-Z blared from his massive system. Immediately I thought of Ishmael. I missed him terribly.

As he sang along to Jay-Z, I wasn't shocked. I knew the type of man he was, still trying to hold on to his youth. He probably had a girlfriend not much older than me. I decided to probe. Why not? I needed something to take my mind off of my problems.

After I gave him my full address, I began with my questions. "Are you married?" I asked.

"No, I've never had them type of headaches." He laughed at his own joke.

"But you have a daughter my age?"

"Yes. Her mother and I didn't get along."

"And you found this out before or after you got her pregnant?"

"Well, aren't we the judgmental type? What about being innocent and having to prove someone guilty? I guess that little spiel of yours was self-satisfying."

"I guess I don't understand how men are always judging their babies' mommas after the fact."

"And you're all of"—he took a sideways glance at me—"twenty?"

"Almost."

"OK, so I'll let you judge me only if I can judge you back."

"Deal."

"I have two babies' mommas. I have a nineteen-year-old son and a sixteen-year-old daughter. I was young back then—"

"So was my father, but he married my mother," I interrupted.

"And I can see how great you're turning out to be," he remarked sarcastically.

Nice stab. I laughed. "Well, as I said, I'm innocent."

"Well thankfully, none of my kids are wielding knives and trying to kill me, so I guess I did right by them."

I thought for a moment. "Hey, I like you," I said.

He made a lemon-sucking face. "I'm not that kind of man. As I said, you're young enough to be my daughter."

"Not like that. I mean, I feel comfortable talking around you, just as I did with my father."

"You speak of him in past tense. Did he pass away? Is that why you and your mother aren't getting along?"

I thought for a moment on whether I should let him in on my father's personal business and realized that my father wouldn't like that. He was a proud man and would hate it if I spilled the beans.

"Yeah. He died of a heart attack last year, and things just haven't been the same since."

"Yeah, death can be hard on a family, but give your mother a chance. She'll come around once she adjusts to not having her husband around." He made a left onto my block. "Where at?"

"In front of the house with the burgundy awning."

He looked at the row of homes. "Nice block."

"Thank you!" I said. "Wish me luck."

"I'll stay here until you get inside safely."

"You don't have to."

"I never said I did."

I hopped out—smelly, hungry, and most importantly, humbled. The whole argument with Jackie and the fight with Julie were in the past, and I was ready to move forward. As I approached I no longer saw my car in the driveway. I wasn't sure what that meant.

I knocked and knocked, but no one answered. I looked through the window and saw Julie sitting on the sofa watching her soap operas. She clearly heard me knocking, but refused to move. I tapped on the window. Nothing. I was desperate.

"Mommy, I'm sorry. I promise that I'll behave," I yelled through the door.

She didn't even flinch. I stood there for a few long moments, but I knew that I had to give up. There wasn't any way she was letting me back under her roof. She had too much to lose, and I was a loose cannon. I swallowed the lump in my throat and held back my tears as I approached the driver's side door of Michael's jeep.

"She's not home yet," I said and lowered my eyes.

"Ummm, is there somewhere else I can take you?"

"No. You've been really great. Besides, she should be home any moment. I'll just wait on the porch."

He persisted. "Do you have any other relatives in the area that you could call, to see where she is?"

"Nah, it's OK for you to leave me here." I just wanted him to go. Any second I was about to lose it and start crying like a baby.

He hesitated, then reached inside his wallet and took out three twenty-dollar bills. "Here, take this."

"Why?"

"Because I said so," he replied and shoved the money in my hands. I couldn't hold back my tears any longer. "T-t-thank you."

Once Michael had safely left my block, I began walking. I had no idea where I was going. And although I was grateful for the money, I knew that sixty dollars wasn't going to get me very far in life. At least it would get me to Ishmael.

Lisa Henderson

The cab driver dropped me off on Park Avenue after I had him circle the block a couple of times. I wanted to see if Ishmaels' car was parked in the vicinity. It wasn't. I got out with eight dollars left in my pocket and went to the Chinese restaurant. I was starving. I also looked horrible and really didn't want anyone to see me. I decided to take refuge in Ms. S's apartment. I was sure she would know how to find Ishmael.

When she opened the door, she was so happy to see me. Her welcome was so warm that for a split second I wondered if I should have stayed with her and not returned to Queens, but that thought quickly faded as I looked more closely at Ms. S. Her face was sunken in and gaunt. Her hair was uncombed and she wore an oversized, dirty housecoat. Immediately I knew she was living like a rock star.

"Lisa, is that you? Why didn't you tell me that you were coming by? I would have cooked something for you. Come in," she said, and moved to the side to offer me entry. The once plush project apartment was practically bare. There wasn't anything of value left. If she could have sold the kitchen sink, she would have.

"I would offer you a seat, but you see . . ." Her voice trailed off and she began to fidget with her clothes. "You know, after they murdered my baby and Timothy got locked up, things done changed around here."

I was frozen. I felt so sorry that this could happen to such a good woman. She'd always treated me like a daughter and when they murdered Shiniqua, she practically begged me to come back and live with her. She had needed me, and I had turned my back on her. Perhaps if I had stayed I could have given her comfort, and she wouldn't be in this position.

"Where's Thomas, Corey, and Kenneth?" I asked, referring to her younger sons.

"They all locked up. All my sons are in jail, serving life sentences." She was truly alone.

"Lisa, I'm glad you got out. This project will suck the life out of you, and you deserve better. I'm glad one of my daughters made it out," she said.

I didn't stay long, but before I left I asked, "Have you heard from Ishmael?"

"He doesn't come around no more. He done turned his back on me, which ain't right. I thought he would hold me down, but you know how people are." She snorted. "He's just a Timothy wannabe, anyway!"

I didn't tell her that he most likely cut off ties with her because of what Timothy and I did, but I just shook my head as if I understood.

We embraced tightly.

"Do you have any money I can borrow?" she asked and my heart broke.

"I'm really fucked up right now. All I got is two dollars and you're welcome to it. That's why I'm looking for Ishmael."

She took the two dollars and said, "He been moved last year. But he comes around here each night about nine o'clock, up on the Marcy side. If he gives you any money, will you promise to come and hit me off? As you can see, I need a little help."

"You know I will."

I left and went to see Nana. I still had hours to waste until nine, and I wanted to take a shower and comb my hair.

I thought that Nana would act indifferent and not let me in, but she didn't. She just opened the door and walked back into her room. I followed behind her.

"Whatchu doin' here, chile?"

"Where's Uncle Billy?"

"He don't live here no more. I put his ass out for good 'cause I don't put up with no nonsense, and I don't want no coppers knocking on my door."

My eyes flew open. "So you know what they did to my father."

She shrugged. "Whatchu doin' here, I asked?"

"I came looking for Ishmael."

"I heard Julie done tossed you out. You can stay here if you like."

Although the thought was inviting, and probably my only hope, I knew that it would be very hard for me to stay here with all the memories of everything that went down in the past ten years of my life. Marcy Projects seemed like a different world to me. As I walked around and looked out her bedroom window, I noticed that the faces had changed. I saw a new set of girls hanging out on the benches, looking cute to attract the new breed of hustlers.

"Thank you, Nana. I really appreciate the offer. And if it doesn't work out with me and Ishmael, then I'll be back for sure."

"You hoping he take you back after all this time? I done seen him with a new redbone chick up in his fancy car. She not from 'round here, either. She look Puerto Rican, and I heard she done earned her master's degree."

My stomach twisted up in knots. News always traveled fast in the

PJs. From what Nana had described, he done traded me in for a new and improved Lisa.

I hopped in the shower and put my same dusty clothes back on when Nana came out of her room and asked, "Is this here yours?"

It was one of my overnight bags stuffed with clothes and underwear. I used to have so many clothes that it was so easy to have left this bag behind. I couldn't believe my luck. I could have kissed her!

My eyes began to get watery.

"Oh gosh, you don't know what this means to me right now. My mother, she threw out all my clothes. All of my belongings were trashed."

"Don't blame her for her ways," Nana stated.

"Well, who am I to blame? Me?"

"No, blame me. I wasn't ever much of a mother. I didn't realize how bad I'd been until I watched how Julie handled you. She didn't do anything to you that I didn't do to her. Growing up, I constantly pit her and Billy against each other. I had a favorite chile each week. Whoever did the most to kiss my ass got treated good, while the other would get ignored until they stepped up to outshine the other. Billy had her beat for years. He'd go out in them streets, rob folks, and bring me all types of shit. It was during these years that he was my favorite and Julie wasn't shit. Soon his robbing streak came to an end and Julie hooked up with your father, and she began to do for me. Now she was my favorite. I did this to my children because my mother did it to me. Manipulating their minds gave me a sense of power. It made me feel smart. I never finished high school, and playing my mind games was like my college degree.

"I was awful. I would lie on my kids to their father right in front of their faces and have them run out of the room in tears. I would feel a sense of victory. Imagine a mother doing that to her own kids. When Julie came back, I felt good kicking your Uncle Billy out of his room and watching your mom kiss my ass, while Billy scrambled to see what he could do to get back in my good graces.

"The night he got locked back up for that robbery wasn't only about getting enough money to score drugs. I knew that he went out there again to rob someone to get back on my good side. Billy had stopped robbing people a long time ago. He could always find someone to get high with. I knew in my heart he did that for me, to get my attention. And he did. I began to look at myself closely and I knew that I needed to break the chain. I called your mother and told her everything I am telling you now. And instead of her embracing what I said and trying to make things right, she hung up on me.

"I had to let my kids go. I've done enough damage to their lives. And I'm having this conversation with you now because I don't want you to have children and turn out to be everything that you despise in your mother. You hear me, gal? You're better than me. You're better than Julie."

I listened to Nana carefully, and I didn't care that she felt responsible. My mother had choices in life and she chose to be that way. All I kept hearing was the people who loved my mother defending her by giving reasons for her actions. And the thing about it was that she never admitted to doing anything wrong, nor was she trying to change. So why should I readily just brush off what she'd done to me? Or to my father?

After I had freshened up, I pulled my hair back in a tight ponytail and took off my old fingernail polish. Luckily Nana had a bottle of clear polish sitting on her dresser. After doing my toenails too, I slipped on an old deep orange Diane Von Furstenburg dress that Ishmael had bought me, and a pair of white sandals. I didn't have any jewelry to bling me out, but I did have lipgloss. I surely looked better than I had in those funky jeans.

Slowly I made my way over to Marcy Avenue, but he wasn't there. It was crowded outside, music was blasting, and I didn't recognize a soul. Nor did I really want to. I guessed the girls my age were past hanging out on benches, trying to be seen. I lingered for as long as I could without feeling too stupid and realized that I would have to take Nana up on her offer. After a couple hours of pacing from bench to bench, I retreated back to Nana's.

I did this for nearly two weeks, alternating the three outfits that I had. Finally, fate intervened. As I walked on the outskirts of the projects looking for Ishmael one day, I ran into Knowledge. He was still chilling. He no longer drove his 2000 black Yukon. He was now pushing a 2004 Phantom. He was a sight for my weary eyes.

"Knowledge!" I screamed.

He turned my way. "Oh, shit, you gonna live a long time! I was just asking about you." He came over and gave me a bear hug. When he pulled back, his platinum jewelry had me mesmerized.

"Liar," I said and softly punched him.

"Nah, for real. I ran into Crystal and Ta-Ta and they asked about you. They told me they heard a rumor that you were back in Marcy, but I didn't believe them."

"Well, I'm not really here for good. I'm just visiting, you know." I looked down so he couldn't read my lying eyes.

"True, true. I feel you. But you looking good, though." His eyes scanned me up and down and then he said, "Do you need anything? 'Cause you know I got you."

He began to dig inside his pockets, but I stopped him. I mean, I did have my pride.

"Can you do me a favor?" I asked.

"Come on, now. We family."

I smiled. "Have you seen Ishmael lately?"

His face got serious. "Yeah, that's my man. Why, what's up?"

I looked him directly in his eyes. "Knowledge, I miss him so much, it hurts. I just need to see him so that I can tell him that."

"I don't know, Lisa. I don't want to hurt your feelings, but I think he moved on."

I knew what he was referring to, but I couldn't accept it.

"Please, Knowledge. I'm telling you that if he saw me again, he'd feel differently. I don't care what bitch he got, she ain't me!"

He began laughing. "Yo, you just reminded me of Shiniqua, all sassy and shit! OK, where you gonna be? I'll give him a message from you. You gonna be at your grandmother's?"

"Why you trying to play me? I thought you just said we're fam?"

"A'ight, I'ma be straight with you. He not feelin' you after you fucked Timothy. That was some real trifling shit. And before Timothy got knocked I had to hear both them niggas' sides, and I can tell you that Ishmael was fucked up behind that. You was his heart, and you did him dirty."

"Yes, I was a real slut. I fucked Timothy for a roof over my head. But before you judge me, you should put yourself in my position and consider my age. I've grown and I'm now grown, and I want my man back. Please, just call him and ask him to come through. I promise I'll just casually walk up, and he won't know you helped set him up. Pleee-assssssse? Do it for me?"

He thought for a second and then said, "OK, but if you get hurt, that's on you."

He pulled out his cell phone and called Ishmael.

"Motherfucker, what you doin'? You don't know how to come through and check a nigga no more? Wifey got you hemmed up all day?"

My stomach flipped.

"Nah, I'm on the block. Why don't you come through?" Knowledge said. After he hung up he said, "He'll be here in thirty minutes."

I knew that meant an hour.

I stood by the pay phone and watched Knowledge a few feet away, politicking with a few of his friends. Girls came and went and I could tell he was loving all the attention he was getting. He'd replaced Timothy and Ishmael. From what Knowledge had told me, Ishmael was no longer pushing weight.

Pop, pop, pop, pop, pop. Shots suddenly rang out and everyone ducked for cover. When I looked up, I realized that Knowledge had gotten hit. I couldn't move. When would it ever stop? From where I stood, he didn't look like he was going to make it. His white tee was soaked in blood and I kept hearing someone screaming.

"Lisa! What the fuck you doing here?!"

I realized then that the screams were coming from my mouth.

"Come on." I felt the strong hand yank me by my arm and toss me into the car.

"They killed him!" I cried. "They really killed him!"

"I told that nigga to give up that block. He'd made enough paper, and it was time to let that shit go."

"Why would they do that?"

"Why? Because they felt like it. Isn't that why people do things, even though they know it will hurt someone? Because they feel like it?"

Ishmael's harsh words jarred me back to reality. He was talking about me.

"I'm really sorry for sleeping with Timothy," I said and looked him directly in his eyes.

He shrugged. "Shit happens."

"Listen, Ishmael, I really wanted to see you so that we could talk. If you didn't know it because I didn't show it, I really love you. And I want us to get back together. So much has happened since we broke up that I don't even know where to begin."

"Yo, which train do you want to get dropped off at?"

"Huh?"

"Train?"

"I'm not leaving you! I just said that I love you, and I know you still love me!"

"Lisa, look at me. I don't love you. I'm in love with my new lady. She's everything you're not. She's smart and classy, and she loves only my dick. You feel me?"

"I don't give a fuck about that bitch!" I yelled.

Ishmael pulled the car over abruptly.

"That you will not do. You will not disrespect her! Get the fuck out!"

"OK, OK, OK, I won't disrespect her. But please, just hear me out! My heart hurts when I think about you. I truly miss you and I want us to at least try. You said that you'd never let me go. What about that? Huh?"

He looked me up and down, taking notice of my cracked fingernails and worn clothes.

He exhaled.

"You love me, huh?"

"I do. I do. I do."

He shook his head. "You got plans for tonight?"

"I just want to be with you."

"All right. Sit back and relax. You hungry?"

"Very."

He shook his head again. Yes, I thought.

Ishmael began driving toward the city and my heart began to flutter. We were going back to his/our apartment, I thought. When we ended up at the W Hotel on Forty-seventh Street. I was a bit annoyed.

"Ummm, I thought we were going back to your place."

"Why would you think that?" he spat. "You coming or not?"

My mind told me to run, but my heart made me stay.

Ishmael got us a room and when we walked in he grabbed me by the back of my hair and flung me up against the wall. My back hit the wall and he began kissing me passionately. He was groping me and murmuring while hoisting up my skirt. We began ripping off each other's clothing in a frenzy. I was so wet that I couldn't wait for him to enter me.

"Did Timothy fuck you this good?" he asked as he rammed his dick in me with force. He was sweating freely as his hands smashed my face into the pillow. He was lifting my legs and pulling them in awkward positions all in an attempt to hurt me. I wanted to scream out, but I didn't want to upset him. I wanted him to get all of his anger and hurt out so that we could move past this.

When he pulled out of me, flipped me over, and began thrusting his dick in me doggy style, I couldn't help but scream out.

"Don't cry now!" he stated. "You wanted this!"

After he fucked me for hours, I drifted off to sleep, only to be awakened by hot piss stinging my face. I woke up gasping and choking. I was mortified.

"What the fuck is wrong with you!" I yelled.

"Oh, I thought you were used to that. Didn't Timothy piss on his bitches?"

"I hate you!" I screamed hysterically.

"Get the fuck out, you slut bitch!"

"I hope you fucking die, you bastard!"

"One day you'll get your wish, but no time soon."

I ran and got in the shower. As the water ran, he came in to humiliate me some more.

"Lisa, when someone tells you who they really are, you should believe them."

I was numb. I remembered saying those exact same words to him so many years ago.

PART III:

THE DOUBLE CROSS...

Lisa Henderson

It amazes me how gullible people are. Last night I'd gone to get
something to eat when I did my same routine, which was pretend
that I didn't have enough money. Instead of the usual male paying for
my dinner, a female did, which was a first. When I ran into her today
and she offered to buy me breakfast, I couldn't refuse. Although I had
close to ten thousand dollars stashed away, I couldn't afford to splurge.
I was on a mission to save enough money to get my father away from
Julie. I couldn't imagine all the awful things she was doing to him, but
I knew that it wouldn't be too long before I had enough money saved
to get a nice home.

Ever since I allowed Ishmael to violate and humiliate me, I'd come
up. No longer was I a female relying on a man to put money in my
pockets and pay my bills. I'd started my own business, LH Enterprises.
I was just as much a hustler as Timothy and Ishmael, only I didn't sell
drugs. I sold green cards! And I was realizing how enterprising citizen-
ship could be.

It all started when I was coming out of a free clinic on Van Siclen

Avenue in Brooklyn. I had just learned that I was pregnant. My first thought was to run back to Ishmael because I knew he was the father, and beg him to support me/us. But his degrading actions toward me kept running through my head. What would my father say if he knew that the love of my life had pissed on me, and I was seriously thinking about begging to be back with him? Wasn't I better than that?

As I walked toward the number three train, I was accosted by a Nigerian man—slim build, dark chocolate complexion, white teeth, and a thick accent. He had been following me for blocks, only I hadn't realized it.

"Excuse me, nice girl," he'd said. I swung around, prepared to give him directions if he was lost, when his next words caught my interest. "You want to make legal money?"

"What?"

"I got a proposition for you. You can make legal money, if you help me out." His shifty eyes began to dart around, surveying the neighborhood, possibly looking for spies.

I examined his clothing—True Religion jeans that fit snugly, a polo shirt that wasn't oversized, and a pair of leather sandals. His hair was nicely groomed and he had on a pair of sparkling diamond studs. He appeared to be in his mid- to late twenties.

"Keep talking," I replied.

He stepped closer to me. "Are you married?"

"Motherfucker, you out here wasting my time like I got all goddamn day to play these reindeer games, and all you want to do is get my number?"

My outburst startled him, but he forged on. "I will pay you to marry me to get my green card. I have money."

I blinked a few times. Was he really serious?

"What do you mean pay me to marry you?"

"I have big plans in America. I need to stay permanently. If you marry me and I get my green card, I will give you lots of money."

"How much is lots?"

"Five thousand dollars. Cash."

"Just like that? All I gotta do is say I do, and that's it?"

"Yeah, yeah, yeah . . . almost," he said excitedly, knowing he had my full attention. "There's more to it. We have to pretend to be married. Do what married people do as husband and wife."

Point blank I stated, "I'm not fucking you. You can forget that!" My days of fucking for money or material things were over. That was a wrap. Besides, I was pregnant.

"No . . . no . . . we will only pretend to do married things in order to pass Immigration. Small things, such as you accompanying me to appointments, if they request that."

I was sure if I would have gone for the fucking part, he would have been only too happy. Instead he settled for what he could get, which was a pregnant twenty-year-old.

"I want my money up front," I said.

"You get two thousand up front, and the balance once my green card is issued."

"How do I know you won't skip out when it's time to pay up?"

"Because you could always report me to Immigration."

I thought for a second. "Nah, I take all the risk. Once you get your card, I doubt if they'll revoke it. I want four thousand up front and the balance when you're certified."

"Now I'm taking all the risk. How do I know that you won't skip out?"

"You should take the risk. You're the one who's in need. I live here. I'm legal."

"Can we compromise and I give you half up front?"

"No."

He paused. "OK, but I make the rules. You got to move in with me so that I can watch you and feel that my investment is safe."

Thinking over his proposition, I wondered where he lived. He could live in some palatial house somewhere. I decided to ask before I turned down that request.

"Where do you live?"

"I live in a two-bedroom apartment on Livonia Avenue, not too far from here, with my six cousins."

"Are you serious?"

"Yes. We save lots of money like that. They all need green cards too."

That was my "A-ha" moment.

"What's your name?" I asked.

"Nigel."

"Nigel, I'm Lisa. How many women did you ask before you met me?"

"I got robbed four times in five months. Each lady take my money, and then I don't see them again." His face twisted in disgust at the painful memories.

"Nigel, I just might be the female version of a knight in shining armor. . . ."

Joshua Tune

I woke up the next morning, fiending. The Black Magic had worked its wonders yet again, and I knew I wanted more. The crawly feeling of my skin and the cramps in my stomach told me that I needed more. Of course, there was the little matter of money, and how I didn't have any. However, I knew that Nikki, Molly, my dear wife, did. She wouldn't have come all this way without the big money on her. I didn't know how much she had, but I knew she had more than the seven grand I'd already stolen. I needed the money more than she did right now.

I looked over at the other bed. Nikki was still fast asleep. I crept to her purse that was on the desk and looked through it. Her wallet only held about twenty dollars, which I took and put in my pocket. I checked the little makeup pouch where she usually kept her cash—nothing. Then I began quietly ransacking the small motel room, peering in every crevice and BINGO! There was one thousand dollars taped underneath the lamp, and I took that as well. I looked over my shoulder and Nikki was still asleep. I quietly opened the door and slipped out. After walking a few blocks until I got to the subway, I rode the A train all the way to East New York, trying not to throw up.

I got on the block and looked for Perez. I found him talking to someone through the partially lowered passenger window of a black S300 Mercedes with super-dark tinted windows. I vaguely remembered the car. The person driving the car must have been his boss. Only someone well connected could have gotten the quality of heroin that was in the Black Magic. Even though I'd never touched heroin until recently, I still knew a quality product when I tasted it. The pull of the drug called me each night. And each time I took a hit, I hoped that I would feel that same rush that I felt only weeks earlier. I was still chasing that same ultimate high.

One of Perez's crew members saw me coming and whistled. Perez looked up, saw me, and grinned. He said something else to the person in the car and a brown paper bag was passed through the window. Perez listened, nodded in response, and walked toward me with the bag in hand. The passenger window closed and the car drove away.

"What's up, man?" he greeted me.

"What's up? I need some more Black Magic."

He chuckled. "Damn, Holmes, you on that shit like that?"

I scratched the side of my neck. Perez noticed and shook his head. "I only got three bundles today."

"I'll take all three."

Perez gawked at me. "What?"

"I want all three bundles."

"You got the loot for three bundles?"

I pulled the cash out of my pocket and showed it at him. He nodded and handed me the entire paper bag. I gave him the money and he counted it before I left. I looked into the bag, already anticipating the rush of the heroin to my brain. Perez nodded at the accuracy of my payment. I thanked him and walked off, but not before he called out to stop me.

"Hey, Holmes!"

I turned around. "Yeah?"

"Be careful with that shit."

I gave a jaunty wave and walked off. I'd seen a little abandoned alley between two stores that would be perfect for a quick hit. I hummed "That Ol' Black Magic" as I hurried to my chosen location.

Minutes later, I was flying high. Gone were the worries of what Nikki was going to do, now that she'd calmed down and gotten some rest. Gone were the thoughts of Parker and the feel of her cold hand as she died. Gone were the demands of Mr. Leventhal to pay up and get out of his fancy hotel. Gone were the cool, assessing, and knowing eyes of Mr. Assam, figuring out why I was unable to pay my bill and why I was nodding off on my feet. All of them were gone, gone in a rush of Black Magic that made me feel, well, magical.

I don't know how I made it back to the neighborhood where we were staying, but I did. I stumbled up the street, talking to Parker and looking around at the bright lights. Well, they weren't that bright since some of the stores seemed to be closed for the night. I stopped into a Popeye's chicken and ordered a two-piece. I devoured it and wanted a snort of Black Magic for dessert. I walked out of the restaurant feeling like I could jog a hundred miles. I jogged up the street as if I were training for a marathon, looking for our motel. For the life of me, I couldn't remember where it was. I stopped and turned around in the street, trying to find a familiar landmark, but everything looked so different.

"Nikki!" I yelled. "Nikki! Come get me!" People looked at me as if I'd lost my mind. One person mumbled something about not taking medications. That person was right. I did need to take my medication, and it was the best thing available without a prescription. I called for Nikki for another block when she suddenly appeared. She put her arms around me and someone else put their arms around me too. I looked at the girl.

"Hey, you're Aaliyah," I slurred. "Back, back, forth, forth . . . let me see you go back, back, and forth, forth," I sang off key.

Pretty soon we were back at the motel and I needed to use the bathroom. The sight of Nikki's irate face had me seeking some fortification for when she cursed me out. Just a little hit of Black Magic, and everything would be all good.

Nikkisi Ling

I truly wasn't feeling how my life was unraveling. It was one thing to be a fugitive. But it was quite another to be a broke fugitive. Joshua had taken every dime I had and squandered it away on drugs. Not only did I hate weak people, but I despised a weak man. In the blink of an eye my life had shifted once again. Each time in my life that I was feeling settled, some negative force always came along and turned my serene world upside down. And the cause of each storm was always a person I loved.

There I was, combing the streets looking for his strung-out ass, and he comes yelling my name like I owed him money! Thank God I had Lisa with me. I'd run into her again in front of the Chinese restaurant, where we struck up another conversation. Again she mentioned that she lived nearby and ate at this spot at least five times a week. She had just come back from the Pink Houses projects in East New York and just wanted to go home and go to bed.

"Did you catch a taxi from Linden Boulevard?" I asked.

"Yes. It would take me weeks to get home if I took the subway," she joked.

"Yeah, I guess you're right," I stated, only half listening. "Nice seeing you, but I've got to go."

She must have seen the frantic look on my face because she asked, "Molly, what's wrong? Is everything OK?"

"No, everything is not OK. My husband is out there wandering the streets, and I need to find him and bring him back to the motel."

"Is he lost?" Lisa looked puzzled.

"Um, kinda," I said. I didn't know her, so telling her about Joshua's drug use was not something I wanted to share. However, if she happened to help me find him while he was running around in what I suspected was a drug-induced haze, she'd find out soon enough.

"Well, if you need help looking for him, let me know. I know this neighborhood pretty well."

"Thank you, Lisa, but you need to go home and get some rest. You look exhausted."

"I'm good."

As we began walking she said, "How long are you and your husband going to stay at the Executive Inn?"

"Well, we should be leaving shortly. We're only in town for a few weeks."

"Right. But I'm sure you're paying a fortune each night. Even if it's only a motel, I heard that the rates are pretty steep. And I also heard that it isn't safe in there. A lot of seedy people rent those rooms by the hour."

"I know what you mean, but I can certainly take care of myself."

Lisa gave me a puzzled look. "Do you mind if I make a comment?"

"Sure, go ahead."

"I know this whole area, from Baisley Projects to Cambria Heights, and I've never seen you around here before. And you talk funny. But I can't put my finger on what type of accent you and your husband have. You two stand out like sore thumbs. Although you seem cultured and reserved, you know things like the Pink Houses is on Linden Boule-vard, and you choose to stay in a less-than-safe motel for weeks. And although I can imagine you eating filet mignon, you seem to have a penchant for chicken wings and shrimp fried rice. I guess what I'm asking is, what's your deal?"

I never realized that while living abroad, Joshua and I had developed an accent. Nor did I realize that our presence was being closely observed. If Lisa was taking notice, who else would? Rule number one when being on the run, never stay in one place too long.

"I lived near Pink Houses as a child, and then I went to college in London, got married, and now we're back because he has to tend to a sick relative. We should be going back to London soon."

"I knew I heard an accent. Wow, London must be great."

"Well, it beats the Executive Inn."

"I'm sure. Hey, just in case you two need to stay longer, I'm renting a room in a house, which is only about two blocks from here. It's pretty decent, and the owner only charges three hundred a month. It's quiet and everyone minds their own business. He still has one room available, but it's in the basement. If you ever want to check it out, the address is 1066 147th Street."

"Well, if we have to stay longer than we'd planned, I'll give it some thought," I replied. Only with no money, I didn't know where we'd be sleeping tomorrow night.

She walked with me up and down the blocks, and it was when we were heading back to the motel that I heard someone screaming my name—my real name, not the alias. Damn that Joshua! Lisa didn't need to know my real name, on the off chance that someone would actually recognize me. It didn't take much to put two and two together, and I could end up in jail within minutes.

I saw Joshua and hurried to him, mainly to shut him up. Lisa helped me guide him back to our motel, which thankfully was only a couple of blocks away. We got him into the room and onto his bed, where I took off his shoes and pulled the covers over him. I turned around and Lisa was still standing there.

"Thanks a lot for your help, Lisa," I said. "I really appreciate it."

"No problem, Molly." She looked at Joshua. "Is he gonna be OK?"

"Yeah, he'll be fine," I assured her. "He just had a bit too much to drink."

Lisa nodded, then left after saying her goodbyes. I turned my attention back toward Joshua. He was sleeping like the dead and didn't even flinch when I checked his pockets and found glassine envelopes full of a powdery substance. I dipped a pinky finger into it and put it on the tip of my tongue. I'd never been one for getting into recreational drugs—I never did anything that I couldn't put down—but I knew enough to know that it was heroin and, judging by the quick escalation of his addiction, it was some good stuff.

I checked his pockets some more and found $272 left—$272 out of over one thousand. I could either use that money to buy two more nights in this sleazy motel and hope that FedEx called, or I could figure out a way to get another thirty dollars and buy a month at the boarding house Lisa had told me about.

I sat down on the bed, head in hands. Shit. Shit. Shit. Shit. Shit! This was a complication I'd hoped to avoid. A strung-out Joshua would never make it past Customs, let alone airport security. I'd get busted for sure. But how could I leave him here in this condition? Despite his faults and weaknesses, I still loved him. I couldn't leave him to be a victim of his sad choices, but I didn't have the time to stick around while he detoxed. It was too dangerous.

What the hell was I going to do?

Lisa Henderson

I was getting my usual Chinese food when I saw Molly walking down the street, looking frantic. We chatted a bit, but I could tell her mind was somewhere other than the conversation we were having. She was really upset because her responses were rather short, like she didn't want to be bothered answering. It turned out that her husband was missing and Molly was crazy worried. I offered to help her find him. At first I could tell that she didn't want to accept my offer, but I guess common sense took over since she was a stranger to Queens. Luckily we found her husband a few blocks away, yelling at the top of his lungs. He seemed to be yelling at Molly, but the named he yelled was Nikki. Maybe Nikki was the sick relative or something.

I helped Molly take her husband back to the motel because he wouldn't have been able to make it on his own that night. He was completely fucked up. I tried to ignore the current of electricity that I felt when I put my hands around his waist. I normally didn't get into white guys, but this one was rather appealing. He had brown hair, an average face, and a pair of blue-green eyes that made me want to pack up and move to wherever he lived.

We got him into bed and Molly thanked me profusely. I stood

around a bit, wondering if she'd break me off with a few dollars as a tip, but she didn't. I still had plenty of my own dough since I had begun arranging marriages, but you could never have enough money. I looked around the room while Molly was putting her husband in bed. The room was definitely not built for long-term comfort, and in the little closet area I saw a small suitcase with wheels and a duffel bag. The suitcase had clothes spilling out of it, like it had been pawed through. The duffel bag was zippered shut.

I gave Molly a hug, went home, and tried not to think about the chemistry I felt with her husband. I knew it was wrong to lust after someone's husband, but, damn, he looked good! And from the tension between him and Molly, it was obvious that Molly wasn't taking care of home like she should have been. But how would I hide my attraction to him and still be friends with Molly? I got into bed and thought about it before I fell asleep.

The next day, I ignored the events of the past few days and went back to Pink Houses to check up on my latest green card bride, Jadora. The little slick bitch had collected her cut of the five grand, which was three Gs, and now she was MIA. She'd missed an appointment with Hassan yesterday and he was blowing up my phone, telling me that I better fix the situation. Unbeknownst to most, those Africans didn't play. My life was on the line. Pregnant and all, I would still whip a bitch's ass.

My green card enterprise expanded from Marcy Projects and Pink Houses, through Jamaica and Cambria Heights. I got two grand a head, and it was easy recruiting young females. I was dangling three thousand dollars in front of young women who could and most likely would fuck for free, and told them that they could earn thousands just by taking someone's last name. To them, it was alluring. I was even lured for a moment. I really considered marrying Nigel until my smarts kicked in. My daddy didn't raise no fool. I thought about how Ishmael would flip the situation and just like that I became my own boss. I found a chick to marry Nigel and took my cut up front. I sold these girls like cattle and stashed all my dough.

I took Pop-Pop, the livery cab driver who took me on all my errands, to Jadora's crib. She lived on Stanley Avenue side and truly fancied herself as a fly bitch. I rode the pissy elevator up seven flights to her apartment. As soon as I stepped off the elevator, I heard Jim Jones blaring from the apartment she shared with her mother and six sisters. She was the oldest at nineteen.

After knocking for minutes, I twisted the knob and walked in. I looked to my right and the living room was filled with her siblings and neighbors. No one said anything to me, or cared much that I had just walked in. I took a right and a sharp left and walked into her bedroom. Flashbacks of living with Nana and Shiniqua came flooding back. Living in the projects was a lifestyle that few were accustomed to.

Jadora had a tight scarf wrapped around her head, and was wearing a wife beater and white Juicy sweatpants. She was ironing her clothes and clearly about to hit the streets.

"What's up, Dora?" I asked.

She jumped and licked her lips nervously. "Oh, shit, you scared me! Who let you in?"

I don't know why I felt so much anger toward her, but I did. Ignoring her question, I got down to business. "What happened with you yesterday? Why did you miss being available for the immigration officer to interview you? This looks really bad. At this point, they're going to be all over your ass, making sure this marriage isn't a scam."

She cut her eyes. "It ain't even that serious."

"No, the fuck it is that serious!"

"Look, calm down. I have big goal and lots of entertainment business on the table. That marriage money wasn't enough for me. Hey, I married one dude. I'm good."

"What the fuck is wrong with you? You sound really dumb right now."

"Oh well." She shrugged.

"Jadora, don't get cute up in here because I will slap the fire out of you!" I barked. "Now you got paid to do a job. Work, bitch!"

I was furious. She was definitely fucking up the game.

"I wish you would put your hands on me!" she challenged. "I will break your bony ass in half!"

Before we could go to blows, several of her sisters came in and stepped between us. At that point Jadora got indignant and began going berserk, as if she needed to be held back. I felt my pressure going the fuck up and I knew I needed to carry my ass out of there, being that I was three months pregnant. But in another place and another time, I was gonna see her. And trust me, she wouldn't like it.

"Bum bitch, sit down with your theatrics! Fear don't pump through these veins," I stated.

"Bum? Bum? Please, I got plenty niggas out here taking care of me, sweetie!"

I guess she was referring to the numerous niggas she'd fucked—rappers, basketball players, and derelicts—and not one of those fucks got her a decent roof over her head. But let her tell it, and she was wifey.

"Taking care of you? Bitch, open your eyes. You live in the ghetto and you're fucking millionaires! You Section-8 trick bitch!"

"Fuck you!"

"No, fuck you, you sleazy tramp!"

"Get her out of here before I whip her ass!"

"Slut, you wanna fight me? Fight your way out the projects!"

On that note, I was out.

My sixth sense told me that she was going to be trouble, but one thing about me was that a person had to get up early in the morning to get over. I already had a backup plan. When I hired each girl, I made sure they brought down their original birth certificate and social security card, which I kept in my filing cabinet. They were all told that once the marriage was complete, they'd get their identification back. I had another chick in mind that would be only too happy to take Jadora's place and play her to Immigration. For a price, of course. I'd just need to figure out the kinks.

As I walked out of Jadora's building, I was heated. I wished Shiniqua was still here, because she would have beat Jadora down for me, since I was pregnant and couldn't do it myself.

Pop-Pop drove down Stanley Avenue toward Linden Boulevard in order to get on the Conduit to the Belt Parkway. Just before we hit Linden, I saw a shiny burgundy Range Rover, which was at the curb. Right behind it was Ishmael's car. Then I saw a man lurking. The fact that he was white man made him stand out even more than the jittery way he moved. He paced around in small steps, keeping an eye on Ishmael's car. I recognized his face as Molly's husband. What was he doing here?

"Pop-Pop, pull over. Here, right here. Stop," I instructed as I got out next to the Magic Johnson Cineplex. I waited for the light and then crossed. My heart was nearly in my throat. Why was I even playing myself?

"Excuse me, mister."

He tried to focus on me. Then he said, "Hey, it's Aaliyah! You're the one who helped Nikki the other night." He scratched his butt and turned his attention back to the car.

I nodded, even though I had no idea who Nikki was. "What are you doing here?"

"I'm trying to get . . . uh, I need to talk to the guy who drives that car." He nodded at the Range Rover. I didn't know the guy who drove that car, but I knew Ishmael's car anywhere.

"You know the guy driving the Range Rover?" I asked in surprise. I wasn't a racist, but the guy didn't look like he had any non-white friends, except for Molly.

"Uh, yeah! I know Perez. He's cool. We're childhood friends."

I frowned. This dude was lying, but why? Unless he was trying to get with Perez to cop. I wondered what Ishmael was doing talking with this Perez guy. I knew for a fact that he was out of the game for good. As if reading my mind, Perez and Ishmael both got out of their cars at the same time. Ishmael looked at us curiously as I tried to restrain Molly's husband from getting too close to Ishmael. Ishmael wasn't a violent person, but I knew he carried, and he would have dropped ol' boy in a heartbeat if he had to.

"Hey, Perez!" Molly's husband yelled.

Ishmael and Perez looked at the man, then looked at each other. Ishmael frowned and said to Perez, "Who the hell is this?"

"Yo, Ishmael, this is one of my customers. I know you out the game, but you remember those days, right, homes?" Perez replied with an uneasy frown.

Ishmael nodded, his eyes still on Molly's husband. "And how the hell do you know him?" he asked me. "Did you bring him here?"

"Hell naw, I ain't bring him here," I snapped. "I met his wife yesterday, when I helped her get him out of a jam."

He looked me up and down and noticed my protruding belly. I know I should have spit in his face for the way he had treated me, but, truthfully, I still loved him. If he would have said he was sorry, even if he didn't really mean it, I would have taken him back in a heartbeat. He was my first love. And he was doing really well for himself. I wanted to tell him that I had my own business and that soon I'd have enough money to start my life over, go back to school, and follow my original dream to be a journalist. Only he didn't ask. He didn't care. His eyes were still filled with disgust.

"I see you're knocked up. Which dirty nigga you let hit it raw and plant their seed?"

Once again, I was crushed by his words. I wanted to say, You're the dirty nigga! This is your baby! I can't wait to tell your bitch I'm having your firstborn! But instead I just said, "You wouldn't know him."

"You sure about that? I know a few niggas you fucked. I just might know him! You never know. It's a small world out here."

"I know you still love me, Ishmael, so you can stop fronting and hiding behind hateful words and actions. Just admit it."

His laugh was maniacal. "You must have bumped your head."

"Umm, no, I didn't. But it's all good. Keep playing dumb."

"Lisa, I'm getting married next week and the reception is at Russo's on the Water on Cross Bay Boulevard, not too far from here. That's why I'm on this side of town. My lady is three months pregnant and I refuse to have a bastard child. I'm happier than I can put into words, and there's not one day I think about you or the past. If Perez didn't damn near chase me down, I wouldn't have stopped on this side of town. I don't know what I gotta do to show you that you're really not that bitch! What do I have to say to get that through your head? If I tell you, you don't believe it. When I show you, you don't believe it. What the fuck I gotta do?"

How about get married? I thought. Those words did it. Those words stopped my heart in its track. I guess there was something with all women where we really felt that we had this connection or bond from almost every relationship. But when that same man up and got married on you, well, the writing was on the wall.

"Please, fuck you, nigga!" was all I could say.

In the meantime, Perez had taken ol' boy aside and was in the middle of a buy. Once they were done, Perez returned to Ishmael's side. The man sat down on a nearby bench and began to snort in broad daylight.

"Yo, stop that shit!" Perez growled. He rushed back over and said, "Yo, man, you can't be doing that here! You gots to raise up outta here." He grabbed the guy's arm and hauled him off the bench and in the direction of the street.

I felt sorry for the man. He was definitely in the wrong neighborhood and he was so determined to get high that he would end up a statistic if he wasn't careful. "I'll help him get back to his motel," I said.

Ishmael looked at me coldly. "How do you know where his motel is?"

"I just told you, I helped his wife get him back to the motel last night. He was high then and could barely walk down the street."

Ishmael shook his head. "Get him the hell out of here." He watched Perez get the guy off Pink Houses property then added, "Do you need cab money?"

I shook my head and went to catch up with Molly's husband. After we got into the cab,

he proceeded to twitch and jump until we got out. When I got him upstairs to his motel room door, I went through his pockets until I found the key. I got him inside the room, where he lay on the bed and promptly went to sleep.

Since Molly wasn't there, I took advantage of the situation to get a better look at the room. I didn't know much about Molly and was curious about her and her white, drug-addicted husband. I noted the bags in the closet area and went over to look. The duffel bag was zippered shut but the suitcase was unzipped. I looked over at Molly's husband and he snored softly. I lifted the lid of the suitcase but saw nothing remarkable, just some folded clothes. Then I saw the corner of a picture peeking out from between the clothes. I eased it out and stared at it, then flipped it over. Me and Noki, July 2000. The picture showed a black girl with straight hair and slanted eyes standing next to an Asian girl. The black girl was smiling while the Asian girl had a frown on her face. I wondered who these people were, and why Molly had this picture. I put the picture back like I found it and let the suitcase lid fall.

Minutes later the room door opened and Molly walked in. Relief flooded her features when she saw her husband in bed, then she noticed me. "Lisa! What are you doing here?"

I explained what happened over at Pink Houses Projects and Molly's face got tight with anger. "How could he be so stupid!" she yelled. "He's going to get both of us killed."

Molly looked a little sick, but I thought it was just the drama of dealing with her drug-addicted husband. She regained her composure and said, "Well, thank you again, Lisa." She laughed a bit. "It seems like we keep saving each other, doesn't it?"

I shrugged. "Maybe we're supposed to be saving each other."

Molly cocked her head and regarded me closely. "Maybe."

Nikkisi Ling

Joshua was going to get us both killed, point blank. Wandering around Pink Houses Projects, of all places, trying to cop! Lisa didn't say much, but she didn't have to. I could tell by what she didn't say that Joshua had been in Pink Houses looking to cop.

I had to get out of the States, but to do that I needed money. I wasn't budging until FedEx located my packages. Once again I thought of my choices, which were woefully limited. I needed to get outside and think.

Walking around the residential area until it became commercial, my mind began to toss around ideas, and then my fingers began to twitch. Old habits die hard. I looked around at my people, faces who looked just like mine, who were in dire need—just like me. It was nine o'clock in the morning, and at noon Joshua and I had to get out of the Executive Inn.

Although I hated to do it, I had no other choice. I contemplated Green Acres Mall and then settled upon Roosevelt Field. I flagged down a livery cab, paid the fifty-five dollars, and was let off in front of Nordstrom. I didn't have much time, nor did I want to linger longer than necessary. But I couldn't be sloppy, either. If I fucked up, then I was going straight to jail, without bail. I didn't know if I could do it. If I was still good. In fact, I used to be great. But that felt like another lifetime.

It was still early, just after ten, and the mall was virtually empty. Mostly workers were walking around and setting up shop. To waste time I purchased a shirt and was grateful for the shopping bag. Next, I bought a cup of coffee and sipped slowly as I surveyed the mall for my mark.

Tall male, late fifties, diamond pinky ring, three-piece tailored suit, hmmm, that's a good look, I thought. I followed him to the register after he picked up a blouse and made the purchase.

"Excuse me, how much is this?" Purposefully I interrupted the sale. The sales attendant looked up briefly and smiled as she swiped his card.

"There isn't a price on that?" she asked politely.

"No, ma'am."

"OK, I'll help you in a moment. Just let me finish with this customer."

"Sure. Take your time."

She didn't need to assist me further. I already had what I needed. There wasn't one greenback in his wallet. He only had plastic, so I didn't waste time lifting it. I realized now that I wouldn't be in and out of the mall. Most people paid with credit cards nowadays.

As the hours passed, I walked up and down the mall, making purchase after purchase, so as not to draw attention to the detectives who were scanning for shoplifters. I hated to do this in the mall where they had more cameras than a movie studio, but I just didn't feel right robbing poor people. When I was younger, that didn't bother me, but I'd grown a conscience.

Finally. There she was. A diva. She had long, flowing black hair, and wore designer shades, a spray tan, and trendy clothes. The woman had a thick Italian accent and a wallet stuffed with cash. She was so engrossed on her phone, talking to someone about a wedding, that she never felt a thing. I saddled up closely to her in the shoe section of Bloomingdales, and steadied my hand as I inched inside her Gucci pocketbook until I felt the sharp corner of a leather wallet. Gripping the edge with my index and middle finger, with the accuracy of a physician, I slid out her wallet, and with one swift movement positioned my back to hers, secured her wallet, and then bounced.

I made my way back into the mall and used the ladies' restroom. At this point, the mall was bustling with patrons. Inside the stall I counted out her money—twelve hundred dollars. I'd hit pay dirt. I tossed the credit cards and identification in the trash, secured my money, put on a hat and shades, changed into the shirt I'd bought earlier, and left. One part of me contemplated making a day of it and getting as much money as I could, since I was already here. And, honestly, the thrill was exhilarating. But the smarter side of me knew not to wear out my welcome. I got what I came for and if I stayed longer, I would be flirting with danger.

I got back to Queens just after two pm. The attendant at the front desk started in on me.

"Mrs. Mathis, you owe $125 for another night."

"My husband and I will be checking out today."

"Don't matter. You've stayed over the twelve o'clock checkout time, and when we knocked on your door, your husband said you'd take care of the bill when you got back."

"Of course I'll take care of the bill, but we don't need another night. We're checking out. So how much for the two hours that we're over?"

"It's $125."

"For two hours? Don't you rent rooms by the hour?"

"That's only if you start off that way. You started off on a daily rate, so that's how you gotta stay. One twenty-five, please."

"You know this is highly unethical? If we have to pay in full, then we're not leaving until tomorrow!"

I knew he was getting over, and I had the nerve to want to preach morals after I'd just stolen someone's money. Talk about hypocrisy.

After I paid for the room, I didn't go upstairs. I knew Joshua didn't have any money, so where was he going? I turned back around and went to find Lisa and rent the room. Hopefully, it was still available.

The cab driver turned onto 147th Street in Southside, Jamaica, Queens, to a row of white homes. One house stood out on the street. It was a small home with brick and black siding, and an even smaller manicured lawn. Most of the homes looked a little worn but for the most part, this would be better than the sleazy motel. I approached the doorbell with reservation. I didn't know what I'd say if Lisa wasn't there.

Before I could ring the bell, an elderly man and his wife came out.

"May I help you?" the man asked.

"I'm looking for Lisa. Is she in?"

"Are you a friend of hers?" the elderly lady asked.

"Yes. Please tell her that Molly is here."

The elderly man turned toward the woman. "You go ahead and get in the car. I'll go get Lisa."

She gave him a quick kiss as she struggled to walk down the steps toward their car. After a few moments, Lisa came hopping down the steps. She was always so energetic, you could hardly tell she was pregnant.

Her grin was wide. She got right down to business.

"Are you here about the room?"

"Y-yes, I am. Is it still available?"

"Yup. This is my landlord, Mr. Keebles." She turned toward her landlord. "See how you didn't want to rent to me, and now I'm bringing you good peoples." She reprimanded him, and he gave her a sly smile.

"Oh, hush, child. Does she know it's in the basement?"

He spoke as if I weren't standing there.

"Yes, I know," I replied.

He turned toward me. "Well, it's an illegal space, but my wife and I need the money. I hope you're not going to give me problems and report me."

"Oh, heavens no! I would never do that."

"She's cool, Mr. Keebles. She's not like that. She minds her business and don't want anybody up in hers. You feel me?"

"Stop all that jive you talking, Lisa. All I know is that she better pay rent on time, or she's out." Mr. Keebles tried to sound tough, but you could tell that he was a softie.

"Well, I'd like to pay my first month today and move in tomorrow. I don't have any furniture or anything, but I could run out and get a bed, I suppose."

"Oh, I thought I told you the rooms are furnished," Lisa replied.

My day was looking better by the moment.

After Lisa showed me the room, which was in the basement—at least five feet underground—with two small windows, white walls, a full-sized bed, a dresser, a nightstand with an old-fashioned lamp, and a musty blue carpet with numerous stains, we went upstairs to the kitchen and she made us a glass of iced tea. I knew that I should have rushed off to check on Joshua, but I didn't want to. It felt good to talk to an American, and it felt good hanging out with Lisa. She truly reminded me of Noki the way she seemed so independent, yet she didn't have a problem depending on someone.

"So what will you do once the baby is born? You mentioned your father. Do you have any other family?" I asked.

"I'm not sure what I'll do yet. I know I won't be living here, though."

"Are you ever going to tell the father that he has a child?"

"No. I hate him," she replied and rolled her eyes as if he could see her.

"I don't mean to sound harsh, but this isn't about you. Your child deserves a father. And unless he's some pedophile or axe murderer, he should be in his child's life. And what about money? He should have to help support the child financially. This shouldn't only fall on your lap. It takes two to make a baby."

I was sure I sounded like someone's mother, and I hoped she didn't resent me for speaking my mind.

"Look who's talking," she stated.

"What do you mean?"

"You're here judging my life when you're married to a dope fiend." She stated the obvious and it hurt. Although she didn't yell or raise her voice, her words still cut like a sword.

"OK, fair enough. How about I don't comment about your personal life, and you stay out of mine? Would that work? I like your friendship and I don't want anything to come between that. You've helped me a lot thus far, and I'm really appreciative."

"Molly, don't trip. I was just being a bitch. It's not that serious, and I don't have much to hide. In fact, I saw my baby daddy yesterday and he doesn't want anything to do with me. He told me that loud and clear. He's happy and about to get married to some trick, and she's having his baby."

"I know how it feels to love someone and have him choose another woman over you. My first love did the same thing to me, only I had to read about it in the newspaper."

"Really? Was he famous?"

"Yeah, rich and famous. I thought we had something special, but all along he never felt I was good enough to be his wife and carry his last name." I laughed bitterly as I thought about Brian.

"Men are so cruel." She added, "But they're real with theirs. When it's over, it's over. They don't have none for you."

"Did you at least get a chance to tell him how you felt? Does he even suspect the baby is his?"

"He don't give a fuck. All he keeps saying is that I'm a tramp and that 'his lady' is better than me. Molly, this is real talk I'm about to say. The night my baby was conceived, that nigga pissed on me. And not like, 'hey, let's do some real freaky shit and I want you to piss on me.' But, 'I'ma piss on you 'cause you're lower than the pavement' type of shit went down," she spewed.

After hearing that, I thought she would get emotional and begin to cry, but she didn't. She just kept shaking her head as if she still couldn't believe the events had occurred. I connected to her immediately. How many times had Brian, Jack, and so many other men made me feel less than human with their degrading acts? I wished I could open up as easily as Lisa, but that wasn't who I was. I was introverted because I lived a life of shame.

Once Lisa began talking, it was like opening up Pandora's Box. She began to tell me about the relationship she shared with her mother and siblings, how her father was now a quadriplegic and her mother was behind all of it, how her best friend was murdered and how being young and desperate she ended up in bed with her boyfriend's former boss. She reminisced on her dream of becoming a journalist, and how life had temporarily snatched that dream away from her.

From what she told me, I knew she had a rough life, but she couldn't hold a candle to what my life had turned out to be. I knew better than to share my life with my new little sister. I couldn't put the pressure of her having to keep my secret on her, nor could I really trust her. Not with my life.

I left Lisa and told her that I'd see her tomorrow when I moved in. She gave me a hearty hug and mentioned she had to go take care of business in Marcy Projects. I hoped she wasn't selling drugs or doing anything illegal, but I decided not to pry. That conversation would just have to wait.

I had a few phone calls to make. FedEx was first. And then I needed to find a fence to get Joshua and I a few fake passports on the black market. I definitely needed my money.

Lisa Henderson

Molly and her deadbeat husband had been living downstairs for over a month now. It was really cool having them around. Most nights we all sat around in the living room, watching rented movies, or Molly would go grocery shopping and cook for the whole house. Since she had moved in, she'd made this place seem like a real home. Even Matt was good company when he wasn't coming down off his high, or when they were not arguing. His drug use was really ruining their relationship, but no matter how many nights she came into my room telling me that she's going to leave him or kick him out, she didn't.

Last week he caught a major beat-down by some corner boys over on Guy R. Brewer, across the street from Rochdale. Rumor had it he tried to score some dope from a kid over in Baisley projects, only he didn't have any cash and when the kid went to serve him, Matt grabbed the bundle and took off running. They had to damn near run thirty blocks before they caught him and whipped his ass. He was lucky they didn't kill him.

Molly was heartbroken when he came home battered and bruised. He hadn't gone outside since. And now that he was home all day, Molly had been running the streets. She left early in the morning and came back late at night. She said she was working in the city at a law firm, but I didn't believe her. I thought she had a little jump-off who was hitting her off with a couple dollars here and there. I didn't blame her for getting her some on the side. I knew I was horny as hell.

LH Enterprises was doing really well. I'd now stashed over twenty grand, and once I got to fifty, I was going to swoop up my father. I was set back five hundred because I had to pay these chicks over on the caveman side of Pink Houses to give Jadora a beat-down. She was all in the PJs running her mouth about how she housed me for my dough, and how we paid her and she told me to kiss her ass. That type of talk could ruin my business. If she started brainwashing these girls that they could get over on me, then word would spread like wildfire. So Pinky and Locksey shut that bitch down. They beat her all upside her bald head. Of course I stood right there as they whipped her ass, and I told her that as soon as I dropped this baby, it was on!

I'd just gotten out of the shower when Matt rapped on the door.

"Who is it?"

"Will you be long? It's Matt."

"I have the bathroom from nine to nine thirty!" I reminded him. I wondered if he was high.

"Yes, of course. I know that, Lisa. I was just asking."

I paused. "I should be out in a minute." Turned out my minute turned into twenty. When I flung open the door, Matt was in full nod. His eyes were tossed back far in his head and his mouth was gaping open. But the shocking part was that he was completely naked. I stood there looking at a rock-hard dick and blond pubic hair. Immediately I got wet and salacious thoughts crept through my mind. Instead of wondering where in the hell he got money to cop from, or how in the hell he got the dope considering he'd been locked up in here, all I kept thinking about was getting dick.

The worst thing Molly could have shared with me was how Matt was in bed. She said he fucked like a stallion now that he was on that shit. She said she couldn't put his dick down, no matter how hard she tried.

"Matt!" I yelled.

"I'm up. I'm up. I'm up." A broad smile came across his face. His baby blue eyes were that of a child. When he smiled, it took years off his face.

"You dropped your towel."

He looked down. "That I did. Oops. Don't tell Molly."

"I won't tell if you won't." I walked over and softly caressed his thick dick.

"We can't," he said weakly. For some reason, that shit kept him horny, and it wasn't hard at all to lure him into my room. He must have really been fucked up to be seduced by my fat, pregnant ass, but oh well. Originally I only wanted him to give me head, but who knew that he had the bomb head game? His experienced tongue had me gripping the sheets and biting down on my pillow.

When he slipped on a condom and eased into me, his thick penis opened and stretched my tight walls to the max. He may have been a dope fiend, but his dick game was serious. He felt so good, and his circumcised head rubbed against my G-spot at just the right angle.

"Oh shit," I moaned. "That's right…fuck this pussy!"

Matt could only moan as I grabbed his flat ass and tried to push him further inside. I opened my legs as wide as they would go, to try and get all of him inside. His balls slapped against the outside of my pussy as I thrust my hips up to meet him.

"Yeah…that's right…yeah…right there! Right there! Oh shit…

right there!"

I clawed his back as I came hard with a scream. I had never come like that before, not even with Ishmael. Soon after, Matt rolled off and lay on his back. His dick was still hard and red, and damp from my pussy juices.

"Suck my dick," he murmured.

My eyes shot open and reality set in. "Huh?"

"Suck my dick. I'm still hard. I need you to put it down."

"Sorry, Charlie. I got mine. If you didn't get yours, then that's on you."

Matt was hardly fazed. He was probably used to women not keeping up with him. He ignored me, turned over on his back, and began to jerk off. And that was where I left him while I went to take another shower. As I washed my body and rubbed my belly, I pushed the guilt of the moment to the back of my mind. Matt was a loser, and Molly deserved better. Anyway, she wasn't going to be with him much longer. Right?

Nikkisi Ling

"How much for an hour?"

"Two thousand," I replied.

"Do you take credit cards?"

"No."

"Are you sure we can't work something out?"

"Goodbye," I said and began to get up from the bar. He gently grabbed my arm.

"Stay put. Let me go to the ATM outside. I'll be back in five minutes."

"The clock starts ticking now."

This was my third client this month. I was a desperate woman. Between turning tricks and jostling people, I had managed to save eighteen thousand dollars. Only that wasn't enough. Passports on the black market cost seventy-five hundred each, and Joshua and I needed two each. Not to mention, we were going to need some pocket money. I needed to save up at least fifty grand before we could leave the States.

I had successfully gotten us one passport each with the money I had earned so far. My new alias was Jennifer Blackmon, and Joshua would be Alexander Pider. No longer would we travel as a married couple. I felt that it would be safer this way: safer for me. If Joshua began nodding at Customs, his ass would be grass. I now only had three thousand left, and I needed at least another thirty-two thousand to leave New York for good.

At first, my decision to go back and sell my body wasn't an easy one. But then I realized that it was about survival, and sitting in a jail cell for the rest of my life wasn't an option. And as much as I tried to hate Joshua for putting me in this position, I couldn't. He traded his comfortable life for me, and I couldn't forget that. He had a bounty over his head, and he did that because of our love. It would be too easy to walk away and try not to regret it, but I couldn't.

My customer made it back with the money, so it was time to get back to work. We left the bar and walked around the corner to the W hotel in Times Square. It was so easy to find clients in this busy, heavy populated, touristy area. The W was a high-end establishment that didn't rent rooms by the hour. Yes, I could go to places like the Executive Inn back in Queens but my safety was my main concern. This establishment had people who remembered faces and security cameras surveying the area. So screams for help wouldn't get confused for screams of passion. For this reason, I made sure to wear a wig and heavy makeup when I turned tricks.

I took my john to the small, neat room, and turned to face him with my hand out. "Cash up front," I demanded. The man's eyes traveled up my toned legs and thighs to my large C-cup breasts. My hard nipples looked the size of nickels underneath the form-fitting spaghetti-strap tank top. He quickly peeled off some hundred-dollar bills. I unzipped my skirt and let it fall to the floor, giving him a glimpse of my trimmed bush. The man's hard dick was visible through his dress slacks; I watched as he fidgeted with his wedding ring. He was just another working stiff who wanted a quick piece of pussy before heading home to his wife and the kids, I deduced. I unzipped his pants, dropped to my knees, and slid on a flavored condom and began to suck him off. When he began moaning, I got up, walked over to the bed, removing my top, and lay on my back with my legs spread. Clumsily he walked over and slid his hard dick into my pussy. I let him do a little work in the missionary position as I stared at the ceiling and gave some halfhearted moans. Then I took over. We fell into doggy style, the frog's position, and finally I rode him. I began to work my hips and ride him effortlessly, while contracting my Kegel muscles. Soon, he moaned, shook, and came. I crawled off and buried my head into the pillow, swallowing the vomit that had begun to rise.

I watched him with flat eyes as he straightened his clothes and prepared to leave. "Uh…thank you," he stammered. "Can we do this again?"

"You know where I'll be…"

I went into the brightly lit, marble bathroom and took a hot shower before I went home.

I got home just before midnight. I was truly exhausted, mentally and physically, and lately I was a bit irritable. Joshua met me at the door, which was a shock.

"Hey, baby, where you been?"

"What are you doing up? Have you been outside?" I asked, immediately suspicious.

"No. I've been in here all day worried about you. Why are you always leaving me here alone?"

Joshua and I made our way into the basement. The funky smell was truly making me want to puke.

"What do you mean, leaving you here alone? You're an adult, and I had to work."

"Well, it's just that I don't like Lisa."

"Really? Why is that? I thought you two were friends."

"I just said I don't like her."

"Well, what has she done? Has she said something about . . . you know . . . your problem?"

"No, no, nothing like that. I just don't like that girl. She's sneaky."

"Well, I like her a lot and I don't find her to be sneaky at all. She's a survivor—"

"Like Noki. I know. I've heard this all before," he snapped.

"Why are you mad at me?" I asked.

Ignoring my question, he asked, "Did our money get here from FedEx?"

I was seething. "Are you kidding me? Do you think I'd still be here risking my freedom if the money arrived? Do you think this is Disney Land?"

"I'm just asking," he said in a cavalier tone.

"No. My money hasn't arrived yet."

"Well when is it arriving? I want to get the fuck out of here," he said as he stuffed a Yankee Doodle chocolate cake into his mouth. All he ate nowadays were sweets. He'd gained at least twenty pounds. His once flat stomach was protruding, his eyes were always swollen and bloodshot and his face was puffy with visible signs of acne. He looked older than his years.

"I'm so sick of you."

"I'm sick of you too!"

After a night of getting a random dick shoved into me and then coming home to this nonsense, I just couldn't take it anymore. I walked into the bathroom, grabbed a towel, and ran my bath water. I could deal with Josh tomorrow.

Lisa Henderson

Today was my father's birthday and I wanted to see him. As soon as I woke up I dialed Julie's house for the first time since I had returned from jail.

"The number you have reached has been changed. The new number is not listed," a recorded message stated.

I wondered if she would care that I was pregnant and having her grandchild? Hell no, I thought. She wouldn't give a fuck. Look how dirty she'd done me and my father.

I sat up in bed with a craving for Captain Crunch cereal. I wiggled off the bed and waddled downstairs in my housecoat and slippers. It was mid-September, but the house had a chill. I had been taking my iron pills throughout my whole pregnancy because I was anemic, but my fingers and toes were still always cold.

"What the fuck?" I gasped. For a split second I thought I saw someone run past the kitchen window. Probably some crackhead. This neighborhood had a few on the low. Then I laughed to myself. What if that was Matt running around here like he stole something?

Boom! Boom! Boom! The thunderous knock on the front door almost sent me into premature labor. My legs began to shake as I clutched my heart.

"Who the fuck is that?" I yelled, angry at whoever was on the outside acting good and stupid. As I waddled closer, I heard again, Boom! Boom! Boom!

"Who is it?" I screamed.

Molly, Joshua, Mr. and Mrs. Keebles and their granddaughter Kia were all up now.

"Who's that?" Molly asked. Her face was frozen with fear.

"It's the police. They have our whole house surrounded with the SWAT team and FBI," Kia remarked. "They're all over the place."

"Sonuvabitch!" Molly yelled.

"Jesus, Mary, and Joseph."

"Well, open the door, child, before they break my good door down," Mr. Keebles instructed.

Walking to the door, I couldn't imagine what Matt had done, because I just knew they were here for him.

"Do you know that it's seven o'clock in the morning?" I asked the officers.

"Lisa Henderson?" the detective asked.

"Y-yes."

"You're under arrest for multiple counts of fraud. Turn around and put your hands behind your back."

"Molly! Help me! They're taking me to jail!" I cried.

As they brought me out of the house, the lawn was littered with law enforcement. All I kept thinking about was that ghetto bitch Jadora. I knew she had snitched.

Nikkisi Ling

Joshua and I must have aged twenty years when the police came up in there. I thought that it was over for me. In a million years, I never would have guessed that Lisa was running a marriage scam. It was no longer safe for me to stay in America. This was really a wakeup call. I needed to cut my losses.

They interrogated everyone in the house for hours, which was truly uncomfortable for Joshua and me. Fortunately for us, the search warrant was only for her bedroom. As they dragged things out of the room, we would clearly see that they had a treasure trove of evidence against her. Not only did she have loads of money, but she also had file folders for each girl with their identification papers, who they had married, the times and dates for meetings, and information on the prospective husbands for each girl to study.

By eleven o'clock, all went back to normal for Mr. and Mrs. Keebles, but Joshua and my nerves were shot.

"We're getting the hell out of here, today!" I said.

"Shit, I'm with you. You don't got to tell me twice. Where are we going to go?"

"I don't know, nor do I care. I'm going to the library to book our tickets online. You should come with me."

"No, I'll stay behind and pack. So, we're going international?"

"Of course. What do you mean?"

"Well, we didn't get the second set of passports. What if something happens with the one we have? Then what? We're better off getting around in America until we can afford a second set."

"That's a chance I'm willing to take. I'm telling you, I have a bad feeling if we stay around here. Something bad is going to happen."

He shook his head. "You're right. OK, go and book our tickets and I'll be ready when you get back."

"Are you sure?"

"Of course I'm sure."

I walked to the Queens Library on Guy R. Brewer Boulevard to have access to the Internet. I tried in vain to get Joshua and I flights out that day, but the prices were ridiculous. The cheapest flight I could get to Cape Town, South Africa was $3,899 per person. When I punched in two days from today, that brought the prices down significantly. I got us two tickets for $2,888, roundtrip. Even though we didn't have any intention of ever coming back to the United States, since we weren't citizens of South Africa, a one-way ticket would automatically bring up a red flag when going through Customs. We had to linger around for two days, but we didn't have any other choice.

On the walk back home, I thought about Lisa. She looked so pitiful and scared as they dragged her out. And the way she called out for me to help her broke my heart. I wished there was something that I could do. I also hated the idea that when she returned from jail, Joshua and I would most likely be gone.

"Molly, this package came for you," Mr. Keebles said when I got back to the house.

"What?"

"This package came not too long after you left."

I ran over and there it was. All tagged up, dirty, and beaten down, but one of my packages had finally arrived. I peered around to see where Joshua was, and then I examined the package to make sure it hadn't been opened.

"Is Matt downstairs?"

"No. He left right after you did."

Joshua assumed we were leaving today and he split? At that moment, I was broken. Our love was broken and our marriage was broken. The disconnect between the old and new Joshua was too much for me to handle. I decided that it was over. I couldn't save him because he didn't want to be saved. God had sent me a sign to get out of here. I managed to open the heavily taped package and exhaled with relief at the sight of the stacks of hundred-dollar bills. I quickly counted it; I now had $350,000 dollars that had weathered a storm and flown internationally to find me in the hood, and I refused to spit in the face of my fate. This was truly God. I knew what I had to do.

My only worry was Lisa. I wanted to leave her some startup money, to get on her feet once she was released from custody. I knew how it felt to walk out of jail without a dime to your name. Not to mention that she had a baby growing in her belly.

Quickly I packed my things. My hands trembled from the events of the day. It was all so overwhelming that I wasn't sure how much more I could take. I called a car service and then changed my mind. I didn't want any traceable records of my whereabouts. I took my luggage with wheels that now held all my cash and walked up to Merrick Avenue, where I caught a gypsy cab to The Hilton Inn by JFK airport. I booked my room for two nights, took a hot shower, and finally relaxed.

I think I was still shell-shocked. I couldn't help but think of how things could have been, and then relive how things were. I wanted to fast-forward my life and be an old woman with lots of children, and grandchildren, and a great husband, sitting on a rocking chair growing old gracefully. Peacefully. That was such a great daydream that I drifted off to sleep.

The next morning I made more calls. I called FedEx again regarding my second package, which was still missing. Then I called the courts and found out that Lisa had been arraigned and remanded back into custody only hours earlier. She'd made the newspapers. Not the front page, as I'd done in my past, but still she was there. One part of me rooted for the teen who had more business savvy than I ever did at her age. Yes, I was a hustler, but I also hustled myself and allowed a man to hustle my body out as well. Lisa had used her mind and hustled others. And to think I thought she was just a misguided, knocked-up girl with no future ahead of her. How presumptuous was I? Her bail was set at fifty thousand. Immediately I called a bail bondsman and began to sort out a few things.

Arriving at the Keebles' home shortly before noon, I kept my cab driver waiting. I ran in and gave Mr. Keebles five thousand dollars and sent him to bail out Lisa.

"Mr. Keebles, do you know the telephone number of the cab driver that Lisa uses?"

He thought for a moment and then his face lit up. He walked toward the kitchen and went to the cupboard drawer. "She keeps his telephone number in here, just in case we ever need him."

"Good. Call him and have him take you down to the Queens Criminal Courthouse on Queens Boulevard. Make sure he waits."

I gave Mr. Keebles an additional two hundred dollars, which should cover the costs of his transportation to and from court. I also ran upstairs to Lisa's bedroom and left her a quick note with twenty-five hundred dollars in an envelope. I wished I could have left her more money, but I just couldn't. I already had to part with more than I had planned.

As I stashed the envelope underneath her pillow, I couldn't help but notice that black power covered all the surfaces in her room—the windows, nightstand, and any flat surfaces. Immediately I looked down at my fingers. The detectives had dusted for fingerprints, but why?

Finally I breathed a sigh of relief because although I had lived in this house for over a month, I never went into Lisa's room. Nor did Joshua. Careful not to touch anything, I backtracked out of her room.

In less than twenty-four hours I would be on a plane to my future, and I was never coming back to America. There was way too much drama and bad memories here.

"So Matt never came in yesterday?" I asked Mrs. Keebles.

"No, we never heard him come in. I know he was upset with the police barging in as they did. We were upset as well. Do you think he's mad with us?"

They were such a cute couple, just trying to make a living. Joshua taking off had nothing to do with the Keebles, and everything to do with his drug habit. His nerves were probably shot and he had needed a hit.

"No, not at all. He had some family business to take care of. When he comes in, can you make sure you he calls me on my cell?"

"Of course, dear."

"Mrs. Keebles?" I began.

"Yes?"

I shoved fifteen hundred dollars into the palm of her hand. "For your troubles."

Her eyes popped open like large saucers. "I can't—"

I kissed her on her cheek and ran off.

In the short car ride to the hotel, I wondered what to do about Joshua. I wanted him to at least have a chance at getting out and not ending up as a strung-out junkie. I contemplated leaving his new passport with the Keebles, but if they saw his picture on a passport with a different name, who was to say they wouldn't report him to the police? And I couldn't leave him any money, because I was sure without someone to monitor his movements, he'd blow it all on heroin. Honestly, my hands were tied.

Lisa Henderson

All I thought about—while being dragged out of my house, stuffed into the back of a police car, interrogated for hours, and then tossed into jail—was revenge. I knew who'd snitched me out, and Jadora was going to pay. I had plans of finding Ishmael, married or not, and letting him know that I was carrying his child. Hopefully that would garner sympathy from him, and when I told him what Jadora had done, he'd take care of her. Or at least have one of his goons do it.

I couldn't sleep a wink that night. That whore's face kept resurfacing. She'd ruined my life, my father's life, and my child's life. Bitches like her fucked up the game. She got paid to do a job. Do the fucking job! How hard was that? I hated get-over, bum-ass chicks like her.

When the corrections officer said I'd made bail the next day, I didn't have a clue who had posted it. Of course, the romantic side of me wanted to believe that Ishmael had heard what happened and came to my rescue. When I saw Mr. Keebles, I was perplexed. I was sure that he and his wife didn't have that kind of money.

"Molly gave me the money to spring you out of custody. That's one classy lady. Can't say the same about her husband, though."

I was only half listening. When Mr. Keebles said that Molly had bailed me out, I realized that the ramblings of a dope fiend might not be ramblings at all. My mind began to race.

"Where is she? Why didn't she bail me out herself?" I asked.

"She's gone. She left yesterday after they raided our house. Her husband left as well. I guess they got spooked. Child, they don't know what you're into or what kind of danger you can bring. Me and Mrs. Keebles feel the same way. We're too old for such shenanigans. I almost had a heart attack. You're going to have to find a new place to live."

"Sure. I understand. I don't want to stay there anymore, either."

Once I returned to my room, it didn't take me long to find the money and note Molly had left stashed underneath my pillow. The note went on to say that she loved me as a little sister and that I should put all my energy into doing something positive with my life; if not for the sake of myself, then for my child. I snorted. The nerve of her.

Joshua Tune

I knew I was too far gone when I went to cop more Black Magic and Perez was nowhere to be found. I stood in front of a cocky black kid who was not as accommodating.

"Yo, man, I done told you that we ain't got no more Black Magic. What you want me to do?"

"But Perez always had it," I argued. I wiped my runny nose with the back of my shaky hand. I had stomach cramps and needed a fix badly.

"Well, Perez ain't here, is he?"

"Look, can't you hook me up? I got the money." I hoped the desperation in my voice would move him.

It didn't. "No, I can't hook you up," he mimicked harshly. "I'ma tell you one mo' time. We ain't got no Black Magic, and I don't know when we getting any more, and Perez ain't here and I can't tell you when he'll be back. So kick rocks!" He put his hand in his pocket with a scowl. He probably had a gun and didn't seem like he'd mind using it on me.

I shuffled away, but not before the burgundy Range Rover came gliding up the block.

"Hey, Perez!" I called out before the car came to a full stop.

The hustlers on the corner looked at each other, then back at me. I could see the frown of disapproval and unease on Perez's face.

"Who the hell is this?" the young black dude asked Perez harshly.

Perez explained who I was, but it didn't seem to help. They still seemed to become rather angry at my presence, especially because I was making a scene.

"I need some Black Magic," I yelled.

Perez ordered the young guy to handle the transaction, then he pulled me to the side and whispered, "Man, what the fuck is your problem, yo? What the fuck you doing over here? You trying to get yourself killed?"

"I wanted some Black Magic, but your partner said that he didn't have any and that he didn't know when you'd be back." I scratched the back of my neck. "I needed some, like, now."

"Man, I don't give a fuck what you need! You don't ever come over here, you hear me? You too fucking hot! Your stupid shit could get the whole fucking block knocked."

"Don't come back no more? After you fucking got me hooked?" I screamed, causing yet another scene. "I'll come back whenever or however I choose. Do you know who the fuck I am? I'm a fucking murderer! I ain't scared of you! My name is Joshua Tune! The Joshua Tune! The infamous Joshua fucking Tune! The whole nation is looking for me! You better watch who the fuck you're talking to!" I warned.

Perez looked at me with menace. "Man, you better take what I got and get the fuck outta East New York, because I ain't above using your white ass for target practice. Feel me?"

I gave him a look like please.

I took my bundles and immediately sat down on a nearby stoop, in between the local bodega and the A-train station, to take a snort. I was enjoying the rush of that first hit when Perez came right back and said, "Yo! You can't be doing that here! You gots to raise up outta here!"

He grabbed my arm, pulled me off the stoop, and dragged me toward the curb where the cab had dropped me off. I bent my head, took a quick snort, then stuck the bundle in my pocket and figured that the one hit was enough to get me back to Queens to meet up with Nikki. I thought I remembered her saying something about leaving.

As soon as I got back to the house, I ignored the questions of Mrs. and Mr. Keebles and went to my room. I fell on the bed to enjoy my rush, especially since Nikki wasn't there.

Once again, incessant banging woke me up from a deep, drug-induced sleep. I jolted awake and stared blankly at the walls in the small room. There was another pounding on the flimsy door. "POLICE! Open up!" someone shouted. Why did law enforcement always like to bang on my door when I was coming down from a high?

I got up, staggered to the door, and there stood two detectives, Mr. and Mrs. Keebles, and Lisa hovering in the background. I guess she had gotten out of jail. Unfortunately, I was too fucked up to care. The two men in suits and sunglasses stood directly in front of the door, exerting their authority.

"Matthew Mathis?" one of the detectives asked.

"Uh, who wants to know? I asked.

"I'm Detective Oldham and this is my partner, Detective Ripton. We'd like to ask you some questions if you don't mind."

"Uh, now is not a good time." I felt the jones coming down and knew I needed to take another hit in order to function properly.

"I don't think you understand," Oldham said. "You don't have much of a choice. Now let's take a ride downtown."

"Are you arresting me?"

The detectives looked at each other. "No, we're not."

"Then I don't have to go anywhere with you. Now, please excuse me."

Once again, I moved to close the door and once again it was blocked, only this time the detectives came in, grabbed me, and pulled my arms behind my back.

"Joshua Tune, aka Matthew Mathis, you are under arrest for aiding and abetting a fugitive, obstruction of justice, larceny, and probably some other stuff we haven't thought up yet." The cold snick of handcuffs closed tightly around my wrists. I could have lived the rest of my life without feeling them again, but I guess that wasn't meant to be.

"You have the right to remain silent. Anything you say can and will be held against you in a court of law. You have the right . . ."

As I was led out to the squad card, wearing only my dirty underwear, the only thought I had was, Nikki is going to kill me!

At the precinct, the detectives put me in an interview room and left me alone. Since I hadn't had a hit, I started getting jittery and nauseous. The detectives would come in and offer me water or coffee, but all I wanted was that Black Magic. As the hours wore on, I became increasingly sick. This must have been what the detectives were waiting for, because they came in and took a seat on either side of me, boxing me in.

"You doing OK there, Mr. Tune?" Ripton asked me. "You're not looking too good."

"I'm fine," I insisted weakly. I wiped the snot from my nose with a damp forearm.

"You want a doctor?" Oldham asked.

"I said, I'm fine."

Ripton looked at Oldham. "So, Mr. Tune, what brings you back to New York?"

"I, uh, I just wanted to come back to visit."

"Really? No other reason?"

"No. What, I can't get homesick?"

Oldham snorted. "Well, there's homesick, and then there's homesick with an arrest warrant hanging over your head."

"You could have gone to Toronto. That's pretty much like New York," Ripton chimed in.

I shook my head. I felt so cold, and my stomach was really hurting.

"You know, Mr. Tune, I find it interesting that you still have not asked us how we knew your identity. That just amazes me. Doesn't it amaze you, Oldham?"

"It boggles the imagination," Oldham said.

I shrugged. I was tired of lying, tired of hiding. "Well, I didn't think there was much sense in arguing."

"True," Ripton conceded, "but the funny thing is that you still haven't figured out how we found out your alias. I looked over your IDs. Good fakes."

Oldham nodded. "Excellent fakes."

"The kind of fakes that you had to pay a pretty penny for," Ripton confirmed.

"They were good enough to get you through Customs," Oldham added. "And Homeland Security."

"So good that we shouldn't have figured out who you really are, if you want the truth."

"Yep," Oldham agreed. "Quiet as it's kept, there are some things out there that can still fool the cops."

"So how did we catch you?" Ripton asked me.

I didn't really care what they were saying. I really needed a hit. My stomach lurched and I bent over and threw up right on the floor. The detectives both pushed back from the table.

"Jesus H," Oldham said in disgust. He left the room, screaming for a janitor.

"You're sick, Mr. Tune," Ripton said. "Let us get you to a hospital."

I shook my head. A hospital meant no Black Magic for sure. I put my head down on the cool table. Oldham returned with a cup of water, a cup of coffee, and a bagel. He put them down in front of me. "Here. You could use this."

I lifted my head and took a sip of water. "Thank you." The liquid revived me a bit, and I drained the small cup. Oldham went back out of the room and returned with a bottle of water, and I drank that down too. I felt a bit better, even though the stench of the vomit was starting to get to me.

"Better?" Oldham asked. I nodded and pulled the hot coffee closer to me, savoring its warmth. I took a sip. It had sugar but no cream, but I could live with that.

"Mr. Tune, where is Nikkisi Ling?"

The coffee sloshed on my hand, but I didn't feel the sting of the heat. "Wh-what did you say?"

"I asked you for Ling." Oldham's eyes narrowed and his voice was filled with hatred and something else—bitterness at having his quarry escape him. He had three years for that bitterness to fester, and he was ready to unleash it on someone. Right now, I was that someone.

"I don't know where she is." I turned my head and breathed through my mouth to avoid the odor of my vomit. Where was the janitor?

"Well, that's not the way we heard it," Ripton replied. "I mean, since you went on the run with her and all, I figured you two were thick as thieves." He laughed at the irony of his joke, and so did Oldham.

I took a sip of coffee and tried to figure out what to say. As much as I hated my fugitive life, that didn't give me the right to force Nikki to give up hers. She'd been through too much already. But wasn't that what I did when I called her, begging for help because I got into some shit I had no business getting into? It was a tremendous risk for her to come back to the United States, yet she did it because I had asked her. Because she loved me. To repay her by ratting her out was not an option.

"Like I said, I don't know where she is."

"Come on, Tune." Oldham leaned in closely. "You and Ling were a hot item three years ago."

"A real Bonnie and Clyde," Ripton co-signed.

"So don't tell me you don't know where she is," Oldham continued. "You probably don't take a shit without telling her what it feels like."

"Did she know about your visit to the late Parker Brown-Battle?" Ripton asked innocently.

"A man going to visit his dying ex-wife, a woman he still had feelings for, even though she'd married someone else. Had to be hard for Ling to watch that."

"If it were me, I wouldn't be able to deal with it," Ripton commented.

Oldham nodded. "Yep. I might be inclined to follow him, make sure he didn't do any last requests, you know?"

"A roll in the hay for old time's sake."

"Especially if she was dying."

"Be hard for a man to turn down a request like that," Ripton sighed.

I shook my head once again. I wasn't going to let them bait me. I got myself into this shit, and I'd get myself out. There was no need for me to bring Nikki down with me. The vomit smell was getting ripe in that closed little room.

Ripton examined me closely. "You know, Oldham, I think that Tune here has some divided loyalties going on."

"Really?" Oldham peered at me. "You know, you may be right. On one hand, he's on the run with a murderess thief—that's gotta be love—but on the other hand, he still loved his dying ex-wife." He shook his head. "Tough situation all around."

"Yep. Especially when they don't deserve his loyalty."

Oldham nodded. "Yep. Especially then."

I tuned them out. Of course they were going to play the loyalty card. They didn't know that Nikki was totally loyal to me. I was the one who didn't deserve it.

"I mean, look at your situation, Tune. You're sitting in here, warrants on your head that weren't there before you hooked up with Ling after you got out of jail. Your record was clean, your debt to society paid, and then you bounced with Ling to parts unknown. And where is Ling?" Oldham leaned in close again. "Not here. Not trying to save your ass."

"She's probably out doing her thing, not thinking about you, living her fugitive life."

"You were probably dead weight, weren't you, Tune? That Ling is a strong-willed bitch. What the hell did she see in you?"

"Yeah. Look at you. You couldn't even stay clean. The minute Parker died, you crumbled like a cookie in the rain."

"Probably mad that his gravy train was gone."

"Two gravy trains."

"You like hooking up with women who take care of you, huh, Tune?"

"That's not true!" I snapped. Inside I had to admit that Parker, then Nikki, did treat me very well. Most, if not all, of my needs were usually anticipated and fulfilled.

"For all that you had a fancy law degree and a high-profile practice, you're nothing but a little boy wanting Mommy." Ripton sneered.

"Fuck you!"

"Wasn't Parker older than you, Tune?" Ripton asked.

Oldham nodded in agreement. "I do believe she was, Ripton. But Ling, she was younger, right?"

"Younger girls don't have the smarts of older women. Easier to fool."

"You sure had them fooled, didn't you, Tune?"

"More like they had him fooled, Oldham."

Oldham chuckled. "Yep." He leaned in as if to whisper in my ear. "Wanna hear a little secret, Tune? Your dear, departed ex-wife was the one who clued us in to your whereabouts."

The shock took my mind off the pain for a moment. "What?"

"Oh, yeah," he continued. "Called us and said you came to visit her house on Long Island. Told us where you were staying, The Plaza Hotel, and your assumed name—all of it."

I wanted to scream that they were liars, but I needed a moment to think. Could Parker have really given me up? She'd continually asked me to turn myself in, thinking that I would be better off without Nikki. Parker also felt that I would still have a shot at a decent life after I served my debt to society. I shook off those thoughts. Parker would have never made a decision for me that was mine to make. I was a grown man.

Then my thoughts shifted to Steven. He, too, knew where I was staying and my alias. I was sure he even knew that Parker and I had made love in his bed shortly before he came home. And that couldn't sit well with him. It wouldn't sit well with any man, even if it was his wife's dying wish. But if Parker or Steven had revealed my information and identity, then why hadn't they caught up with me earlier? I'd been at The Plaza for weeks after I'd left Parker's house. And how did they find me now?

"Seems like Mrs. Battle-Tune never could quite forgive you for running off with Ling and leaving her here," Ripton said.

"You're lying! I don't believe any of it. It she turned me in, then you would have caught me back at The Plaza."

"You know the hands of justice are slow," Oldham commented. "It took time to process your fingerprints and put a warrant out under your alias. We had to make sure that an innocent man wouldn't get hauled in.

When we went to arrest you, you'd already skipped out on a hefty bill. I guess Nikki's thieving ways are rubbing off on you."

"Stop it, all right? Just stop with your mind games. Let's not forget that I'm an attorney and I know all the games that detectives play."

"No, you were an attorney," Ripton said. "Now, you're nothing but a common criminal with criminal friends. Now you're hooking up with girls half your age who run illegal green card operations. Is that your baby the girl's carrying?"

"I don't have anything to do with Lisa! You can't tie her mess in with me!"

"Imagine the excitement when we get a call from Detective Slade, stating that they got a hit back on the fingerprints from Lisa's room. The prints connected to a case we'd been working for the past three years. I couldn't believe our luck. Could you, Ripton?"

"Nope. Sure couldn't. I kept thinking, how dumb is this guy to still be in New York? I thought for sure you were gone again, that we'd lost you, let you slip right between our fingers . . . but no! You were still here, and we were guessing that you wanted to get caught so you could help yourself by helping us get Nikkisi Ling. We're only going to entertain this offer for a few more minutes. Then we're going to haul Lisa Henderson in here and offer her a plea on her fraud cases. And if she knows any information on Nikkisi Ling, well, you know what they say. Hell hath no fury, and all that."

"She doesn't know shit," I spat. "And neither do I."

"Cut the bullshit! We want Ling, and we think you can give her to us," Oldham said.

"Do it and we can make this all disappear," Ripton promised. "The warrants, the jail time you're facing—all of it."

"Think about it, Tune," Oldham urged. "You'd be back in the States, near your family and friends. You won't have to keep looking over your shoulder. You could live your life as a free man." He paused. "And we could get you into a good rehab program, get that monkey off your back."

"Just tell us where Ling is," Ripton said. "If you work with us, we'll work with you. You were a lawyer once. You know how the game is played."

I did indeed know how the game was played. They had me cold on the warrants, and there was no way I was getting out of those without a fight. But to give up Nikki? Was I really that weak that I couldn't take the weight for her? Then I thought about everything. All I'd been doing for the past three years was taking the weight for her. Her weight, weight I shouldn't have taken on in the first place. I should have listened to Parker, and then I wouldn't be sitting here today. I shook my head yet again and let a tear spill down my face. I'm sorry, Nikki. "I want a lawyer."

Lisa Henderson

After the drama with Matt was over, I decided to call Ishmael. "How did you get my number?" he asked.

"I have my ways," I replied.

"But why are you calling me? I thought I made myself clear the last time I saw you, that it was over."

I was silent. "I, uh . . ." Silence on the other end, like he was waiting for me to say what I had to say. "I need some money, Ishmael. I got myself into some real trouble."

"I heard about your troubles, and I don't give a fuck." When I started to speak, he cut me off. "Listen, I'm not an ATM, Lisa. We don't roll like that no more."

"But it's for the baby," I protested.

"You must have bumped your head. You want me to give you some paper to help you raise another nigga's baby?"

"The baby is yours."

He laughed sarcastically. "The only baby I got is the one coming from my wife! You just keep the lies coming, don't you?"

I was speechless, but I also felt a pang of guilt for the lies I'd told him in the past. "Why would I lie about something like that, Ishmael?"

I put as much indignation in my voice as possible.

"Maybe because Timothy got knocked and you don't have anyone to keep you laced anymore," he shot back.

"That's not true," I said heatedly.

"Then why didn't you come to me when you first found out you were pregnant?"

"Because you never returned my calls!"

"Just like you found me when you needed money, you could have found me to tell me you were pregnant."

I didn't have anything to say to that. He was right.

Ishmael sighed deeply. "Lisa, I need to know if that baby is mine. Do you understand that? You were with"—he hesitated—"with Timothy right after I got knocked. I need to be sure." He paused. "Does Timothy know you're pregnant?"

"I haven't talked to him since . . . since we broke up, but this isn't his baby. I'm one hundred about that."

"Lisa, until I can get a paternity test and know for sure that the baby is mine, I'm not giving you a dime."

I panicked. I needed money to get my father! "But what am I supposed to do, Ishmael? This is your baby too!"

"They got community clinics where you can get the baby checked out or whatever. You can get WIC and shit like that. Don't try to play a street nigga."

"Those places aren't any good, Ishmael. You know that."

"They were good enough for you when you lived in Marcy, and good enough for my moms. You'll be a'ight." He fell silent again, like he wanted to say something. Finally he said, "Look, Lisa, I want to ask you something else."

"OK."

"Word on the curb is that someone snitched on Timothy so that he got knocked. It kinda makes sense, since he'd been out in the streets, on the low since that little boy's murder, and they weren't able to catch him. But shortly after messing with you, he gets sent up."

"So what you saying?"

"I'm saying that it's an awful big coincidence, Lisa. And I don't believe much in coincidences."

I was shocked—and scared. It seemed that I'd underestimated Ishmael's reasoning skills. "You trying to say that I'm a snitch?"

"I'm saying that the timing is interesting. And if you did have something to do with it, then you're a fucked up, trifling, snitch bitch. That's all I'm saying." Before I could say anything else he said, "I gotta go. Let me know when you have the baby so we can arrange a paternity test. Take care of yourself, Lisa." Click.

The distance I felt between us hurt me to my heart, even though it was partially my fault. Still, I wouldn't have been with Timothy had I known that Ishmael had gotten locked up. I thought that he'd left me and was somewhere on the low with Toya. If only we hadn't gotten into that argument the night before, none of this would have happened, and I'd still be living the life I'd become accustomed to, thanks to Shiniqua.

Tears filled my eyes at the thought of her. I missed her so badly, and I wished she was here to tell me what to do. I looked back at the TV screen, which now showed a rerun of *The Golden Girls*.

I turned the channel to the news. There was a breaking news alert about a Nikkisi Ling, a murderer of some businessman three years ago. Apparently she'd been on the run ever since, and took a million dollars with her when she ran. Her man was on the run with her too, and his name was Joshua Tune aka Matthew Mathis. Pictures from three years ago flashed on the screen—a black woman with slanted eyes and straight hair, and a white guy with blond hair and blue eyes. A warrant was out for her arrest, and a reward was being offered to anyone who had information on her whereabouts. The authorities suspected that she was back in the New York area.

The reporter also mentioned the suicide of this Nikkisi's sister, Noki. Her picture flashed on the screen and I paused. I remembered the picture I'd found in Molly's suitcase at the motel, the one of two girls, one black with slanted eyes and one Asian. The Asian girl looked just like the picture on the screen, and the name was the same as the one that had been scribbled on the back of the picture.

Was Nikkisi Ling Molly Mathis? I recalled Molly's face and it wasn't the same as this Nikkisi. Molly's face was rounder, and her hair was different, and she didn't have slanted eyes. But if she was on the run, she had enough money for plastic surgery, especially with a million dollars, I thought. And it's real easy to cut and dye your hair. And since I now knew Matt was really Joshua Tune, I was pretty sure Molly was Nikkisi. Matt had kept referring to a Nikki, but I thought he was just too high to remember who he was with.

I finished watching the news and sat back, deep in thought. What would Shiniqua do? Shiniqua would have recognized an opportunity and gone for the money. Or would she? Despite her money-loving ways, Shiniqua put a high price on loyalty. All of the Ships, and the people who worked for them, did too. She wouldn't have turned on someone who had been good to her, especially someone who bailed her out of jail when she didn't have to and even left a bit of pocket change.

Molly, or Nikki, or whatever her name was, ain't do nothing to you, a little voice in my head said. She ain't been nothing but nice to you. How could you even think about ratting her out?

True, Molly had been nice to me from jump, but the truth was that I didn't know her from the man on the moon. And I didn't care how many meals she bought me, or how much money she left me in a letter,

I had a baby to think about now, not to mention helping my daddy.

I remembered how whenever Matt was high, he would ramble on about how he and Molly were rich and that they didn't need to live as they were. He told tales of being a spy for the CIA and traveling internationally, trying to catch double agents in espionage. He said sometimes he had to go deep undercover into seedy neighborhoods to catch these criminals. These ramblings, coupled with small things that Molly would say or do, made me certain in my conclusion that Molly and Nikkisi were the same person. And she wasn't a spy. She was a murderer.

I was only three hours fresh out of jail, but a plan had already formed in my head. If all went well, then I would have all the money I needed for my baby and my daddy, and I wouldn't have to do anything illegal to get it.

I went downstairs, unplugged the house phone, and then told Mr. Keebles that the police had inadvertently cut the telephone wire before they came in to arrest Matt.

"Don't worry, Mr. Keebles. I'm going to call Verizon and have someone come out and repair the line. OK?"

"Lisa, thank you. I don't know how much more we can take. Mrs. Keebles and I are thinking about moving out of this neighborhood and going south, to Florida."

I felt sorry for the weary couple. They'd been through a lot in the past few days, most of it my fault. Moving away would probably be the best thing for them.

My next move was to use my cell phone to call Molly.

"Molly, this is Lisa," I gushed. "I'm home. I just got here. Thank you so much for bailing me out. You really didn't have to do it."

"Of course I did. We help each other, remember?"

"Yes, I remember. And thank you for the money. I'm really going to get myself together and go back to school."

"I'm so proud of you."

"Molly, I'm so afraid to stay here tonight. I need a place to calm my nerves. This isn't good for the baby. There are news cameramen all over, trying to get me on film."

"Where's Matt?"

"I haven't seen him. He's still gone."

She breathed a sigh of relief. "Well, where are you going to stay? Are you going to call your family? Your mother? Family is important in times like these."

"I already tried. They won't help me. I was hoping that I could stay with you. Where are you? Are you at the motel?"

"Heavens no, I'm not there. But I won't be here for much longer. I'm going back to London."

"Without Matt?"

"Unfortunately, I have to."

"But where's here? Where are you? Can I come over, if only for a few hours of sleep. You don't know how it is in jail."

She hesitated before she finally gave in.

I had Pop-Pop take me to the Hilton at JFK Airport and told him to wait for me a few blocks up. I had a gut feeling that I was about to solve a mystery.

Once off the elevator, I began talking on my cell phone. As I knocked on the door, I pretended to be engrossed in a frantic conversation.

"Are you kidding? Of course I'll tell her. Is he all right? Yes . . . yes . . . please help him!"

Molly pulled me into her hotel room and saw the frantic look on my face. "What's happened now?" she asked.

"Molly, it's bad. I'm not sure if I should tell you."

"Tell me what?" She looked on the verge of a nervous breakdown.

"It's Matt. He's been stabbed. He's back at the house. He told Mr.

Keebles to find you and that you'd know what to do. He specifically said for them not to take him to the ambulance, or call the authorities."

"Oh, my gosh!" she shrieked, and then began to cry. "How bad is it? Is he going to die?"

"I don't know. What are you going to do? Are you going over there?"

Just as I thought she would, she dialed the house, but the phone just rang and rang. She did this for several minutes as she paced.

"Why aren't they answering the damn phone?!" she yelled.

"They're probably helping your husband, and dodging calls regarding my arrest. Reporters have been calling all day."

"I suppose you're right. Lisa, I need you to do me a huge favor—"

"Oooowwww." I gasped in pain, clutching my stomach. "Ooowww-ww."

"Are you OK?"

I sat on the bed. "Please, I can't take much more stress. I need a hot bath and a nap."

"Jeez, OK. I wanted you to check on Matt, but I guess I'll have to do it. He's my husband and my responsibility, not yours. I should only be gone an hour. If anyone comes to the door, don't let them in. You have my telephone number. Call me if anyone suspicious comes around."

"What do you mean, suspicious?"

"Just call if anyone knocks on my door. OK?"

"I'll probably be asleep, but OK."

I waited a full ten minutes before I made my move. And it didn't take me long before I hit the jackpot. I had located Molly's stash of money.

Next, I picked up the phone and dialed the Crime Stoppers number. "Hello? Yes, I just saw the news, and I have some information about Nik-kisi Ling. Yes, I want this call to remain anonymous. And, yes, I want the reward."

Nikkisi Ling

It was early evening when I arrived at the Keebles' house. My gut kept telling me to turn around and go back to the hotel. I felt uneasy leaving Lisa there with my money, although it was hidden in my suitcase, but I assured myself that A: she wouldn't snoop around my room and, B: she thought that Joshua and I were a poor couple from England. Besides, I would only be gone long enough to give Joshua his passport and a couple thousand dollars, and then I would wash my hands of him. Hopefully his injuries weren't grave. He must have either tried to steal some dope, or owed a dope boy some money.

I had the cab driver drop me off around the corner from the house so that I could case it first. Lisa said the place was crawling with news reporters, and I didn't want my picture on the news, even if I did have a different face.

My walk was slow, steady, and distinctive. Up ahead, I saw a man—another person who had an equally distinctive walk was Joshua. I'd know that walk, body frame, and those blue eyes from any distance. Why was he being let off around the corner from the house? I thought. What was he up to? He certainly didn't appear to be injured. And then it hit me like a ton of bricks. Lisa had set me up! But before I could process that information, I noticed two detectives from my past—Oldham and Ripton—conversing with Joshua.

Joshua and I made eye contact. I continued to casually walk toward him, and our eyes spoke to each other. Was he going to sell me out? Was he part of the setup? He dug his hands deep into his pockets and never made a gesture. His eyes hit the ground and I knew I was safe. As we passed each other I bumped him, and kept it moving.

As Detective Oldham lowered himself into the front seat of his undercover squad car, he and I made eye contact, and for a second he hesitated. My bowels became watery. And then he resumed his position. He didn't have a clue that I was the fugitive he was looking for. Once I hit the corner, I took off running for my life. I kept calling Lisa on her cell phone, hoping that she wasn't in on it to, but I knew she was. And now there wasn't any way I could go back to the hotel and get my money.

I had about five hundred dollars and my passport left on me after I had slipped Josh his passport and the money I brought for him. That was just going to have to do.

I was sitting in a burger place in Penn Station when the news bulletin scrolled across the screen.

Accused murderer Nikkisi Ling has been confirmed as being in the New York City area under the alias of Molly Mathis. There is a warrant out for her arrest, and anyone with information on her whereabouts is encouraged to call crime stoppers at 1-866-555-TIPS.

The French fry I'd been nibbling on stuck in my throat as I stared at the letters. Soon a reporter repeated this bulletin and my mugshot from three years ago was shown on screen, along with the mugshot of Joshua. There was also a picture of Noki, and the sight of her young beauty broke my heart all over again.

The reporter gave the pertinent facts of my case, starting with my marriage to Jack, his death—which was ruled a homicide—and ending with Noki's suicide and my escape with a million dollars of my dead husband's money. And now they somehow knew I was in New York, and they knew my complete alias. But how? Lisa only knew my name was Molly, so the only way I could think of was Joshua. I knew they had caught him, since I saw the detectives with him outside of the house, and the only way they could have gotten my full alias was from him.

But why would Joshua snitch on me? Was he that unhappy with our life together? Did he regret going on the run with me that much? Maybe Alessandro was right, and Joshua didn't care about me. Sure, it was fun and thrilling when we first left the States but as time went on and the thrill left, he wanted out. He was like a kid who'd gotten over the novelty of a new toy and wanted to take it back to the store.

I just knew this had something to do with Parker! The bitch was dead, so I couldn't tell her what I thought of her in person. But Joshua just had to come back to the States to be with her. And the drugs. Joshua falling off the wagon couldn't have come at a worse time. He wasn't the swiftest of men on a good day, despite his law degree, and the drugs made him downright careless. He tended to ramble on, then black out when he was high. Who knew what he might have said, and who he said it to?

I remembered him yelling my true name on the street when he was high. He may have let it slip to the wrong ears, especially if those ears were in any way associated with Detectives Oldham and Ripton. They were burning to nail my ass to the nearest wall, and I was sure that being successfully on the run for the past three years had just fed that fire until I'd be lucky to get the needle if those two ever caught me. That Oldham motherfucker would tell them not to give me tranquilizers, and then he would push the poison into my veins himself very slowly, just to prolong my agony.

I shook my head. I couldn't dwell on that now. I had to get the fuck out of New York ASAP without Joshua. My original plan was to fly out of JFK in the morning with my new identify, Jennifer Blackmon, but I felt antsy. I didn't want to wait. I wanted to get out of New York now.

I hated the fact that Joshua was busted and being forced to work with the detectives to apprehend me. Yes, he could have given me up at that moment when we saw each other at the house, but he didn't. And that proved that he still loved me, even if he was no longer in love with me.

I put some cash on the table, grabbed my purse, and slid out of the booth, careful to keep my face averted. The news didn't have a picture of me in my current reincarnation, but I still couldn't be too careful. They had my name, and it was only a matter of time before someone gave a description of how I looked now.

Penn Station was crawling with National Guard soldiers armed with M-16s. Cops strolled through too, since there was a police substation there. This was not the place for me to be. In the wake of September 11th, things had changed regarding national security.

I took the nearest set of stairs to 34th Street and walked quickly to the corner. I hailed a cab and asked him to take me to the Port Authority. If I could get a bus to Washington DC, I could fly out of Dulles International and hopefully be in Cape Town within twenty-four hours.

That plan got nixed when I got to Port Authority and saw that there were even more cops there than at Penn Station. The word must have been out to watch the buses, trains, and planes, and to arrest Molly Mathis if she showed up trying to buy a ticket. That didn't worry me. I had already tossed that old passport. I turned around, left the station, and lost myself in the noise and light show that was Times Square. I needed to think.

I let myself get carried along the human river of tourists, businesspeople, and random New Yorkers just doing them. I passed the carts of hot dogs, Italian ices, pretzels, and New York souvenirs as I walked in the direction of uptown. I had no idea where I was going, I just put one foot in front of the other. Soon I left Times Square behind and ended up near Columbus Circle. I walked past Lincoln Center to Central Park and sat down on a bench to think.

Joshua Tune

I couldn't do it. Not once I looked in her eyes. I couldn't turn Nikki in when I saw her. I thought my shock would have given me away, but it didn't. Her coming out of nowhere, casually strolling down the block in the middle of a police undercover sting operation to find her, was unreal. And even in the midst of the lies, betrayal, and confusion, she had managed not to think just about herself.

When she first bumped into me, I thought it was because her nerves were bad. I should have known better. When I walked around the corner and entered the Keebles' house, I reached into my jacket pocket and found my new passport and two thousand dollars in there. I read the name: Alexander Pider. She had given me another new beginning.

My job as a snitch was to sit and wait at the Keebles' house and act normal until Nikki showed up. The police would keep watch on the house by posting undercover detectives on the block and in a five-block radius. They also tapped the telephones. When she came looking for me, I was supposed to blow the whistle and flag her down. That was all I had to do, and then I would have my life and freedom back.

That night, a neighbor of the Keebleses knocked on the door, putting the police on high alert.

"Is that her?" Detective Oldham asked. He had called me on my cell phone from the van where he was watching the house. "If it is her and you can't speak, simply say, 'I'll see you tomorrow.'"

"It's not her. It's a neighbor," I replied and hung up.

"Matt, she has a message from Molly," Mrs. Keebles said. I looked at the timid-looking black girl. She was no older than sixteen.

"Are you Matt?" she asked.

"Yes, I am."

"I'm supposed to tell you something in private."

"Sure. Follow me."

I led her to the backdoor and we stood on the deck. "Molly said to tell you that Jason has left the nest. Her out has been compromised, Lisa is Conklin and she intercepted the overnight bird."

I processed the information.

"Did she say anything else?"

"No, that's it."

"OK, thank you for that. Don't repeat that to anyone else, you hear me?"

"She's already paid me enough to keep my mouth shut."

"Good girl."

Jason and Conklin were characters from my favorite movie, The Bourne Identity. Jason had to flee his surroundings because he was constantly being set up by Conklin, who pretended to be a friend. That message simply meant that Nikki was gone for good, and that somehow Lisa had stolen our money. Lisa was a traitor and not to be trusted.

Lisa Henderson

After meeting with Detectives Oldham and Ripton, I sat with a police sketch artist at the police station. He took down my description of Molly/Nikkisi and would use that sketch to make flyers, which he told me would be distributed across New York City. The news stations ran her picture every day for a few weeks and then she was old news.

I couldn't be too mad at Molly/Nikkisi, though. Getting away with a cool million was nothing to sneeze at, and on a motorcycle at that! And she had been living it up overseas. Detective Oldham said Joshua confided in them that she'd been in Italy, which was hot. I would have liked to live in Italy. I wondered if what the rest of the news reports said about her was true—that she was half-Japanese and used to be a prostitute. And apparently Matt, aka Josh, used to be this big-shot attorney who'd married a rich wife, then divorced her over some bullshit, then got with Molly/Nikkisi. Now he was a dope fiend, risking his life to cop in Pink Houses and get his fix. I shook my head. The world was a crazy place, and people were even crazier.

When I finished giving my statement and got ready to leave, the detectives stopped me in the hallway. They ushered me into an interview room.

"Ms. Henderson, we just want you to know how much we appreciate you coming forward with this information," Oldham said.

"You did us a great service," Ripton added. "So great that we're going to speak with the district attorney and have your case dropped."

I smiled. "Well, that was a part of my plea agreement, wasn't it? Didn't my attorney request that stipulation?"

Oldham nodded.

I wasn't about to let these cops pretend like they were doing me a favor out of the goodness of their hearts.

"Another stipulation was my father. I need him out of the care of my mother, and I want my allegations investigated."

"Sure. We're working on that. But in the meantime, where will you be staying? We could have you set up in the Witness Protection Program for your safety. With two fugitives on the loose—"

"Two? I thought her husband was apprehended?"

Detective Ripton let out a nervous cough. "He was. But he's a slippery little sucker. He somehow managed to get past our guys in the wee hours of the morning during a shift change. The rookie cops on duty decided that it wouldn't hurt if they took a quick coffee break, leaving Tune unattended for twenty minutes. Apparently, that was more than enough time."

I couldn't worry myself with their foolishness. Their problems were their problems. I had moves to make. I was now $340,000 richer! And I couldn't wait for Molly to be apprehended, because there was a $250,000 bounty on her head.

Oldham continued. "We've confirmed various sightings of Ms. Ling in the Queens neighborhood you mentioned, and also at Penn Station. A cab driver mentioned taking her to Port Authority as well." His smile was meant to be encouraging, but it was just eerie. "We are much closer to making an arrest, and we have you to thank for it."

"Especially the picture of what she looked like now," Ripton said as he shook his head. "I tell ya, I would have walked by her on the street and not known who she was."

"That was the whole point. A million can get you some good plastic surgery, and they have good places overseas," Oldham mentioned.

"Especially Ibiza." The two detectives exchanged a look. I was lost. What was the big deal about Ibiza anyway?

"Anyway, Ms. Henderson, we just wanted to get your contact information so that once she's apprehended, we can get your reward to you," Oldham said.

"You said my tip would be anonymous, right? No one is going to know that I talked, right?" I still felt slightly guilty and should Molly/Nikkisi ever be caught, I didn't want her to know that I was part of the efforts that had gotten her knocked. I mean, she would assume that, but I didn't want her to know for sure. I didn't mind her knowing I'd taken her cash. Anybody would have done the same thing, in my position. Shit. She was a thief. She would have done the same thing too. But being a snitch just wasn't cool. I pushed back memories of calling Crime Stoppers on Timothy, but told myself that that was just revenge. This thing with Molly/Nikki was strictly about survival; it wasn't personal.

"That's right," Ripton reassured me.

"OK, it's been real, but I need to go. And don't forget that once I'm settled, I want my father. I'll call you in a couple weeks."

I sauntered out of the station after making my deal with the devil. You would think that Oldham and Ripton were old pals of mine, the way they smiled as I left.

Lisa Henderson

Three months later

I owned this—my new life. I had a sense of tranquility as I maneuvered my Michelin tires on the newly paved road. The new Lexus GS 350 hugged the road and bent corners as if it were a train hugging the tracks. I looked in my rearview mirror at my daughter, Bria Shiniqua Henderson, who was sleeping peacefully in her car seat. She was only four weeks old, but she looked just like me.

I pulled into the cul-de-sac and parked in my driveway. Could a girl who suffered through all I had gone through really be living like this? Could all of this really be mine? Today was my first day in my new home. For the past three months I had been living in protective custody, but once the heat died down—courtesy of a nightclub fire, from which they recovered the body of a Molly Mathis aka Nikkisi Ling—I decided to leave and start my new life. I took a small portion of Molly's money and purchased a 2300 square-foot home in New Jersey. Considering how the market had been plummeting, I got it for a steal. I was told that my father would be brought to my home the following day, and that should satisfy most of my heart's desires.

As I stepped out of my car, an uneasy feeling came over me. I peered over my shoulder, but saw nothing. I exhaled. I leaned into the backseat, unclasped Bria's car restraints, and hoisted my little angel out, kissing her cheek as I inhaled her baby scent.

The hairs on the back of my neck stood on edge and my stomach plummeted. I felt the presence before I saw the figure. The shadowy object loomed over me and my mind raced to find a way out. Could I run with my daughter and get away? If I screamed, would anyone help me? How did I mess up? How did I get caught slipping?

I turned around to face my past.

"You know what this is about."

His voice was gruff, but his eyes were what sent chills down my spine. I tried to read him. Would he allow me to walk out of here if I promised to give back the money?

"Is there any way out of this?"

"No. Don't make it any worse than it is."

"My daughter—"

"Go quietly and she won't be hurt. I give you my word."

Stoically, I followed him into my home. The home that was only a few moments ago my pride and joy would now be my coffin. I held onto Bria tightly and whispered a million apologies into her young, sweet ears. I told her I was sorry for not being a better mother, that if I had to do it all over again, I would do things differently. I would have protected her better. Then I said a silent prayer for Bria and for my soul.

"Put the baby down on the sofa and lie face down on the floor."

I put Bria down and then turned to face him. My eyes filled with tears, but I refused to beg. I had chosen this path, and now my time was up.

"I didn't know she'd die," I began.

"Hurry up. Move!"

"She was my friend too!"

"Shut the fuck up!" he said through clenched teeth.

"I figured that you two liked living in poverty and that you wouldn't need the—"

"Fuck you! Fuck you! Fuck you!" He went berserk.

His calm persona was replaced with hatred and pain. I knew I wasn't dealing with a stable, sane person and when Bria began crying, I did as I was told.

I dropped down to one knee.

"Where are you going to take Bria? Her father lives in Brooklyn, but he doesn't—"

"Lie face down," he said again.

I still had important information regarding my child that he needed to know, before I allowed him to take my life. The firm kick in the middle of my back startled me as I fell forward. I let out a little gasp, but held in most of my pain. I didn't want to scare Bria.

"Could you at least take me into another room? My daughter . . . I don't want her in here."

"You got two seconds to get up and go into the other room, or I'll splatter both y'all's brains on this fucking rug."

The threat wasn't idle. I got up, ran into the family room, and assumed the position. These are my last seconds on earth, I thought as I inhaled the new carpet scent into my nostri—

"Joshua!"

I heard the familiar voice and felt somewhat relieved. It was Molly.

"Nik?" Matt asked in disbelief. "I thought you were dead."

"Joshua, put down the gun. She isn't worth it."

"Is that really you?"

Slowly Nikki walked closer to Joshua and continued to speak. "I'm not dead. The person who burned in the fire wasn't me. Soon the authorities will know that, I'm sure."

"But it was all over the news."

"Joshua, you need help for your addiction. You're my husband, and I love you. Let's leave from here and make this right. We don't have much time. She's a government informant. For all we know, the police could be here at any second."

"But what about our money? This bitch stole all our money!"

She pointed toward the satchel of money that I'd stolen. "It's here. We still have two hundred thousand dollars. We can still make it."

"How did you get that?"

He asked the same question that I wanted to ask. How did she get inside my house and find my secret hiding place?

"I'm a thief, remember?"

Joshua didn't want to leave or put down the gun. He was higher than a kite and my life depended on whether he'd listen to Molly, or Nikki, or whatever her name was. I needed him to see me as human.

"Molly, please get him to stop. Please tell him that I have my baby to look after. She needs a mother, Molly. You know how hard it is for a child without her mother. Look at what happened to you and Noki," I pleaded.

As I was talking, I was buying minutes. Detective Oldham had been given me a cell phone for emergencies. This phone couldn't dial out, but once I cut it on, it alerted authorities that my life was in danger, and they'd send squad cars immediately. It was sort of like an Amber Alert, or a silent burglar alarm.

"Joshua, listen to her. Listen to me. This isn't right. Let's split the money and both have a new beginning."

"I've missed you, Nik. I've really missed you!" He began to cry like a little baby. "And I need to confess that I slept with Parker ... and I really did that . . . with her . . . I did that to us. . . ."

"Joshua, that's the past. I don't care about things like that. I just want you to have a shot at a better life. You need to put down the gun and walk out of here. You're not a murderer any more than I am."

"Why are you taking up for this bitch? I slept with her too! Lisa and I were having sex while you were out trying to get money to save us! You looked at her like she was your sister!"

"Killing her won't fix us. We're done. I'm not going with you, Josh, but I don't want to leave you here. Put down the gun . . . please."

I continued to look for a vulnerable moment where I could grab Bria and escape while these two lovers sorted out their differences. I looked up and realized that I wasn't the only one with plans of leaving the scene. Nikki was slowly backing out of the room as Joshua continued his babble.

Her actions made me panic. I didn't want her to leave me alone with him.

"Joshua, will you listen to her?" I screamed. My voice must have scared him because he turned around quickly to face me and then BOOM!

Nikki Ling

We were fugitives. We'd always be on the run. I had to decide if my love for Joshua superseded my love for myself. I begged him to leave Lisa's house because we had what we had both come looking for, only I couldn't get through to him. As I backed out of the doorway, I realized that he wasn't the man I'd fallen in love with. And that his drug addiction would always compromise our freedom. My freedom.

I whispered, "I love you, Joshua."

But I loved myself more.

I didn't stay long enough to witness what happened between Joshua and Lisa.

After I had dumped my Molly Mathis passport when I saw my alias on TV, fate would have it that my actions gave me a few months of going undetected. Someone must have pocketed my discarded passport and gone to a club. Sadly, the club was set on fire by an unknown arsonist, and once my passport was located in the rubbish, the news speculated that I couldn't take the pressure of being on the run for murder, and not only had I killed myself, but I also took the lives of 187 people with me. Since most of the people in the club were illegal immigrants, it was taking quite some time to do DNA testing on everyone who had gotten burned in the fire, and that gave me even more time to plan my next move.

As the taxi drove out of the cul-de-sac toward Newark International Airport, I finally exhaled. I didn't know what life had in store for me, but I knew it had to be better than what it had offered in the past.

"Will I ever see you again, Nikkisi?" Pop-Pop asked. At this point, he knew my life's story.

"Not if I can help it." I gave him a kiss on his cheek. "But if I'm ever in New York, I'll definitely look you up."

Nikki Ling

I sat on the balcony of the little villa that I had rented on the outskirts of Tuscany. Alessandro, that sweet, funny, flirtatious man had managed to get it rented to me. The villa was owned by the cousin of his sister-in-law, and had been uninhabited for a long time. The cousin was all too happy to get a rental income from the villa, since property taxes were taking a bite out of his income.

I'd hated leaving the home I'd built with Joshua but I knew that if I stayed there, someone might come for me. Italy had a formal extradition treaty with the United States, but the police near my old home didn't go looking for trouble. Still, I didn't want to stick around and see what happened when trouble came looking for them in the form of the FBI and New York Police Department.

It took me three days to get back to Italy. I flew out of Newark International Airport to Charlotte, North Carolina, then from Charlotte to Atlanta, then from Atlanta to Trieste, Italy with a stopover in Rome. In Rome I called Alessandro, and played damsel in distress. He graciously came to get me. He now visited me often, and he was glad to hear that "Matt" had remained in the United States. He liked to remark that I no longer looked like "a puppy."

Slowly, I began to open up about my past. I needed an ally and Alessandro proved to be just that.

I was a fugitive. I would always be on the run. I had enough money to last me for a long time, if I was careful. And I had companionship in Alessandro, who seemed to be grateful just to be in my presence.

Sometimes I would think of those final days in Queens. I would remember Lisa, and I wondered what started her on the path of a train wreck lifestyle. As always, I would think of Noki and once again wonder how our lives would have turned out if I'd taken better care of her, or if she'd taken better care of herself, or if our mother had worked in a department store instead of as a prostitute.

Of course I would also think about Joshua and our life together, before and after we ran. I thought about his addiction and wanted to weep. So much promise, and he threw it away for a few ounces of a drug that would kill him anyway. I would always love Joshua Tune, especially for what he'd risked for me. But for once in my life, I loved myself more. As I stared at the leafy green olive trees that swayed in the sunny breeze, I finally felt that loving myself was more than enough.

The ringing of my cell phone startled me. I hesitated, and then looked to Alessandro. I never used that phone, yet I kept it on just in case Joshua ever called. It was my American telephone number. Finally I picked up.

"Hi, this is Stacy Compo from Federal Express. We've just located a package for a Miss Molly Mathis. Is she available?"

"No, she's not. Can I take a message for her?"

"Yes. Can you tell her that we've located her last package, that has been missing for quite some time. And if she could give us an address, we can have it shipped to her. Or if she would like, she can come pick it up."

"OK, I'll give her the message."

"Do you want to give us an address?"

"I think you should speak to the rightful owner. I'll have her call you."

"Do you need the telephone num—"

"I'm sure she has all of that. Thank you."

I turned to Alessandro.

"They've found me!"

Detective Oldham

"Do you think she suspects anything?" I asked. The call to Nik-kisi was being traced and recorded while one of our detectives posed as a FedEx agent.

"I think she isn't a dummy," Detective Alana stated.

"Didn't I fucking tell you she didn't burn in a fire?" I asked. "It's just a matter of time before I fucking capture her ass! I've already contacted *America's Most Wanted.* They're going to do an episode on her. She's gone from prostitute, to thief, to murderer, to kidnapping, and then to murder again! You know she did the Henderson girl and her—"

"What about Tune? He could have had a hand in it too," Ripton asked.

"I don't give a fuck about Tune! I want Ling. And she's still out there somewhere! I'm telling you, she must have a box of Lucky Charms shoved up her ass!"

"Well, although she didn't stay on the call long enough for a proper trace, as soon as we get the information from her cell phone company regarding which cell tower the call hit, she's done. It's over!" Detective Ripton chimed in.

"I tell you, I will never get tired of chasing down that black widow!"

EPILOGUE

"Spin me around again, Daddy!"

"Lyric, Daddy is tired now, honey. Can we go home now and have dinner? Daddy will make you your favorite," I said, bribing my little girl.

"Chicken?" she squealed. "Oh, yes, I love chicken!"

"How do you say it in Spanish?"

"*Pollo*!"

"Correct. Come on, let's go," I said and then looked down. "Let me tie your sneaker."

"What a lovely child," a woman said. I looked up and saw a nice-looking, slim, white female. I looked around to make sure she was speaking to me.

"Thank you."

"I noticed she called you Daddy. Is she adopted?"

"Excuse me?" I stood quickly. "The nerve of you!"

"I'm sorry. I didn't mean to offend you or your daughter. But we see you here all the time. My son and I." She pointed toward a dark-skinned boy. I knew him from the park. His name was Banda, and he was Ethiopian. "He's adopted. And since your little girl looks black, I was speculating. I just thought she was adopted."

"She's bi-racial, not that it's any of your business. Have a good day. We have to go."

Five years ago, I made a huge mistake and took the life of Lyric's mother. Since then, I've spent every day trying to make it up to a child who I renamed Lyric. My first instinct was to take her. But I was high. Hours later, she was still in my arms and everything seemed natural.

We left America under my alias, Alexander Pider, and have been living in Cape Town, South Africa ever since. I came here because I kept thinking that Nikki would find me. And when she did, I'd be ready. I'd finally kicked my drug habit for good, and I had a lot more to offer her than I could have in the past.

If our love was truly meant to be, we'd definitely meet again. If not now, then in the next lifetime. That I was most sure of . . . .